LOVE'S A CALCULATED RISK

Atlanta Skyline's benched goalkeeper Brendan Young would have been happy to ride out the end of his contract after his gambling addiction was splashed all over the news media. Instead, his teammates' injuries have unexpectedly put him back in the game. A new face in his weekly Gamblers Anonymous meeting provides another surprise spike—of pure attraction. Why is Erin Bailey, former world champion women's soccer player, at this meeting? And why can't he stop thinking about their red-hot one-night stand?

Six months ago, one reckless night in Vegas ended with Erin in Brendan's bed. She's sworn off dating athletes, especially those whose reputations could destroy her new career as the Championship Soccer League's Director of Ethics and Advocacy. But the secret they share—and the crazy heat they generate—makes it impossible to keep her distance.

Both have choices to make about the future, but no matter how steeply the odds are stacked against them, walking away could be the riskiest move of all . . .

Visit us at www.kensingtonbooks.com

Books by Rebecca Crowley

Atlanta Skyline
Crossing Hearts
Defending Hearts
Saving Hearts

Published by Kensington Publishing Corporation

Saving Hearts

An Atlanta Skyline Novel

Rebecca Crowley

LYRICAL PRESS
Kensington Publishing Corp.
www.kensingtonbooks.com

First Electronic Edition: March 2018
eISBN-13: 978-1-5161-0266-2
eISBN-10: 1-5161-0266-5

First Print Edition: March 2018
ISBN-13: 978-1-5161-0267-9
ISBN-10: 1-5161-0267-3

Printed in the United States of America

Chapter 1

The folding chair creaked as Brendan eased into it. He crossed his arms and stretched his legs, wrinkling his nose. August had started dry and hot, but the church basement smelled damper than usual.

He returned the nods of a few regulars as they took seats around the circle and gauged the expressions of the newcomers to see if any recognized him. He didn't usually expect to be known by sight, particularly now that he had a full-time seat on the bench. But since his extracurricular activities had garnered more headlines than his goalkeeping, occasionally he ran into unexpected recognition.

Anyway, none of the new faces showed any sign of familiarity. He leaned back in his chair, mentally bracing himself for the worst hour of his week.

"Let's begin with a recitation of our twelve steps." Lenny, the heavyset, bearded group leader, opened his well-worn pamphlet.

The sound of flicking pages filled the room before Lenny's voice intoned, "We admitted we were powerless over gambling, and that our lives had become unmanageable."

Brendan's pamphlet remained closed on his lap, unneeded after nearly six months of weekly meetings. He rolled his eyes to the ceiling as he muttered, "We came to believe that a power greater than ourselves could restore us to a normal way of thinking and living."

He mumbled his way through the other ten assertions, then waited patiently while Lenny took the two new attendees through the twenty questions designed to determine whether someone was truly a problematic gambler. By all accounts the first person was—he'd blown his entire retirement savings on slot machines.

The second newcomer seemed to be more addicted to personal drama than the lottery tickets she claimed were ruining her life. Brendan narrowed his eyes in judgment as she answered yet another question negatively, then launched into a detailed explanation about why her weekly lottery tickets were a huge problem nonetheless.

The door behind him banged open. He glanced over his shoulder—and froze.

Five feet and ten inches of red-haired, blue-eyed velocity personified stood in the entrance. She wore an unrelentingly tight skirt and an unapologetic expression.

Erin Bailey. Of all people. The last time he'd seen her she was—

"Sorry I'm late," she breezed in a tone that clearly broadcast just how sorry she wasn't. She glided around the periphery of the circle, totally unimpeded by her sky-high heels, and dropped into the chair opposite his. She curled her strawberry-pink lips in a smile he bet no one realized was fake.

Then their eyes met. Her insincere smile vanished as instantly as it appeared.

Considering he'd spent the last ten years being paid exorbitant sums to think faster than his opponents, he probably should've come up with a better reaction. Some slow-running part of his brain tossed up suggestions too late for him to act on—a smug smile, maybe. A coyly arched brow. A subtle tilt of the head.

Instead, he stared at her dumbly, barely able to keep his jaw from dropping as a wave of memories slammed into him with the force of a two-hundred-pound striker.

Their polite greeting at their mutual friend's New Year's Eve wedding in Las Vegas. Her pleased smile as he slid into the seat beside her at the reception. The scent of jasmine, reminding him of the tangling, flowered vine climbing up the side of his house. Champagne. More champagne. Her admission that she'd had a crush on him in college. His pretense that he hadn't known. Soccer gossip. Champagne, again.

The images blurred as the night went on. The casino floor. Slot machines. Poker tables. Blackjack. Champagne, champagne, champagne.

When he looked at her in that harshly lit basement room he saw the view from the hotel balcony, fireworks exploding above the sweeping, glittering expanse of the Vegas strip. The pale peach contours of her body against the crisp white linen. Her bright green dress discarded on top of his dark gray suit. His fingers threading through red hair as vivid as a desert sunset. The line between her eyes as she moaned his name and clamped her hands on his hips to force him deeper, harder, faster.

When his vision came back into focus she stared at him. He wondered if she saw those things, too, or if she was too busy panicking that he was aware the Championship Soccer League's newly appointed Director of Ethics and Advocacy was a gambling addict.

Maybe she was regretting that phone call in February after his name had been one of several high-profile athletes whose gambling habits had become painfully public when online betting site SportBetNet was hacked and lists of its professional-athlete members appeared in the press. Maybe she wished she could take back her frosty insistence that their one-night stand couldn't possibly lead to anything more—not even friendship—and that she trusted he'd understand the position this put her in and be suitably discreet.

He finally found a hint of a smirk.

The lottery ticket enthusiast answered her last question, barely managing the seven of twenty "yes" answers that supposedly qualified someone as a gambling addict. She leaned back in her chair, satisfied, and Lenny turned to Erin.

"Welcome," he said warmly. "Would you like to introduce yourself?"

"Sure." She ripped her gaze away from his, and the lighting in the room seemed to dim at the lost contact.

Her too-bright smile was back in place as she offered the circle a little wave. "My name is…" She stole a glance at him, and he could read her backpedal as easily as a debut striker's first attempt on goal.

She would've lied about her name. Now she had to tell the truth.

"My name is Erin. I'm a compulsive gambler," she announced decisively. "It's been three weeks since my last bet."

"Hi, Erin," the group chimed in unison.

"Is this your first meeting?" Lenny asked.

She shook her head, and Brendan thought Lenny looked slightly relieved at not having to run through the questions for the third time.

"Well, you're very welcome," he repeated. He turned to a lanky, well-dressed man with graying temples. "Jeremy, you're our speaker today. Are you ready to share your recovery story?"

Jeremy began by recalling the pressures of law school and Brendan zoned out almost immediately, fixing his eyes on Erin—the last person he ever expected to run into at a Gamblers Anonymous meeting.

He shifted in his seat, attempting to redirect his attention to Jeremy's story. As he angled his body he met Erin's gaze again. She looked away as rapidly as she had earlier, but not before he saw the flash of blue-flame heat in her eyes.

Brendan exhaled, trying to calm the sudden increase in his heart rate. In that moment he knew she remembered everything. The bright lights. The pumping adrenaline. The blazing lust.

The scalding, breath-stealing connection that was as bright and beautiful and fleeting as the fireworks that had popped overhead.

* * * *

Brendan took his time stirring milk into the cup of coffee he didn't particularly want, hovering beside the oversized carafe and keeping Erin in his peripheral vision. As he anticipated, a handful of the meeting's male attendees descended on her as soon as the session finished. He'd already overheard two offers to be her sponsor and now Jason—who'd lost his college tuition money on online poker—had practically pinned her against the wall as he pumped her for details.

Brendan waited just long enough to hear her fabricated backstory— she told him she was a marketing executive for a bottle manufacturing company—before moving in, the second cup of coffee in hand.

"Sorry to interrupt." He edged around Jason, extending the orange ceramic mug to Erin. "Skim milk, no sugar."

Erin gave him the first genuine smile he'd seen all evening as Jason glanced between the two of them.

"You know each other?" he asked, giving Brendan a reassessing once-over.

"For more than ten years."

"We went to college together," she explained.

"Cool," Jason replied insincerely. He eased away but kept his attention on the two of them for a few moments longer than necessary.

Comfortable Jason was out of earshot, Brendan turned to Erin. "Hi."

She took a long sip from her coffee mug, her gaze never leaving his over the rim. Eventually, she lowered the mug and flashed him a sheepish grin. "Hi, yourself."

"I didn't know you moved to Atlanta."

"League headquarters are here."

"Didn't think that meant you had to be. Can't you supervise our ethics from New York City?"

"Apparently not. What?" She arched a brow in challenge. "Were you expecting me to call you when I landed?"

He couldn't stop his smile. That was the Erin he knew. Sharp, smart, sexy as sin.

"Be nice to me or I'll tell Lenny you want to share your recovery story next week."

"Don't worry, there won't be a next week." She glanced over his shoulder at the mingling crowd, then back at him. "Let's get out of here. I'm feeling less anonymous"—she bracketed the word in finger quotes— "by the minute."

He put his untouched coffee on the table and pushed open the door. "After you."

His gentlemanly gesture was self-serving, and he enjoyed a front-row view of her rear end as he followed her up the stairs, through the musty lobby into the humid summer night. They stopped halfway down the path toward the parking lot. He glanced down at the moths clustering around the ankle-height lights embedded in the grass, then back up to find her watching him.

"So." She shifted her weight. "How've you been?"

"Great, if you ignore the three-month suspension and my permanent seat on the bench."

She cringed. "Do these meetings help?"

"If I needed help, maybe, but I don't. I only turn up because it was one of my manager's conditions for staying on the team."

"But don't you think that—" She stopped herself, rephrased. "You had a lot of activity on that betting website. Huge sums of money in and out. All on soccer games."

"Soccer games in Europe," he corrected. "I never bet on my own league. Gambling never interfered with my career or my personal life, and I won far more than I lost. Everyone at these meetings talks about hitting their rock bottom and realizing things had to change, but that didn't happen to me. I had a hobby—a hobby that certain people decided was in violation of some dubious moral code."

He drew breath to say more, then reined himself in. Those certain people were her bosses, now—the Board heavyweights at League headquarters. He shouldn't hold her responsible for their actions.

And he shouldn't assume anything he said wouldn't get back to them. Which reminded him to ask, "What are you doing here?"

She glanced away and back, a sure sign that whatever she was about to say wasn't true. "Oh, just checking it out, seeing how it all works. Some of the league execs want me to start up an anti-gambling task force so I thought I should know what resources are available for players with problems."

He didn't believe a word of it, but he didn't need to say that. She was smart enough to know he saw through her. "Congratulations on the new job, by the way."

"Thanks. And sorry."

"For what?"

"Anything I've done that deserves an apology."

She didn't look away this time. They shared a gaze across the short distance, in the deepening dark, the church grounds hushed and empty.

He weighed what had gone between them, allocated fault like poker chips, assigned each mistake with as much fairness and objectivity as he could muster. In the end, he supposed their piles were pretty equal.

"You're fine," he said quietly.

She exhaled. "Good. We've known each other a long time. Now that I'm here in Atlanta, it might be nice to see each other occasionally. As friends," she added.

He shoved his hands in his pockets. "I'm moving at the end of the year."

"You're leaving Atlanta Skyline?"

"I'm leaving soccer."

Her eyes widened in shock. "Are you serious? Don't tell me Roland fired you over this gambling thing."

"My contract was up at the end of this season anyway. Roland's been looking for a reason not to renew it since the day he inherited me from the previous manager."

"But you could sign with another team. I can think of five other managers who'd love to get you on their roster. You're the best American goalkeeper in a generation."

"Except I'm thirty-three, and there's a whole new generation of players hitting their prime." He shook his head. "I'm done. Time to retire."

Her expression was solemn. "That's really sad, Brendan."

He shrugged. "I've had a good career. Longer and better than most. Everything ends eventually."

"What are you going to do?"

"Head home to Nebraska. I bought a house I'm going to renovate. I'll focus on my family, and on my sports foundation. My brother has—"

"—Down syndrome. I remember. I met him once during college."

He smiled, recalling the confident, ambitious girl she'd been even then. "Of course. Anyway, that's the plan. My house is already on the market."

"Well. I guess we'll have to make the most of the time we have, then."

"I guess we will," he agreed, knowing with absolute certainty they probably wouldn't see each other again for years, if ever.

Soccer was the loose tie that had occasionally tightened to throw them together, but he was stepping out of its range while she got closer to the center with every professional move she made. Within six months she'd be a go-to pundit, the public face of Championship League Soccer, with more hours clocked on news shows than in her brief career as a professional player.

He'd be the guy sitting alone at the bar, pointing to the hot redhead on the screen and telling anyone who'd listen that he used to know her.

"So," she said, articulating in a single word the sense of closure that had suddenly descended on their conversation.

"Good luck in the new job."

"Thanks. Maybe we'll bump into each other before you go."

"Maybe," he offered noncommittally. "Can I walk you to your car?"

"I'm good."

He nodded. Yes, she was. She always had been. "I'll see you around, then."

"Bye, Brendan."

He lifted a hand, then watched her cut across the grass to the parking lot. The headlights of a brand-new sports car flashed and chirped as she unlocked it remotely. A door slammed, an engine revved, and she was gone.

He took his time on the walk to his own car, parked at the other end of the lot. This would be the first of lots of goodbyes, he reminded himself, and probably one of the easiest. No sense in getting maudlin about it.

Still, he lingered beside his car for an extra couple of seconds, enjoying the warm air, the clear night sky, the knowledge that tomorrow he would train with the best soccer team in the CSL.

In three months everything would be different, but tonight he knew exactly where he belonged. He might as well enjoy it while he could.

Chapter 2

"And that's how we can significantly increase match attendance and ticket sales with relatively little capital expenditure. In time, I truly believe this could elevate the profile of the women's game worldwide and expand opportunities for female soccer players for generations."

Erin clicked to the last slide in her presentation: a photograph of three preadolescent girls of different ethnicities, arms linked, soccer balls at their feet, broad smiles on their young faces.

She turned to face the boardroom table, lined on both sides by white men—and one woman—all over the age of fifty. The Executive Board of the Championship Soccer League.

Her heart ran at a pace competing for a hundred-meter world record. Her whole body trembled with nervous excitement and adrenaline, and her stomach informed her there was a very real possibility she might throw up. But she smiled as though no one had told "no"—as though she hadn't spent her entire career hearing that word over and over.

"We have a few minutes left, and I'd be happy to answer any questions."

She looked from person to person. The chief marketing officer smiled encouragingly but said nothing. The deputy commissioner glanced at the clock on the wall. The HR director—the only other woman in the room—stifled a yawn.

Randall Morenski, the chief financial officer, and her line manager, finally broke the silence. "What's happening with the gambling task force?"

She blinked. "Uh, well, I'm reviewing the work that's been done by the regulatory affairs and compliance teams."

He wrinkled his nose. "We can't put that in the annual report."

Had the floor just dropped slightly, or was it her imagination? "I wasn't aware you required any content on the task force for the annual report." Randall smiled wanly as everyone shifted their attention to him. "I know you've only been in the job a couple of weeks—and that your job has only existed for a couple of weeks—so don't worry about not being up to speed on everyone's expectations. Thing is, after the big gambling scandal with that betting website in February, we need to make it clear to our sponsors, our regulators—everyone—that the CSL is taking gambling seriously. It's important for us to show we're cracking down on unethical behavior."

"Understood," she agreed. "Happily, from what I understand of the investigation so far, player gambling doesn't seem to be a pervasive problem. On the other hand, the women's game—"

"But there was that one guy, the local. Plays for Skyline. The leaked data showed he was winning tens of thousands of dollars betting on soccer. What's his name?"

"Brendan Young," she supplied grimly.

Randall snapped his fingers. "Brendan Young. You should speak to the Skyline manager, the Swedish guy—Roland Carlsson. Find out how Roland punished him. Maybe we can include something on that."

"I certainly will," she offered brightly. "But it might be worth bearing in mind that the data breach was six months ago, at the beginning of the season. As far as I'm aware, Brendan completed his suspension and hasn't been off the bench since. I'm not sure there's much more we can—"

"But was that enough?" Randall challenged, brows raised.

"If Roland Carlsson felt his—"

"We need a big bust," he decided. "Something splashy for the annual report, proving the CSL is tough on gambling and tough on players who violate the code of ethics. Take the investigation deeper. See if you can root out any other major gamblers. If not, let's make Young do his penance in a full-color spread."

"Perfect," she lied. "If we can quickly go back to my presentation, I really believe there's still time left in the season to lay the groundwork for a focused women's game promotion campaign next year, and—"

"Sorry, I'm going to have to step out," the executive vice president for Communications announced, rising from his seat.

"I also have a hard stop at eleven." The general counsel was on his feet, and soon the entire Board began to file out of the room.

"Feel free to email me with any questions, or if I can clarify anything further," Erin told the line of departing executives.

"I'll ask Lizzie to find time for us to meet about the task force." Randall gave her a thumbs-up, then followed the others out of the room.

"Fantastic, thanks," she muttered, turning to close down her presentation and unhook her laptop from the projector.

She made her way back to her office with significantly less spring in her step than on her walk into the boardroom an hour earlier. She left her door half-open, dropped into the big leather chair behind her desk and swiveled to stare out her floor-to-ceiling windows at downtown Atlanta. The sky was a brilliant blue and the bright, high summer sun glinted off the skyscrapers. By all accounts, it was a beautiful day.

"Fuck," she whispered. "Fuck, fuck, fuck."

The Board wanted quid pro quo. Fine. She'd taken this job knowing she'd be alone in her fight to improve the women's game, and that the creation of the Director of Ethics and Advocacy position was the league's response to a couple of iffy news stories over the last year. She expected to face ambivalence. Opposition. Even suspicion.

She never expected to face Brendan Young.

The resistance, the lack of buy-in, the full awareness that her appearance probably helped her land this job as much as her experience—she was used to it. She'd been underestimated by people in positions of power since she was ten years old, hovering outside her father's home office while he phoned every boys' traveling soccer team in New Jersey until he found one that would give her a tryout.

Not that it made her special. Every successful female athlete she knew had run a gauntlet of skepticism and pushback. Leaving the game and transitioning to the business side of sports only made it worse. Goals on a scoreboard were indisputable, but professional competence was a lot harder to prove.

Still, she made it. From a low-ranking policy analyst at a think tank to a talking head on major news networks, and now an executive director with a sprawling office and a paycheck to match. She should be delighted. Even if she had to give the Board what they wanted in order to get what she wanted, she couldn't be in a better position to marshal the resources and exposure to finally give women's soccer the boost it deserved.

"Except for Brendan fucking Young," she muttered.

She wasn't the type of woman to have an Achilles' heel, but damn if he wasn't as close as she got.

She leaned back in her chair, remembering the first time she saw him. A naïve freshman in her third week of college—and the product of a parochial, all-girls private high school—she'd had one amaretto sour too many at a soccer party. She was running her mouth, on a tangent about women's soccer, totally oblivious to the predatory attention of two sophomores when Brendan pushed a bottle of water into her hand and led her away.

He'd been kind but slightly aloof that night, and through the next two years they overlapped at Notre Dame before he graduated. She developed a ferocious crush on him but even then she'd had no time to waste on relationships or romantic dramas. When she wasn't sleeping, studying, training or playing...actually she was always sleeping, studying, training or playing. A few seconds of swoony fantasy usually accompanied the rare occasions when she ran into Brendan, but every other minute of her life was dedicated to building her future around soccer.

Erin bit her lip, transposing the cool-headed twenty-year-old he'd been then with the man she'd slept with on New Year's Eve, and then the man she saw last night in the church basement. He still commanded every one of the six feet and four inches that made him especially attractive to a tall woman like her. His ash-blond hair was still thick, his green eyes still piercing, his body the same lean perfection she'd enjoyed over and over again in Las Vegas. But as a college kid, even as a one-night stand, his characteristic calm had always been underpinned with a glimmer of humor. A flash of the unexpected. The potential to be totally surprising.

Instead, he'd seemed weary last night. Drained. Resigned.

Yet not quite defeated.

She exhaled, propping her tablet in its docking station and shaking her mouse to bring the screen to life. Brendan had just about scraped through the gambling scandal with his personal legacy intact. Randall Morenski wanted to change that—and she was responsible for making it happen.

"Can I come in?"

Prinisha, the whip-smart Head of Advocacy she'd pulled over from the think tank, stood in her half-open doorway. Erin nodded.

"How did it go?" Prinisha asked, settling into a chair.

"About how I expected."

Her face fell. "Then they weren't tossing confetti to celebrate the bright future of women's soccer."

Erin shook her head. "No, but they didn't set up roadblocks either, which I saw as tacit approval." She reconsidered. "There is one roadblock."

"What?"

"Morenski wants a big piece on gambling crackdown in the annual report."

Prinisha frowned. "Why? They've already done a four-month investigation that shows gambling isn't a major problem."

"I don't know, but I believe the words he used were 'big bust' and 'splashy'."

"That sounds more like a *Sports Illustrated* swimsuit edition than a year-end report."

Erin shuddered, picturing Randall's beaklike nose and liver-spotted bald head. "Amazing, thanks. Now, whenever I see him I'm going to wonder about the stack of magazines he keeps under the bed."

"Or in the toilet," Prinisha added. "I bet the pages are all stiff with—"

"I can't unthink that and he's my boss, so let's not."

"Sorry," Prinisha offered, although her grin suggested she was anything but. "So, it sounds like if you get Randall his gambling piece, we can expect support for the women's advocacy program. Is that right?"

"That's that gist. If we can't get anything else from the investigation, he wants me to go after Brendan Young."

"Brendan Young," Prinisha repeated, her eyes brightening as the name registered. "The online betting dude. Didn't he get fired from Skyline?"

Erin shook her head. "Suspended, then benched. He's still there until the end of the season."

"So we hang the guy out to dry. Sucks for him, but if that's what Morenski wants, then." She lifted a shoulder.

Erin nodded slowly, her mind working. That was what Randall wanted, and if she gave it to him, she might gain an ally where she had few. She and Brendan hadn't been friends for years, not really—not since he graduated and became one of the most successful American players in the game, signing first for a major club in England, then in Spain. There was no shortage of money and opportunity and attention for a player like him.

But for her? She'd fought for everything she had. There were no lucrative international contracts waiting for her when she graduated, despite being one of the highest-scoring strikers in the history of the college game. She slogged through a few years in the women's side of the Championship League before the microscopic pay rises and empty stadiums became too depressing. Then she traded the dressing room she'd struggled so hard to get into for an office where she was right back at the bottom.

Brendan wouldn't know anything about that. He became a multimillionaire at the age of twenty-two.

She owed him nothing. He had money and an apparently profitable gambling habit he could resume with gusto once he left the sport. He was leaving Atlanta, leaving soccer, leaving the world where she was finally getting a foothold. Even if she had the remotest interest in dating, Brendan would be at the bottom of a long, long list of potential candidates, if for no other reason than it wouldn't exactly behoove the Director of Ethics to be on the arm of the sport's biggest ethical shit-show.

There was no good reason why she shouldn't give Randall his punitive pages and secure her future at the league.

Except for Brendan's smile. That reluctant, almost sheepish quirk of his lips. And the way he'd looked out for her when she was an eighteen-year-old he'd never met before. And his expression as he'd slid inside her in Vegas, that flash of awe and disbelief and sheer delight.

And, of course, that he might be the only person in the world with enough clues in hand to realize that she was a gambler herself. A compulsive gambler. Maybe even a problem—

"You're right," she told Prinisha firmly, shutting down that line of thought. "Brendan's career is over. We might as well dig what we can out of the ruins."

Prinisha grinned. "Where do we start?"

Erin took out her phone and began scrolling through her contacts. "Leave it with me."

* * * *

Brendan returned the security guard's friendly smile as he signed in on the ground floor of the towering building that housed Championship League Soccer.

"Long time, no see." The guard leaned over the side of his desk to buzz Brendan through the security gate. "I thought they were done hauling you in here."

"Apparently not."

He pressed the button for the eleventh floor without having to be told. He'd been to league headquarters more times in the last six months than most players racked up in their careers. The only difference on this occasion was who'd summoned him.

Erin Bailey.

He looped a tie around his neck as the elevator swished up. He'd debated whether he needed it but decided he was better safe than sorry. Who knew, she might spring the commissioner on him.

He wouldn't put it past her. The Erin who lied about why she was at a Gamblers Anonymous meeting wasn't the Erin he knew—or the one he thought he knew, anyway.

The elevator doors slid open, revealing another set of glass doors bearing the CSL logo. The receptionist barely looked up as he entered.

"I'll let Erin know you're here," she informed him. He took a seat on the low couch opposite her desk.

He didn't wait long. He'd barely taken out his phone when Erin appeared in the doorway behind the receptionist.

She wore a tight black dress and her hair was smoothed into some kind of high, complicated knot. Her eyes flicked to his tie and he instantly regretted wearing it.

"Come on back." She nodded for him to follow her, flashing her fake smile.

He trailed her around the edge of the open-plan area to what he gathered was her office. She shut the door behind them and he stopped short, taking in the sweeping view of downtown.

"Nice digs," he remarked as she took a seat behind her desk.

"Thanks. Sit."

But he decided to treat himself to a tour instead. He moved along the wall, studying the framed pictures. Her senior-year college team. Her professional team, New York's Empire Ladies. Her national team, next to which hung—"Wow, you've got it here." He took the frame down from the wall, studying the Olympic gold medal up close.

"Figured I might as well put it where I can see it."

"I never got one of these." He tilted the frame, watching the light play over the gold surface before replacing it on its hook.

"Don't worry, I think your name found its way onto a couple of big trophies in Europe. And from the way the season is wrapping up, maybe onto this year's CSL championship trophy too."

"Doesn't really count if you spent the championship season on the bench." He turned to face her. "Is Donald coming?"

"The commissioner? No, why?"

"Just checking." He unknotted his tie and shoved it in his pocket.

"I thought that was for my benefit."

He shook his head and finally dropped into the chair in front of her desk. "What's this about?"

Her fake smile returned. His heart sank.

"As you know, as the league's Director of Ethics it falls to me to assure our stakeholders—sponsors, staff, even the fans themselves—that Championship Soccer is above reproach when it comes to conduct on the pitch and off. The SportBetNet data breach raised a lot of—"

"Cut the shit," he interrupted. He'd seen her naked—he was entitled to curse in her office. "What do you want?"

Her amicable façade fell away. She sat back in her chair, taking his measure with narrowed eyes.

"I'd like to run a profile on you in our year-end report. The Board wants to show the league is tough on ethical violations, but I think we can spin it to be redemptive. I spoke to your manager this morning, he said you completed all—"

"What do you want from me?" he clarified, impatience tightening his muscles. How many times was he going to be punished for something that only dubiously qualified as an ethics violation?

"I'm doing you a favor," she snapped. "The Board would happily vilify you in high-gloss color. I'm giving you the right of reply and an opportunity to help me help you. If you're not interested, you can leave and I'll give them free rein."

"A favor?" he repeated in disbelief. He shoved his hand through his hair, trying to tie down the heaving fury that threatened to cut loose. "I didn't do anything wrong."

"The Code of Ethics says—"

"The Code of Ethics prohibits match-fixing."

"And it's been amended to say—"

"Amended after the data breach," he pointed out, leaning forward. "Why is the league so fixated on this gambling thing? They allow online betting sites to sponsor teams, so why is it so terrible that I won some money on European fixtures?"

"You didn't just win 'some money,' Brendan. You won thousands of dollars a week. I'm amazed the site didn't cut you off."

Actually, he had a system of rounds so he never withdrew too much from any single site to avoid account closures, but never mind. "You didn't answer my questions."

She sighed, exasperated, signaling she didn't know the answers either. "I'm trying to help you. We're on the same side. As your friend, I want—"

He laughed, and it sounded as cynical and harsh as he felt. "Really. Now we're friends."

The steel in her expression cracked for a split second before firming right back up. "We don't have to be. It's up to you."

"So what happened in Vegas—"

"Stays in Vegas," she confirmed coldly.

He regarded her steadily, trying to come to terms with this new, adversarial dimension in their relationship. He couldn't decide whether this was a professional veneer or really who she was now: an unquestioning enforcer of decisions she knew were wrong.

It didn't matter either way. She'd chosen her position. He had to protect himself.

"I'm disappointed that it's come to this," he told her quietly. "I've paid my dues to the league and don't deserve to be scapegoated further. But if the Board wants more—if you want more—I guess I have no choice but to participate."

Her posture eased with relief. "Thank you. I don't know the details yet—maybe it'll be some kind of community service project we can photograph or an event. I wanted to get you on board first, but now that you are I'll think about how we can illustrate a journey of redemption. I want you to retire with the legacy you deserve," she said earnestly. "I'll make sure that whatever ends up in the report doesn't compromise that."

"Thanks," he said mildly. "It's good to know I have a friend at the league."

"Of course you do." She smiled, maybe more warmly. "Any progress on the move? Is your house still for sale?"

"The first showings are this week." He stood up. "Do you need anything else from me?"

She shook her head, also rising to her feet. "Thanks for coming in. Let me walk you—"

"I know where I'm going."

He got all the way to the door before he reached into the inside pocket of his jacket. He'd hoped he wouldn't have to do this. In fact, he'd hoped he'd be proven totally paranoid about this meeting, and that she'd called him here for a lingering cup of coffee, a few traded memories, maybe even a dinner invitation. He'd hoped he'd been wrong to arrive suspicious and prepared.

He cringed as he withdrew the triple-folded piece of paper from his pocket. Sometimes being right sucked.

"I know you want what happened in Vegas to stay there," he began, pivoting to face her. "But there is something that came back with us."

He recrossed the room, unfolded the page and smoothed it open on her desk.

"I found this on the floor when I was checking out," he explained. "It must've fallen out of your purse. If you want your Gamblers Anonymous cover story to hold water you should probably switch to paperless statements. Or at least leave them at home when you travel."

Erin's eyes widened and her cheeks flushed as she saw what he'd put in front of her: a credit card statement showing ten thousand dollars of debt, most of it generated from a slot-machine app.

To her credit, when she met his gaze and spoke again her voice was calm and even. "Let's be clear. Are you blackmailing me?"

"Absolutely not. Just letting you know what I know."

"And?"

"That's it."

She tilted her head. "That's not it."

He raised his hands in innocence. "I promise. I'll trust you to do right by me with the league, and you'll trust me to keep this between us."

She propped her elbows on her desk, her eyes never leaving him. "I thought you were one of the nicest guys I knew. I had no idea you were such an asshole."

"The feeling's mutual." He nodded to the credit card bill. "You can keep that. It's a copy. I'll show myself out."

He turned and stalked out of her office without a backward glance. He rounded the open-plan desks, giving each person he saw a mental middle finger.

And fuck you, and fuck you, and fuck you...

The receptionist barely acknowledged him as he crossed the lobby and pressed the button for the elevator. When it arrived he stepped aside to let two people out—*and fuck you both, whoever you are*—then punched the button for the ground floor.

As soon as the doors slid shut he raised both middle fingers in a vehement salute. Four years ago the Championship League had coaxed him home from Europe, showering him with praise and money and promising his career would fly just as high in the States as in Spain. That he'd be a big fish in a small pond, and that even as a late-career player he'd get as many games as the young up-and-comers.

Now they wanted to make him the poster boy for players behaving badly. Slap him on the wrist so hard his arm broke. Shatter what was left of his career and mark his retirement not by remembering his achievements but by slamming him for his mistakes.

They could go fuck themselves. He was done bending over. If they insisted on shoving him down, then so help him he'd take their pretty new Ethics Director with him.

Chapter 3

"And the training facilities," Skyline Ladies' left-back added. "I get that the women's game doesn't generate enough money from ticket sales to justify a load of top-of-the-line machines, but some of the stuff we get isn't just secondhand, it's straight-up broken. I don't know the numbers, but it seems like we must be spending so much on maintenance, wouldn't it be cheaper to buy new?"

Erin nodded and glanced at Prinisha, who briskly tapped notes on her tablet.

"Thank you." Erin acknowledged the left-back, then swept her gaze over the room. The full complement of Skyline's women's team sat in various postures around King Stadium's boardroom table, their expressions distributed between eager, expectant, and skeptical.

"I hugely appreciate you all meeting with us and the honesty with which you've shared your concerns." Erin folded her hands on the table. "As a former pro myself, I hope you know that I've experienced most, if not all, of what you're unhappy about. Much of what I'm hearing, though—low salaries, substandard equipment, and facilities, a poor scouting network, limited scholarships—can be traced back to the same thing. Money."

She shifted in her seat. "The ugly fact is that women's soccer generates less revenue through ticket sales than men's. It becomes a vicious cycle. With fewer people in the stadiums, fewer channels are willing to televise games, and fewer companies are willing to sponsor teams."

"So fewer people know about the sport, and even fewer people buy tickets," one of the wingers volunteered.

Erin nodded. "Exactly. Butts in seats, ladies. That's what it all comes down to. So the first step in my plan for next season is to increase visibility.

Not just more publicity for the women's league, but better, smarter exposure. And I want all of you to be part of it."

She leaned back in her chair. "Skyline is one of the best teams in the league in the men's and the women's game. We have Roland to thank for that—he has invested more funds into improving the women's team than any other manager in the league. That makes Skyline the best place to test new marketing ideas."

She glanced at Prinisha, who tapped her tablet to pull up a graphic showing four different campaigns on the wall-mounted screen behind them.

"These are some of the ideas we'll try next year. It's important to target young girl fans, but I want us to reach farther, too," Erin explained. "We're going to launch Dads and Daughters Day, to get more dads active in bringing their kids to games. We're also going to offer group ticket discounts to schools, as part of an overall rethink around pricing strategy. Right now all of the tickets are relatively inexpensive compared to the men's game, but I think we can do more nuanced incentives to increase match attendance."

A chorus of approving murmurs rang around the table. Erin smiled but hesitated to give herself too much credit. She'd have no trouble selling these women on her ideas. The other teams and their sponsors—that was a different story.

Simone Adeolu, Skyline's champion striker, raised her hand. "I guess you've already spoken to Roland about this?"

"Of course. Although he's not technically the women's team manager, that person does report to him so it was important I had his buy-in."

"And he's fine with it?"

Erin grinned, recalling the Swede's earnest insistence that Skyline would commit wholeheartedly to whatever she recommended. "More than fine."

Simone looked hesitant, and Erin gestured for her to say what was on her mind.

"I have a lot of friends at other clubs," the young striker ventured. "I hear what they go through compared to us. I think this is a great plan and I don't want to be Debbie Downer, but what's the likelihood the other teams will get behind this enough to make a difference?"

"That's a totally fair question, Simone. Actually, I'm glad you asked."

Erin took in the attentive faces turned her way as she considered how to phrase her answer. What would she have wanted to hear when she was in their seats?

The truth, probably.

"I'm not going to lie," she stated. "This is an uphill battle. I'm expecting resistance. I'm also expecting to be pretty unpopular for a while. We all know how much teams love the league barging in and telling them what to do and how to do it, so I don't expect a red-carpet reception when I start informing managers they need to spend more on promoting their women's teams."

The players exchanged knowing glances across the table as she continued. "I didn't take this job with the CSL to sit in front of TV cameras looking pretty and toeing the party line. I took it because, like all of you, I've been told 'no' my whole life. Now I'm finally in a position to start saying 'yes,' and I'm going to make sure others do too."

She caught Simone's intake of breath and held up her hands. "I know what you're thinking. It's not always about the will—sometimes it's about the way. Thanks to Roland, Skyline will be getting the best of the best when it comes to executing these campaigns. Glossiest marketing material, most expensive promo slots. But we've developed three tiers for each campaign, depending on how much each club is capable of allocating. The third-tier version is so stripped down, there's no team in this country that can make a case not to afford it."

Simone raised her hand again. "Can I make a suggestion?"

"Please do."

"Again, going off what I know from my friends, have you thought about visiting each team in person? Not that I'm saying they would, but… I wouldn't like to see any of these nice campaign materials stuffed into a trash can because no one understood the big picture."

Erin narrowed her eyes, her mind working. "That's not a bad idea. A prelaunch road show."

"Winning hearts and minds," the goalkeeper chipped in.

Erin glanced at Prinisha, whose expression suggested she was already outlining a travel schedule.

"If we have these meetings before next year, it also gives us a chance to tweak or customize the campaigns," Prinisha mused.

"A face-to-face meeting is always more palatable than a phone call," Erin agreed. "Fantastic thought, Simone." She turned to the rest of the players with a grin. "Keep 'em coming, ladies. What else have you got?"

* * * *

Erin knocked briskly on Randall Morenski's half-open door. His reply was muffled, so she pushed inside on the assumption he'd said, "Come in."

She flashed her most practiced, winning smile, trying to ignore the vastness of his corner office. The walls were busy with photos of Randall posing with famous people, punctuated by a row of degrees. "Can I interrupt you for a minute?"

He turned from his computer and focused on her, seemingly taking a couple of seconds to remember who she was. Then he smiled and motioned for her to take a seat. "By all means."

"I wanted to talk about next year's marketing program for the women's game. I was with Skyline Ladies this morning and they had some great ideas. In particular, I want—"

"Slow down." He raised a palm, giving her one of those self-deprecating smiles that men in positions of power deployed when they were about to be incredibly patronizing. "My memory's not quite as young as yours. Remind me—what marketing program?"

Erin took a calming breath. No problem, let me just sum up my hour-long presentation in thirty seconds since you clearly weren't listening. "The three-tiered publicity campaigns to increase attendance at women's games nationwide next season. I presented it to the Board last week."

He snapped his fingers in recognition. "I remember. I signed off your budget proposal on Monday. You're all funded for next year. Unless you didn't get the email? You may need to remind Lizzie to add your address to the loop."

"I got the email," she assured him. "I wanted to talk to you about—"

"Now that I think about it, Lizzie never put in our rolling meeting about the gambling task force." He scribbled a note on a Post-It, then looked up at her hopefully. "Unless that's what you want to discuss now?"

Her smile faltered, then recovered. She may have dragged her feet in giving Lizzie availability. "I think Lizzie sent me some dates. I'll make sure we get that on the schedule."

"Okay." He folded his hands on his desk. "Shoot."

She sat up straighter, recapturing the courage she'd walked in with. "I know I have budget approval for next year, which I'm looking forward to putting to use. After meeting with Skyline Ladies this morning, though, I'd like to make a case for a small travel budget for this year."

He arched a gray brow. "It's already August. The season ends in October."

"That's why it's important for me to get on the road as soon as possible."

She watched the amiability draining from his expression like water circling a drain. "The road to where?"

"I'd like to do some in-person outreach to the clubs with women's teams. Lay some diplomatic groundwork. Help them understand the value of the campaign while they still have time to get to grips with it, so it's more of a collaboration than a command."

His eyes narrowed behind his wire-framed glasses. "There are ten women's teams in the league. Are you saying you want a budget to cover flights and hotels to visit all of them?"

"Nine. As I said, I met with Skyline this morning." She tried a cheeky, charming grin.

He exhaled. "That's a lot of travel at short notice, particularly approaching year-end. Money is tight this quarter now that we've parted ways with our airline partner."

The airline that decided to distance itself from the league after three of its flight attendants made sexual harassment claims against a CSL player. Yeah, cry me a river.

"Don't worry, I don't expect business class and five-star accommodation."

He snorted. "Somehow I doubt that."

She opened her mouth to protest but he continued, "I know we're waiting for an official meeting, but since you're here, has there been any progress on the gambling task force?"

Her posture stiffened as she recalled her meeting with Brendan. "Some."

"Any breakthroughs? Or is Brendan Young still our number-one offender?"

"I can't give you a conclusive answer at this point," she replied tightly.

He dropped his gaze to the surface of his desk, and when he raised it to hers again his expression was all business.

"The task force is important to me. The success of the women's game is important to you. I'm sure there's a way we can ensure both are given equal priority."

"That was always my intention," she responded evenly.

"Let's not over-commit to your women's-game initiative before we've ascertained whether or not pervasive gambling is a bigger issue in the league. I'll approve each trip on a case-by-case basis, in parallel with updates on the task force. If the investigation is progressing well, I'm sure I'll have no problem signing off on funds for you to travel for meetings with women's team coaches." He smiled. "Will that work?"

It wasn't a question—it was a condition. She gave him the gambling busts he wanted, she got money to travel.

She had no choice but to nod her agreement.

"I'll ask Lizzie to find time for us to meet on Monday. I'll bring a provisional travel schedule and our first formal update on the task force."

"Fantastic," he proclaimed. "I look forward to it."

"Thanks for letting me interrupt."

"Any time." He actually winked as she stood to leave, and if she hadn't spent years practicing her unflappable smile she probably would have gagged. She stormed back to her office, anger building with every step. She managed to shut the door with enough civility not to attract attention, then slammed her fist into her palm as she flopped into her chair and swiveled to face the windows.

Randall's tit for tat was annoying, but nothing new. Every rung she'd mounted on the professional ladder had required some measure of compromise. In college she agreed to participate in a bachelorette auction for the campus newspaper on the condition they dedicated an entire sports page to the women's team. At New York Empire she repeatedly butted heads with the manager about including the Empire Ladies in publicity events until he said, fine—she could appear in a bikini in the men's team's topless calendar.

Moving to the corporate side of sports made the exchanges more subtle but even more frequent. Swiftly ascertaining that the squeaky wheel tended to get fired, she worked twice as hard as her male peers yet shared equal credit and kept her mouth shut when their promotions came more quickly than hers. She trusted that patience and diplomacy were the best routes to the top, bit her tongue so often she couldn't believe it wasn't severed and delivered what her superiors wanted while stockpiling favors.

She'd only been at the league a couple of weeks, though, and her well of loyalty and goodwill was empty. That shouldn't have been a problem—in principle she had no issue with Randall's request and would've eagerly dumped some hapless gambler in his lap to secure her travel budget.

But the only candidate she had was Brendan Young. Who also happened to be the only person in the world with the ammunition to destroy her hard-won career.

She gritted her teeth as for the millionth time she regretted shoving that stupid credit card bill in her purse. She'd flown to Vegas from New Jersey after Christmas at her parents' house. Her mom presented her with a stack of unopened mail as she was leaving for the airport, and after seeing the first bill she'd panicked—she thought she'd switched to paperless statements and had no idea evidence of her compulsive gambling was being delivered to her parents' doorstep on a monthly basis. She'd stuffed the bill in her purse, then paced in front of the boarding gate as she argued with a customer service rep who insisted her paper statements had been canceled and couldn't explain why they were still being mailed.

An uneasy mixture of guilt and relief trailed her all the way to Las Vegas. On one hand, she knew the best way to avoid a repeat of this situation was to finally pull herself together, delete the slot-machine apps from her phone, and begin paying off her credit card debt. On the other, she was triumphant with the heady elation of getting away with it yet again—of keeping her secret and making another narrow escape.

Clearly, that thrill made her careless. She pressed her palm over her eyes and groaned as she imagined Brendan's reaction when he found it. She'd like to think he hadn't cared at that point, particularly after everything they shared that night. But the fact that he'd kept it all this time—waiting, quietly holding on to it, securing himself against some future betrayal—assured her there had never been anything between them except mistrust, foolishness, and a dash of lust.

She exhaled. What was done was done. The fact remained: Brendan was both lock and key to the future of her career.

Now she had to find a way around it.

Around him.

She stared at her magnificent view for ten minutes, not seeing an inch of it as she weighed, measured, and discarded idea after idea.

Erin had to fight fire with fire, she decided, dismissing once and for all the potential for this to be resolved amicably. She tried to be nice and keep their friendship intact. He responded with hostility, so now she would do the same.

She crossed her arms, thinking about their night in Vegas. She kept trying to persuade him to stick money on roulette spins but he resisted, drifting back to the poker and blackjack tables, his easy smile belied by his ferocious skill at both and the towering stack of chips he took away.

It made sense, she supposed—goalkeepers were trained to read the game more deeply than any other player, and to predict their opponents' movements before they made them. If he could read the intentions of a world-class striker, reading an amateur poker player should be a no-brainer.

Not that it did her any good—casino gambling was perfectly within the league's ethics code. Only sports betting was off-limits.

If the articles were to be believed, the sums of money he'd won on SportBetNet were staggering. How did he do it?

More importantly, what was the likelihood he'd actually stopped?

That's where she could get him. He'd paid for his past transgressions, but anything new she dug up would be the weapon she needed to rebalance the scale.

She smiled. She knew just where to start looking.

Erin swept up her tablet from her desk and typed "Brendan Young house" into a search engine. Immediately a gossipy article in one of the local papers popped up—a feature on the grandiose abodes of Skyline's players. Five paragraphs in was a photograph of a handsome, beige-clad house with a generous front porch, accompanied by a description of goalkeeper Brendan Young's Craftsman-style home in the affluent neighborhood of Virginia Highland.

Another few taps on the screen and she found the real estate listing. Six bedrooms, five bathrooms, high ceilings, close to all local amenities.

"One-point-five million," she read aloud.

Nice work if you can get it.

She picked up her cell phone and dialed the number on the listing. A woman answered in two rings.

"Hi, I've just seen a house on your website, a Craftsman-style in Virginia Highland? I'd like to make an appointment for a viewing."

Chapter 4

"We've looked at a couple of other schools. Iveta thinks it'll be too hard for Adela to move in the middle of the year, but I want her out as soon as possible. This anorexia fad amongst her friends scares me to death."

Brendan shook his head sympathetically, pulling on the rowing machine in sync with Skyline's first-choice goalkeeper, Pavel Kovar. "They're only, what, ten? Eleven? How do they even know about that stuff?"

"The stupid internet, I guess," Pavel replied, the words sharpened by his Czech accent. "I had no idea having a daughter would be this complicated."

For a few minutes, they continued their workout in silence, the swish of the rowing machines the only sound in the empty gym.

Brendan considered Pavel's predicament but had nothing to add, and he knew his teammate preferred silence to unnecessary chitchat. On paper he should dislike Pavel, who took his first-team slot when Roland joined and brought the Czech keeper over from Europe. Instead, he resented Roland's decision, not Pavel himself, and over time they'd become solid friends. A steady family man, Pavel always had a litany of domestic stresses ready for discussion, which Brendan found a welcome window into a life much less lonely and isolated than his own.

"How far have we gone?" Pavel spoke first, squinting at the display on the machine.

"Five miles. Keep going."

The Czech keeper groaned but pulled with renewed vigor. Skyline's team training session had ended more than an hour earlier, and they were both eager to wrap up their workout and head home.

They'd made it another half-mile down the imaginary river when the gym door opened. Brendan didn't bother to look up—lots of players stopped in for a workout after training—but when Pavel glanced over his shoulder and then stopped mid-pull, Brendan did the same.

Roland approached them wearing a grim expression, forehead creased behind his stylish plastic-framed glasses.

Brendan groaned inwardly as he let the seat go slack and flexed his calves. He'd never had a bad relationship with a manager until the Swede arrived a year into his Skyline contract. Even then, he thought Roland's reputation for bringing European excellence to American teams would make them fast friends—after all, Brendan had spent years playing in England and Spain.

Yet they'd disliked each other from the moment they met. Roland clearly resented inheriting an expensive player on a long-term contract, and Brendan wasn't thrilled to go from starting every game for Skyline to being displaced by Pavel.

But there was more to it. Brendan chafed under Roland's intense training programs and admittedly could've been more tactful. Even after he'd adapted his style and began shutting his mouth he still felt the manager's suspicion every time they interacted. As though Roland never quite believed the hype around this great American goalkeeper but didn't have enough evidence to do anything about it.

Like now, as the Swede's gaze darted between the mileage on the two rowing machines.

"We're not cheating, I promise," Brendan assured him dryly.

"I've just spoken to Tony," Roland replied, ignoring Brendan's comment as he named the team's medic. "Peter went in for an MRI today."

Brendan's attention sharpened at the mention of Peter Lucas, the young, second-choice goalkeeper Roland pulled up from the academy after the SportBetNet debacle in February. Peter had limped off the training field yesterday and hadn't turned up for this morning's session.

"It's not good news," Roland continued. "He ruptured his Achilles tendon." He and Pavel cringed in unison.

"He thought it was just a sprain," Pavel said, wincing.

Roland shook his head. "Much more serious. He'll be out until next year."

The fact and its implications settled between them with the weight and subtly of an eighteen-wheeler. Upside down. And on fire.

"So," Brendan said unnecessarily.

"So," Roland echoed. "Looks like you'll be watching the rest of the season from the sideline instead of the stands. Be prepared to dress for Saturday."

Brendan fought to keep his nodding reply calm and neutral. "I hope Peter makes a quick recovery. He has a long career ahead of him."

Roland made a sound that seemed to be the vocal equivalent of a sneer, then left the room without another word.

Pavel grinned as soon as the door shut behind their manager. "Congratulations. You've just been promoted to second-choice keeper."

"Apparently." Brendan repositioned his feet on the rowing machine, processing the bombshell that had just fallen into his lap. His elation felt wrong, coming at his teammate's expense.

He'd spent the last six months coming to terms with the reality that he wouldn't retire in the blaze of glory he'd imagined during his eleven years playing professional soccer. His last match wouldn't be marked by a legendary save, a clean sheet, or a guard of honor applauding him on his final trip down the tunnel. Instead, he'd be in the stands with the rest of the squad, anonymous and forgotten, his locker already cleaned out, his cleats hung up for good.

Not anymore.

"Unfortunately for me you have the constitution of a prize bull," Brendan remarked, taking up the rowing-machine handle again.

Pavel shook his head. "I don't understand."

"You never get injured."

His teammate grinned. "For you, I'll make an exception."

"Please, don't." He indicated their twin machines. "Come on, another ten minutes."

Pavel groaned but repositioned himself on the machine.

Within seconds the swish of their workout pervaded the gym. Brendan tried to focus on the sound, on his form, and on the satisfying use of his body. He tried to narrow his awareness, maximize his workout, and push himself as hard as he could, as always.

But his thoughts clamored for attention and his hands trembled and his heart insisted on an erratic, too-fast-too-slow rhythm.

It's not over, he repeated with every pull. It's not over.

* * * *

"Very nice," Erin remarked approvingly as the real estate agent led her through the front door of Brendan's home. On a quiet, residential street, the house occupied a big lot made private by lots of mature trees. As Erin crossed the threshold into the pristine, open-concept living room, she realized the million-plus price tag reflected more than the good location.

"The house is just shy of six thousand square feet," the agent, Marsha, explained, her heels clicking across the wooden floorboards as she led Erin into the kitchen. "Hardwood floors flow throughout. The kitchen was totally redone two years ago, then hardly ever used as far as I understand. Granite counters, stainless steel—"

"Why hasn't the kitchen been used?" Erin interrupted.

The agent smiled, her heavily made-up eyes crinkling at the corners. "The owner's a confirmed bachelor. Luckily he has pretty good taste so it isn't all man-caves and game rooms."

"Big house for a single guy."

Marsha leaned in. "Between you and me, the owner is a professional athlete."

Erin made what she hoped was an appropriately impressed face before returning her attention to her surroundings.

Tick. Definitely the right house.

Erin scanned each room intently as Marsha showed her the rest of the ground floor and then led her upstairs, alert for anything incriminating. The living room, dining room, and first couple of extra bedrooms were all frustratingly bland. In the third bedroom—which had obviously been professionally staged, unless Brendan had the unlikely habit of decorating unused rooms with fresh flowers—she began to wonder if this was a pointless exercise. His house was on the market and open for viewings. Not exactly the context in which he was likely to leave scandalous personal materials or recently dated betting slips lying around.

"And here's the master," Marsha said grandly, pushing open the double doors.

"Finally somewhere that looks a little human," Erin muttered, stepping inside.

The master bedroom was big, so big that one end had been divided into a seating area by brackets of open shelving. As opposed to the boringly neutral choices elsewhere, this room was palpably masculine. Beige carpet, bluish gray walls, and on the large bed a gray duvet folded down over white sheets.

She skimmed her fingers across a pillow, taking in the details of this personal space. She'd known Brendan for years and she'd known him physically, intimately, but as she drifted around his room she realized she didn't really know him at all.

She wandered into the seating area, where an Eames chair was positioned in front of a wall-mounted flat-screen TV. Maybe he spent most of his time in here, and that explained why the living areas downstairs seemed so sterile.

She stood beside the chair, imagining his long frame stretched in front of a soccer game, legs crossed at the ankles.

Her gaze slid to the bookcase. Maybe he was more of a reader.

The shelves were certainly packed. Fat travel guides for countries across Europe, Spanish-language textbooks and a few books actually written in Spanish. Not too many novels, but lots of non-fiction, mostly about sports.

She squinted at a spine on the bottom shelf. *The Zen of Gambling.*

Not exactly damning, but she mentally filed its presence nonetheless.

"I like this." She stood in front of the glass doors leading out to a small terrace overlooking the backyard.

"Wait until you see the bathroom," Marsha promised.

Erin stepped into the en-suite. Like the bedroom, it was oversized and minimal in a manly way, with navy-and-gray mosaic tiling, a huge tub, and a separate, equally large stall shower.

His scent hit her when she opened the shower door, setting off memories strong enough to rock her back on her heels.

Bright yellow lemon. Freshly stained wood. The hint of a distant bonfire carried on an autumn wind.

She closed her eyes, overwhelmed by vivid flashes of recollection. That same scent on his skin when he hugged her at the wedding, her nose brushing his neck above his crisp collar. In the crowded elevator, when he quietly took her hand and she squeezed his big palm, confident the signals she'd sent him all evening had been received. Feeling safe and satisfied as she rolled over in the tangled sheets to find his lazy grin, his mussed hair.

And back in New York, unpacking her suitcase, lifting the dress she wore that night. The smell of him overpowered her then exactly as it did now and she'd dropped to the bed, expensive silk clutched in tight fists as she braced herself, breathed to quiet her racing heart, crossed her legs to ease the sudden pressure between them.

"Did you notice the floating vanity?"

Marsha's voice slammed through her thoughts like a bus running a red light. She propped her arm against the floating vanity in question as receding adrenaline left her weak and unsteady.

Ever since Vegas, the thought of Brendan incited a strange, not totally unpleasant but heart-pounding and then draining physical response. Sort of like stepping off a roller coaster, knees wobbling, jaw tight, totally pumped to ride it again.

Belatedly she realized Marsha was waiting for a response.

"It's great," she enthused hollowly.

"I know!" Marsha pressed her hands together. "Wait 'til you see what he's done with the basement."

As Erin trailed Marsha through the hall, down the stairs, and across the kitchen to the basement door, her adrenaline spike gave way to guilt knotting so fiercely in her stomach she almost doubled over.

What the hell was she doing, spying on Brendan's house, trying to dig up blackmail material? Yes, he'd undermined her favorable impression of his hard body and gentle hands and—focus, Erin—and turned out to be a backstabbing son of a bitch instead, but that didn't mean she should sink to his level.

She reached deep into her stores of empathy, driven by the intimacy of seeing his bed, touching his sink, inhaling his scent.

Maybe he felt cornered when she brought up the year-end report. Maybe he truly believed he did nothing wrong. Or maybe she hurt him more than she realized when she called to insist their one-night stand could never be anything more.

Either way, he didn't deserve this. And she was better than this.

Time to tell Marsha she might buy a condo instead and haul ass out of here.

The excuse was on the tip of her tongue when Marsha pushed open an antique-looking, glass-paneled door at the bottom of the stairs.

Erin took two steps inside and froze.

"Here's where he hides the bachelor vibe," Marsha explained.

"Wow," was the only response Erin could muster.

He'd converted the expansive basement into an authentic English pub. A polished-wood bar ran along one end, complete with a row of taps and shelves of spirits. The floor was carpeted in muted evergreens and clarets and dotted with low, round tables and matching stools. Pennants from his former clubs in Liverpool and Valencia dotted the walls, and although a few high slit windows let in some natural light the space had a pub's cozy fireplace smell.

She moved further inside, then stopped.

On the wall to the right past the bar was a whiteboard, so clinical and huge that its incongruity jarred in the otherwise dim room.

It wasn't the decorating choice that widened her eyes. It was the tight, neat handwriting in bold black marker—and the words didn't advertise drinks specials.

The handwritten grid probably wouldn't mean anything to most people— maybe even to most gamblers. He used acronyms for leagues and teams, abbreviations or initials for players. But she knew the context, and she knew her sport. She knew exactly what she was looking at.

Betting odds.

"Gotcha," she whispered.

"This could easily be converted into a home gym." Marsha appeared at her side. "Or a fantastic cinema room."

"It's perfect exactly as it is. In fact, would you give me a minute? I'd like to soak it all in."

Erin could practically hear the cash register springing open in Marsha's mind. "By all means. Take as long as you'd like. I'll wait upstairs."

The agent's high heels echoed up the stairwell. When she heard the upper door close, Erin focused on the whiteboard.

She shouldn't touch it. Or take a photo of it. Or acknowledge it anyway. She shouldn't even be down here. She should've left five minutes ago.

But if she wanted to march enthusiastically down that road, she shouldn't have scheduled this viewing at all. She shouldn't have dropped her credit card bill in his hotel room. She shouldn't have slept with him in the first place.

Except she had slept with him. And she couldn't un-see this.

What could she do with it? She tapped her finger against her lower lip. It wasn't ironclad proof—he could just be tracking the odds without placing any bets. Not sure what the point of that would be, but nonetheless, it was possible.

She took a step back, physically and emotionally. What did she want? And how far would she take this?

Even if she found something that would ruin Brendan's career, in her heart she knew she'd never use it, not the extent she probably could. She might threaten and allude, but she wouldn't go so far as to share something with her superiors that would see him banned from the league. Not this close to the end—not when she wasn't sure herself that he'd done anything so terribly wrong.

She wanted to scare him. Not destroy him.

But he didn't need to know that.

She picked up one of the black markers in the tray below the whiteboard. The surface was crowded with his precise handwriting and immaculate gridlines, so it took her awhile to find a spot with enough space to make an addition.

Eventually, she found somewhere. One of the matches had been rescheduled, so instead of successive columns for the odds on a home win, an away win, a draw, and whether or not both teams would score, there was a white rectangle labeled with what she assumed was the new date the match would be played.

She crouched in front of the board, uncapping the marker. She wrote carefully, trying to match his handwriting, confident he'd notice the addition but Marsha wouldn't.

Eight letters and a dash. She straightened, pleased with her handiwork.

Hopefully, this would be enough to send him a message and scare him into compliance before things between them got any more complicated.

She replaced the marker and bounded up the stairs, grinning an awful lot for someone about to tell a Realtor she'd decided she couldn't afford such a beautiful house.

* * * *

"Didn't she know she couldn't afford it when she called for the viewing?" Brendan cradled his cell phone in the crook of his neck as he yanked his sports bag higher on his shoulder with one hand and opened the door from the garage into the kitchen with the other.

Marsha sighed. "I'll be honest with you. I think it was the pub."

"The pub?" he repeated incredulously, slinging his bag on the kitchen island and unzipping the top. "The pub is great. Why would anyone not buy the house because of the pub?"

"I warned you it could be a deal-breaker."

"It shouldn't be. It's in the basement. If she doesn't like it, she can pretend it isn't there." He tugged his balled-up workout clothes from the bag and threw them into the washing machine.

"I told you that for this price people want something special. A gym, or a home theatre. Even a guest suite. This was a single lady. Corporate type. What's she going to do with a pub?"

"Drink in it," he suggested, removing his empty water bottle and shoving it in the dishwasher, then moving to the fridge. "Anyway, I'm not sure single ladies are my target market, even if they are the corporate type."

"Really," Marsha said dryly. "Then who is your target market?"

"Families." It was a perfect family home. That's why he bought it.

"And what's a family going to do with a pub?"

Good point, but not one he planned to concede. "I'm not turning it into a gym."

"But you have all that equipment in the spare bedroom. If you just took out the tables and moved in one or two—"

"I'm not doing it. Find another buyer."

"I'll try, Brendan, but—"

"Talk later." He ended the call before she could protest further and shoved the phone in his pocket.

He opened the fridge and stared unseeingly at the shelves.

Were people really put off buying his house because of his pride and joy in the basement? It hadn't been on the market that long and it was something of a specialist purchase at the price, but still...

Brendan shook his head, selecting a bottle of water and a tangerine. Then he pulled a spiral-bound notebook out of his gym bag and tucked it under his arm.

He couldn't think about his house sale right now, not after the bombshell he'd had at training. He still wasn't sure how he felt about Peter's injury, and he needed to clear his head.

He needed to work his odds.

He jogged down the stairs into the basement, his favorite place in the too-big house. He'd built it to look exactly like a down-market pub he used to frequent when he played in Liverpool—one of the few pubs he could enter without being swamped by soccer fans. The regulars knew exactly who he was, but no one bothered him, and it became his oasis in a city—in a country—that was soccer mad.

His chronic, background anxiety and feverish thoughts eased every time he stepped inside his own private public house. If only he could make it smell slightly mustier and pay some grumpy old dudes to slump at the bar all day, he'd never know he was in Atlanta instead of England.

He placed his water and tangerine on the bar and took a seat on the last stool, perfectly positioned to glance between the whiteboard and his notebook. He flipped through pages creased and indented with dense handwriting to the one he'd started that morning. He picked up a pen from beside the bar mat and settled in to study his odds, hand poised over the paper.

He flexed his hand, his whirring thoughts already slowing as he scanned the board. His shoulders relaxing, he mentally stepped into the methodical, long-standing routine of calculating and recalculating odds that had been better for his anxiety than anything a psychiatrist ever tried.

"Anxiety"—that was his favorite diagnosis of the several he'd had since he was a teenager and his cyclical, ultra-focused thought patterns became so intense and intrusive that he stopped sleeping. For as long as he could remember he'd had hyper, scrolling thoughts, like an unending stock ticker running behind his eyes. He unconsciously and instantaneously evaluated every angle of a situation and calculated the probable outcomes. As a child, he knew which slice would be biggest from the slant of his mother's arm as she cut a cake, and immediately called dibs. If he crossed an intersection he instinctively took stock of how many cars were approaching from which directions and the likelihood that any of them intended to turn without signaling, based on a snap scan of their positions in their lanes.

Sometimes it was useful. His immense capacity for concentration meant he was an outstanding student, and his naturally heightened awareness and super-fast reaction times made him a star athlete from a young age. He first excelled as a Little League catcher but found his true love when he joined a rec soccer team. After only a handful of games his coach told his mom to find him a real club, and a week or two later he was the youngest player on a highly competitive traveling team. Assessing his height, speed, and uncanny ability to read his opponents' intentions, his coach immediately put him in goal.

More often, though, his unusual thought patterns meant he lived with a veering, uncontrollable brain and a constant sense of worry. Because he could predict a full range of outcomes for any given circumstances, he often had negative, fearful thoughts. In the car he braced himself for what felt like inevitable crashes. He'd anticipated fistfights around every corner at school, and he developed an irrational paranoia about failing to complete an assignment or study for a test and spectacularly flunking out.

After turning in three weeks of math homework early—and then falling asleep in class—his teacher called his mother, who took up the cause of his suspected mental illness with the same gusto she'd used to fight for his older brother's dyslexia diagnosis and champion his younger brother, Liam, who had Down syndrome.

He and his mother completed a circuit of every psychologist and psychiatrist in the greater Lincoln, Nebraska, area and received verdicts ranging from adolescent hormones to obsessive-compulsive disorder. He began to resist his mother's attention and downplayed his symptoms. Steadily she backed off, and he transitioned from hiding his problem to developing techniques to control it, to maximize the upsides and minimize the downsides.

By the time he graduated from high school he'd become a master of mental self-regulation. For the most part, he simply matured enough to be able to talk himself out of his worst thought spirals, and when the noise in his head became too much he quieted it by working ahead in his calculus textbook, channeling his focus onto the complex equations. In college he took his first statistics class and was instantly hooked, gulping down modeling theories, filling entire notebooks with calculations while setting records on the soccer pitch.

He finished college in May and in July he was in England, twenty-two years old, with more money than he knew how to spend and fiercer competition on the pitch than he'd ever imagined. He bought advanced statistics textbooks but still struggled to control his increasingly intrusive thoughts—until he walked past one of the storefront betting shops that were legal in the UK.

That afternoon he sat in a pub for three hours, drinking juice, analyzing the players in the Italian league, researching their past performances and assessing their chances in that weekend's match schedule. He filled out a betting slip and handed it into the shop with a modest wager.

He tripled his money.

Of course, his system didn't have the same soothing effect now that he couldn't place any real bets. As soon as the data leaked from SportBetNet he shut down all his accounts and hadn't wagered a cent since. He'd thought about it, and he'd gone as far as entering his credit card details into one site or another, but always changed his mind in the end, reminding himself the day after his contract expired he could gamble every hour of every day if he wanted.

In the meantime, he had his homemade pub, his notebooks full of calculations, and his master fixture chart on his whiteboard.

He scanned a page as he unpeeled the tangerine, looking at the anticipated team sheets for upcoming English matches. He popped a segment into his mouth and chewed thoughtfully, opting to look at one of the London rivalries first. His thoughts settled into a calm hum as he went down the lists of players, weighing each one's recent performances, injuries, intersection with other players, long-term records against this opponent, track record of conduct in emotionally charged pairings like this one...

He decided it would be a draw, either 1-1 or 0-0. He glanced up at the whiteboard to see the odds bookies were offering on both scores, squinting at the chart—and dropped the tangerine on the floor.

Gotcha—EB

He ground his teeth as he put the pieces together.

A young, single woman viewing his house.

EB.

Erin fucking Bailey.

He snatched up his phone and redialed the Realtor, then stormed up the basement stairs as he listened to it ring.

"Hi again, Brendan."

"What color hair did she have?" he demanded, stalking across the kitchen.

"I beg your pardon?"

"The viewer today. Was she a redhead?"

"Actually, yes. Why? Do you know her?"

He ended the call without another word and turned his phone upside down on the counter, ignoring its buzzing as Marsha called back.

He paced a directionless circle around the kitchen, shoving his hand through his hair as his anxiety amped up from a background hum to a breath-quickening whine.

Less than two hours ago his career had gotten its biggest boost in months when he'd been promoted to the second-choice keeper. Now it teetered on the edge of failure again, with Erin poised to push it off the cliff.

He couldn't believe she had the audacity to sneak into his house and spy on his personal space in some sick attempt to double down on this antagonistic game they'd fallen into.

Scratch that—yes, he could. He should've known she'd retaliate. He was stupid to think this had ended in her office.

He stopped pacing and forced himself to pull his thoughts into a coherent line. There was no defense he could use without implicating himself. He couldn't call her boss, he couldn't call the press. Any effort to expose what she'd done would send her straight to the league with what he guessed was photographic evidence of an ongoing gambling habit. He'd never be able to convince them he hadn't actually placed any bets—how could he prove a negative? That would be the end of any sliver of redemption he might grab over the next couple of months.

He had to hand it to Erin. She was smart, strategic, and knew exactly what she was doing. She'd made a brilliant move in their personal chess match. He never saw it coming.

It would've been kind of sexy, actually, if it wasn't so infuriating.

He flattened his palms on the counter as he made a decision. He couldn't out-connive her, nor did he especially want to. But that didn't mean he would give up.

He retrieved his phone, swiping to dismiss Marsha's three unanswered calls. He scrolled to a number and tapped to call.

"Good afternoon, Erin Bailey's office, Suzanne speaking."

"Hi, Suzanne. This is Brendan Young."

"Mr. Young, hello. I'm afraid Erin's in a meeting, may I take a message?"

He drummed his knuckles on the cool granite. "No. But you can do something else for me."

Chapter 5

With the air of a warrior preparing for battle, Erin reapplied her lip gloss, then fluffed her hair. Satisfied her armor was fully in place, she snapped shut her compact mirror and shoved it in a drawer, then checked the time.

Four minutes until her meeting with Brendan.

She hadn't even flinched when the meeting appeared in her diary, nor did she bother to give Suzanne a hard time when her young assistant revealed that she'd forgotten to ask what it was about. She knew exactly why Brendan was coming to her office, and she was ready for him.

She didn't have a plan, but she had a goal. She wanted the scales to tilt back in her favor. For him to back down, quietly go along with her concept for the annual report and slink off into oblivion.

Surely that wasn't too much to ask.

The phone on her desk rang. She punched the speaker button.

"Mr. Young is here to see you," Suzanne announced.

Mr. Young. Erin rolled her eyes. "Send him in."

She moved to her wall of windows, crossed her arms and turned her back to the door. A clichéd posture, yes, but for good reason. It exuded superiority.

Behind her the door clicked open and shut. She didn't bother to glance over her shoulder, knowing full well who was in the office with her.

"Brendan," she stated evenly.

He laughed, and she spun at the derisive sound.

"What is this, *The Wolf of Wall Street*?" he asked, arching a brow.

Her cheeks heated but she kept her expression cool—no easy feat when she took in a full, sweeping view of the man before her.

Damn, he's hot.

He'd ditched the formal attire and wore slim-fitting jeans and a thin T-shirt that hugged the contoured muscles in his arms and shoulders. His hair was slightly mussed, his eyes hard and clear as emeralds, his mouth set in a tight line.

She ached to kiss him.

"What can I do for you?" she asked instead, gesturing to one of the chairs in front of her desk as she took her seat behind it.

He remained standing. "You crossed a line yesterday."

She tilted her head. "Which one, exactly?"

"Don't play dumb. I know what you did."

"There's the rub. I know what you did, too. Are still doing, I think it can be fairly assumed."

He shook his head. "I work the odds. That's all."

"You don't bet on them?"

"Not for months, no."

"That's hard to believe."

"Doesn't matter. It's true."

She sighed in exasperation to cover her surprise. She expected him to come in and insist that gambling wasn't immoral, not that he wasn't doing it. What was the point of all those detailed, meticulous, crazy-person-handwriting calculations if there was no money involved?

Yet for some bizarre, gut-level reason, and despite practically catching him red-handed, she didn't think he was lying.

"All that work, all those probabilities—you're telling me they're just for fun?"

His expression faltered slightly, then toughened again. "Yes."

"That's insane."

He lifted a shoulder.

She sat straighter, regrouping. This wasn't about his motivation or even whether or not he wagered money in contravention of league rules. This was about making him do what she said.

"Frankly, it doesn't matter. Anyone who sees what I saw will assume you're betting. It's more than enough evidence to get you booted out of Skyline and discredited forever. No one reads the follow-up stories, they just remember the headline. Do you want to go down in history as a goalkeeper or a gambler? This is your moment to choose."

"I've been choosing for eleven years," he insisted, taking a step closer. "It's my legacy. Not yours, not the league's."

Guilt bleated at the back of her mind. She shoved it aside. "It doesn't work like that, I'm afraid. Maybe they'll remember you differently in

Liverpool or Valencia, but unless you're planning to move back to Europe I suggest you get on board."

"With what, my own scapegoating?"

"Not if you cooperate. I'm willing to pitch an idea to the Board that will focus on your service, not your mistakes." She leaned back in her chair, preparing to elaborate on the plan she'd formulated last night. "I know you've done a lot of work with people with intellectual disabilities. If we can spin that into some kind of—"

"You're not spinning a goddamn thing," he demanded, his tone suddenly harsh and sharp with anger.

She rose from her chair. "May I finish?"

"No." His entire body was stiff, his brows drawn together. "I've been advocating for sports for players with intellectual disabilities since I was an undergraduate. It's more important to me than any trophy I've ever won. I will not let you turn it into some bullshit public-relations drivel."

"It's not bullshit," she replied testily, her heart rate increasing as she stepped out from behind her desk. "And it's the best offer you're going to get."

"Shoehorning fifteen years of volunteering and investment and dedication into an article about how I'm so sorry I placed some bets online is no offer at all."

"Beggars, choosers," she spat back.

He inhaled to speak, then seemed to second-guess himself. She crossed her arms and propped her hip against the desk, waiting.

"Why are you doing this?" he asked finally. "You know me. You know I'm not who the Board is trying to make me out to be."

Fury exploded into her chest like a burst pipe. She stepped up to him, fists clenched, their bodies inches apart.

"Are you kidding me?" she demanded. "You're the one who kept my credit card bill like a stalker, then waved it in my face when I was prepared to go to bat for your shitty reputation. I don't know you at all. You brought us to this point, not me."

"I'm a stalker?" he asked, incredulous. "You snooped my house."

"Because you pushed my back against the wall," she countered. "You lit the match. I just fought fire with fire."

He snorted. "Is that what you tell yourself? Does blaming me make you feel like less of a vindictive psychopath?"

She met his cold stare without wavering. She couldn't believe she'd slept with him. Couldn't believe she'd been stupid enough to give him that power, even if only for a night. Couldn't believe she still thought about doing it again every single day.

"Be careful," he warned, his voice barely above a rumble. "Your career is just taking off, but mine's almost over. Don't underestimate a man with nothing to lose."

They stood in mutual antipathy for one, two, three, four long seconds, each poised for the other to break first. Then she made a terrible mistake.

She looked at his lips.

He saw it.

The atmosphere in the room changed completely. Heat overran hostility, and the charge between them shifted from rancor to crackling attraction. Delicious tension fisted in the center of her chest, then worked its way down through her stomach, her lower abdomen, and settled tightly between her legs.

He held his aggressive stance, but lust flickered in his eyes. She recognized it, remembering the first time she saw it in Vegas. She'd cajoled him into putting twenty dollars on a roulette spin. He started verbally working through the probabilities of landing on one number, two numbers, three numbers, so she grabbed the twenty, plunked it on black and told the croupier to spin.

She doubled his money. He turned to her, mouth slightly ajar, eyes wide, lust burning in their green depths. At that moment she decided to have sex with him. Her New Year's gift to herself.

Her nipples tightened inside her bra as she recalled the warm press of his hands, the solid weight of his body, the heavy, stretching fulfillment of him between her thighs. She swallowed.

He saw that, too.

His gaze dropped to the hollow at the base of her throat and made a slow, lazy ascent back to her face. His jaw was looser but his expression more focused, and as he dipped his head almost imperceptibly closer she wondered what he was thinking about.

Maybe—like her—he remembered that first kiss in the elevator, the insistence with which he'd pushed her against the wall the second the doors banged shut after the last guests stepped off.

Maybe he was reliving the way he'd shoved the cups of her bra out of the way and scooped her breasts out of the V-neck top of her dress before lowering his mouth to taste each one in turn.

Or maybe he was thinking about what happened in the shower when she'd stroked him so slowly, so lingeringly, with such stubborn refusal to give him what he wanted that he had to brace himself against the tile and repeat her name in a broken, pleading voice.

She heard his breath quicken in the silent office. She stole a glance at his zipper and permitted herself the hint of a smile at the strain she saw there.

She inched closer, her skirt whispering against the denim of his jeans. She arched her back slightly, giving him a faint view of the now achingly hard points of her breasts.

He moved swiftly, decisively. Raised his hand to cup the back of her neck, the skin bare below her upswept hair. Her breath caught in her throat and the complexities of their situation, the games and maneuvers and goals and highest of high stakes all vanished from her mind.

She wanted to kiss him. She wanted him to touch her. She wanted him inside her and she didn't care where or how or when as long as it was soon, very very soon.

He brought his cheek against hers. She closed her eyes at the faint scrape of stubble, drowning in the scent of him, wood smoke caught in denim on a crisp fall morning.

His lips brushed her ear and he whispered, "Neither of us deserves this."

Her eyelashes fluttered shut as she luxuriated in the deep, warm vibration of his voice. "Speak for yourself."

"You know it as well as I do." His lips skimmed the line of her jaw and her hands found his waist, twisting her fingers through his belt loops.

"We're sinners, you and I," he murmured. "You saw my chart. I saw your debt."

She shoved him away, his words sizzling across her nerves like ice-cold water tossed on glowing coals.

"We're nothing alike," she clarified sternly, taking two big steps backward. "You put your career and reputation on the line for a stupid vice. I had to build an image—an expensive image—without ever having pulled down the sort of money you did as a player. Not because I wasn't as talented or as successful, but because even the best woman doesn't get paid anywhere close to the worst man."

He crossed his arms, slamming the door on whatever accord they'd briefly shared. "Four hundred dollars on a slot-machine app in one day. Are you blaming that on systemic inequality?"

Shame closed an icy fist around her neck. Over the last few years what started as a fun, diverting stress reliever with the added benefit of occasionally pocketing some extra cash had spun completely out of control. She knew that. She also knew she was getting it back under control, one day at a time. She hadn't even opened the app since… Okay, yesterday had been a stressful day so she'd taken a couple of spins at lunchtime, but before that—anyway, it wasn't relevant to this conversation.

"Let's be clear that you're referring to my personal, private information which you had no right to access," she reminded him primly.

"The personal, private information you left in my hotel room."

"And which you held on to for six months."

He shrugged. "You said you didn't want to see me again, so I didn't have a chance to give it back."

A bolt of guilt raced toward her heart but she halted it mid-trajectory. He wanted her to feel bad. She wouldn't give him the satisfaction.

"Why are you here?" she asked instead. "What do you want?"

"For you to back off."

"Not happening."

"You know if you don't, I'll—"

"You're not in control anymore, Brendan. Deal with it." She dropped into her chair, resuming her position of power in the room. "You have nothing more on me than I have on you. And to be honest, you probably should've thought of that before you waved that credit card bill in my face. It's not a good idea to threaten to open other people's closets when your own is packed full of skeletons."

He shook his head slowly, his face settling into an expression so cool and composed that a kernel of worry formed in her chest. Had she missed a move in this game?

"You still don't get it," he said quietly. "The stakes aren't even. We have different bets on the table. You have a hell of a lot more chips to lose than I do."

She rolled her eyes to disguise her sudden uneasiness. "Make life easy for yourself. Go along with the plan for the year-end report. Just cooperate and I'll make sure you come out looking good. I promise."

He shoved his hands in his pockets, silently studying the floor. He stood like that for so long that she was tempted to tap her foot under her desk or drum her fingers, but she knew that's what he wanted. He may be a great goalkeeper, but she'd been a hell of a striker. She was trained to keep her next move a secret from him as intensely as he was trained to spot it.

So they remained, in unmoving deadlock, for nearly five minutes. At least she gauged it to be about five minutes—she didn't dare glance away from him in case she gave away her impatience.

He broke the stalemate, dragging his gaze up from the carpet to meet hers. His eyes were unreadable, but determination set his shoulders.

"Don't push me," he told her finally. Softly. Evenly.

She didn't blink. "I'll push as hard as I want."

They sized each other up for another handful of seconds, two masters of inscrutability facing off across sky-high odds. Then he turned abruptly and left her office, the door closing behind him with a gentle click.

She exhaled so heavily her head spun. She rushed to her feet on a surge of adrenaline, walking back to the windowed wall and crossing her arms over her chest.

She'd won that round. She thought. Hoped.

He had a point about their respective chips to lose, but she was pretty sure he was bluffing. If he didn't care about his legacy he wouldn't have bothered to go this far to protect it. He had, so he did, and that meant the scale was still weighted in her favor.

The risk was whether she'd missed something, but there was nothing she could do about that now. She had to believe he'd do the right thing. Agree to her terms and let them both move on relatively unscathed. If not, the consequences were unthinkable.

So she wouldn't think about them, she decided, returning to her seat and clicking to open her inbox. She wouldn't think about her disgrace if that credit card statement became public, or the tailspin into which it would throw her career, or the abject shame of her parents finding out...

He sees everything, her traitorous thoughts reminded her.

She flattened one bracing palm on the surface of her desk, waiting to feel something—anything—at a level appropriate to the situation. Fear. Anxiety. Anger. At least one of them should be surging through her body at this point.

Nothing.

She swiveled away from her desk and picked up her phone, scrolling to the same slot-machine app that had gotten her into this trouble in the first place. She should give up, she knew, but these were exceptional circumstances. Stressful circumstances. Unprecedented, unlikely-to-be-repeated circumstances for which she could justify a few minutes of playing.

Five spins, she assured herself as she scrolled to her account details, double-checking that she'd loaded a credit card that hadn't reached its limit. Just enough to get that rush. To put a crack in this icy, numb wall.

She navigated back to the main screen and tapped to spin.

No matches.

One spin down, four to go. She tapped again.

Two cherries and a seven. Closer.

She tapped again. Three more spins. Or until she'd lost five dollars. She'd skip her fancy coffee on Monday morning.

Or seven dollars. Seven wasn't much. She'd skip her coffee on Monday and Tuesday.

Okay, until she'd lost ten dollars, but no more. The free coffee in the lunchroom was fine, anyway.

Or fifteen dollars. Fifteen dollars was her hard limit, not a cent more...

Chapter 6

"Clear it! Goddammit, Kojo," Brendan muttered to himself as Skyline's right-back headed one of Miami's passes dangerously close to his own goal. One of the academy players—also on the bench for the first time this season—looked at him warily but said nothing.

It had been a hell of a reintroduction to the Skyline rotation. His warm reception in the dressing room eased any nerves he had about whether he'd be accepted in the squad after so long on the sideline. Every one of his teammates made a point to shake his hand, slap his back or otherwise acknowledge his return as he dressed in his teal uniform, a deliberate contrast to Skyline's brick-red and navy. He had no reason to suspect any of them would be less than thrilled to see him—he'd been training with them all year—but nonetheless, it was nice to have his own muted delight reflected in the men around him.

He wasn't a bad guy, despite how the league—and Erin—wanted to portray him.

Any lingering preoccupation about how exactly they were going to resolve the nagging issue of the year-end report had been soundly eradicated by the insane events of the match at Skyline's King Stadium. Miami were strong opponents and it had been a closely fought game. Then shortly after halftime, some unhinged spectator threw road flares onto the pitch in what had subsequently been determined to be an Islamophobic attack on Skyline's left-back, Oz Terim.

Brendan had surged to his feet alongside his teammates, with only the potential for penalization and Oz's own waved assurances keeping them from storming the pitch. Although play resumed, the mood in the stadium was a taut mix of fear and fury.

Unsurprisingly given the disruption, Skyline's performance in the final thirty minutes could generously be called uneven, and more accurately called shit. The players were clearly shaken, their concentration shattered, and while Brendan admired Oz's decision to finish out the match he was, quite frankly, useless. Thankfully Miami had the decency to more or less play around him, but as a linchpin in the back half of the team, his mental absence was palpable.

With twenty minutes still on the clock and the score at a thinly held one-one, Roland nodded for three of the reserve players—two defensive and one attacking midfielder—to start warming up.

Brendan registered slight disappointment as the three men bounced up from their seats. Their inclusion made sense—Skyline was in no position to score again and both players would bolster Oz's weakened left side—but on some consciously unlikely level he'd had a sliver of hope he might get to see a few minutes' action.

Why Roland would substitute his superstar goalkeeper for the inadvertent second-choice option he didn't even like, he had no idea. But he'd hoped nonetheless.

The manager called over the fourth official as the three midfielders stripped off their neon substitutes' vests. The referee raised the electronic board, calling off his exhausted attacking midfielders, Nico Silva, Laurent Perrin, and Rio Vidal, and sent three sets of fresh legs into the fray.

Brendan leaned back in his seat, shoving aside the closed door of that opportunity and focusing on the match. His gaze darted left and right, forward and back, taking in Miami's formation, assessing his own teammates' positions. From between his goalposts, Pavel shouted and gestured, organizing the new players and instructing the center-backs to pull in to support them. Brendan cringed as Pavel called a question to Oz—one of the best left-backs in the league—only for the defender to turn too late to answer, his dazed expression confirming that his thoughts were a million miles away.

Fifteen minutes to run and Miami redoubled their efforts to score a second goal, clearly seeing a chance to win a match in which a draw would otherwise have been a decent result for these two top-ranked teams. They had a high-profile, American striker whom Brendan had briefly played alongside in the national team, and although he was quick and powerful, he was as subtle as a low-flying police helicopter.

"Shift up," he commanded his teammates under his breath. He could already see the path through which Miami could route the ball, the angles left uncovered by sluggish Skyline players, the striker's positioning to head one into the net. Yet one of Skyline's Brazilian center-backs, Guedes, threw himself downfield at a Miami midfielder.

"You're too late, Guedes," he insisted, wringing his hands between his knees. "Forget him, the ball will be halfway up the pitch by the time you get there."

Unfortunately, he was right. Guedes slid into the midfielder with a sloppy tackle that was so late the referee had no choice but to call a foul.

Brendan slapped his hands over his face. A collective groan rippled along the bench. The Miami players arranged themselves to take a free kick.

A quick sweep of the two teams' formations—including Oz's blank stare and the two Miami forwards' totally readable efforts to conceal which one of them would take the kick—and he knew this wouldn't end well. He slid his hand over his eyes and listened to the reaction of the crowd. The sharp intakes of breath and exhaled sighs of relief suggested the ball got dangerously close to finding its mark.

Eyes open again, he watched Miami press hard into Skyline's area. He fisted his hands and drummed his cleats on the concrete slab beneath the substitution seats, his gaze moving restlessly. Skyline and Miami were likely choices for the league final, and a one-one finish meant both teams walked away on equal footing.

"Don't drop a point now," he urged his teammates, glancing between the dwindling time on the clock and the tight, consolidated play in Skyline's half. "Ten minutes. You can hold them off for ten more minutes."

Ten minutes plus extra time, he considered grimly. But surely the referee wouldn't give too much for the disruption earlier. That would be a distinct advantage for Miami, considering Skyline were the victims in that incident and their traumatized, targeted player was still staggering around the pitch. The ref couldn't possibly—

"On your right," he shouted uselessly, anticipating Miami's winger's run toward the goal half a second before Pavel did.

Pavel raced out to meet the winger, diving to stop the ball as it left his opponent's foot. In the same instant, one of Miami's central midfielders broke free from Kojo's effort to mark him and hurtled toward them.

Brendan saw the impact before it happened, practically felt it in the millisecond between knowing the midfielder's momentum was unstoppable and then watching it happen.

Pavel caught the ball on the ground and curled over it. The Miami midfielder twisted to avoid him but caught the goalkeeper with his boot, inadvertently kicking him squarely on the side of his head.

Brendan shot to his feet, his nerves alight with concern. He craned his neck to get a glimpse of Pavel, who lay flat on his back, unmoving.

The midfielder responsible for the blow waved over the medics, who jogged across the pitch wearing latex gloves. Both teams stood in loose, idle formations, worry for the goalkeeper obvious in their stiff shoulders and nervous glances. There were two injuries that haunted players more than any others: broken legs and kicked heads. No one could stand at ease on the pitch or the sideline, as each one of them realized it could just as easily be their body prone and motionless on the grass.

"They're taking a long time," the academy player on his right remarked. "Is he okay?"

"I don't know," Brendan muttered, worry tightening his chest.

The clock ran down to single digits and still the medics didn't give the signal for play to resume. With their backs facing him, Brendan couldn't tell what was happening, but he suspected it wasn't anything good. A glance at Roland's face confirmed his fears. The manager frowned deeply behind his glasses.

Finally, one of the medics twisted, but instead of nodding to the referee he motioned for a stretcher.

If the mood in the stadium had dropped any lower it would've been underground.

The match resumed listlessly as four medics carried Pavel off the field. Brendan stood at the edge of the substitutes' area, trying to get a glimpse of his friend as he was taken down the tunnel, but all he could see between the medics' navy jackets were his teammate's gloved hands folded on his chest.

The substitutes eased into their seats as center-back Paulo took Pavel's place in goal. Both teams were visibly shaken and even though the referee added six minutes of extra time, neither side made much use of it. Skyline passed backward amongst themselves and Miami didn't press for possession. Between the Islamophobic attack and what looked like a catastrophic injury, it felt like everyone in the stadium just wanted to go home.

A ripple of hushed murmurs began at the other end of the sideline at the same time as one of the assistant managers stepped up to Roland's elbow and muttered something in his ear. Players shifted and fidgeted as information spread down the line, and after a couple of minutes, Brendan twisted to look at Nico Silva, seated behind him.

The Uruguayan midfielder's face was white.

"Skull fracture," he said hoarsely. "They had to call an ambulance. He needs emergency surgery."

"Jesus Christ." Brendan crossed himself and closed his eyes, taking a second to send up a prayer that Pavel would be okay. He thought of his teammate's wife, his preadolescent daughter, the domestic niggles Pavel always complained about in training. Only two days earlier Brendan heard all about the problems he was having with algae in his pool.

It hadn't been a terrible tackle, a late challenge, or even one of the accidental but harmless collisions they all had with other players, including their own teammates. By all accounts the angle was innocuous—a midfielder running down a ball, a goalkeeper leaning out to stop it.

A second's calculation. A fluke impact. Now Pavel's life may be changed forever.

He shared a sickened head shake with Nico, then turned numbly back to the pitch, where a minute remained on the scoreboard. As he redirected his gaze he happened to make eye contact with Roland. The manager's face was stony but resigned.

They both knew what this moment meant.

Skyline's number-three goalkeeper was now number one.

* * * *

"Oh my God." Erin set down her glass with such force that red wine sloshed over the edge. She bent forward to mop it up with the wad of paper napkins that arrived with the Chinese food while keeping an eye on the TV.

Her sister glanced up from her phone. "What happened?"

"Atlanta's goalkeeper just got nailed in the head." She sucked in air between her teeth, watching medics rush out onto the pitch.

"This game is totally wild," Maggie decreed, putting down her phone and picking up her glass of wine. "We're still going out after this finishes, right?"

"Sure," Erin promised distractedly, her gaze fixed on the screen. Maggie had flown down for the weekend, ostensibly to check out her older sister's new home, but mostly because her newlywed husband was away for a two-night bachelor party. They'd relocated to St. Louis for his biotech career a few months earlier and although Maggie insisted she loved it, Erin knew even before their boxes were unpacked that she hated it. She missed her friends, her job, and her horse, and although she was halfheartedly looking for a new role in events management and her husband was working on the logistics of relocating her champion show jumper, she seemed to be striking out in the friend-making initiative.

Now that Maggie realized Atlanta was only a ninety-minute flight—and that her sister had a reasonably comfortable pullout couch and a host of nightclubs on her doorstep—Erin suspected she'd be having a houseguest fairly often.

"He looks really badly hurt," Maggie commented as the goalkeeper stayed on the ground.

"Getting kicked in the head like that is every player's worst nightmare." Erin shuddered at the thought.

"Will he be okay?"

"I hope so."

For a few minutes, they watched in silence, sipping their wine as the goalkeeper was carried off on a stretcher, picking at what was left of their Chinese takeout until the game finally reached its conclusion.

"And news from the Skyline camp is that goalkeeper Pavel Kovar has been taken to the hospital by ambulance with a suspected skull fracture," the announcer shared grimly. She and Maggie winced in unison.

The camera swung to show various players from both teams shaking hands over the one-one score, the managers embracing briefly, and then a quick shot of the substitutes' bench as the sidelined players stood to exit down the tunnel.

It was barely a second's glimpse, but it confirmed the suspicion that had gnawed at her from the moment Skyline's goalkeeper went down.

Brendan had sat in reserve for this match. Peter Lucas must not be expected back this season.

And with Pavel Kovar appearing to be seriously injured, that automatically bumped Brendan into the starting lineup—the starting lineup of a team on a nearly certain trajectory to the league final.

Power streamed through her, heady and intoxicating. In her office Brendan said she couldn't take anything more from him than was already gone. He had nothing left to lose.

Now he had everything. She could take it all.

"See that guy?" Erin pointed to Brendan's distant, departing back. "I went to college with him."

Maggie squinted at the screen, then leaned back in recognition. "Oh, yeah. Bradley Young?"

"Brendan."

"I remember you talking about him. I think I met him at one of those family things on campus. And didn't you see him at that wedding you went to in Vegas at New Year's?"

"I did," Erin affirmed. "I didn't realize I'd mentioned that."

Maggie nodded enthusiastically. "You definitely mentioned it. In fact, I believe you said he was even hotter than in college."

"So hot." Erin unlocked her phone and quickly searched for photos of him. She swiped to a good one and passed it to Maggie, who whistled her appreciation.

"He's tall, too. Like six-foot-four."

"Nice." As above-average-height women, they shared an appreciation for sky-high members of the opposite sex.

"Sad news, though. He's a gigantic dick."

"He has a gigantic dick? Why is that sad? And how do you know this?" Maggie demanded, passing back Erin's phone.

"No, he *is* a giant dick. We had a professional run-in this week. He's the guy who was caught up in that gambling thing at the beginning of the year."

Maggie waved a dismissive hand. "Soccer crap, not interested. You should sleep with him."

Erin nearly choked on her wine. "Excuse me?"

"You should," her sister insisted. "You don't want commitment anyway, right?"

"No, but—"

"So he's hot and local and you can ignore his personality."

Erin shook her head, marveling at her sister's characteristic failure to take almost any element of life seriously. "No way."

"Why not?"

Erin almost laughed out loud at Maggie's unknowing question. Because he'd all but blackmailed her. Because he was an obsessive gambler oblivious to the severity of his addiction. Because she'd already slept with him and hadn't stopped thinking about it since.

Good reasons. Why weren't any of them convincing?

She twirled her wineglass by the stem, sitting with her surprising lack of distaste for the idea. Brendan was in a position to singlehandedly derail her entire career, and on some level she hated him.

Then why was another level toying with the notion of recruiting him for duty as a friend with benefits?

An enemy with benefits, she corrected.

She thought of his big, empty house. Sterile room after sterile room eventually giving way to a few signs of life like the thumbed books in the bedroom, the ridiculous pub in the basement. That crazy chart, the time and expense that must've been required in building such a personal, private place to pursue such a destructive hobby.

Then again, if the figures leaked in the SportBetNet scandal were any indication, it wasn't destructive for him at all. His replica pub and handwritten chart generated some decent income.

Quite the opposite of her compulsive, frivolous spins on her slots app.

She sat back on the couch, aware of her sister's curious stare as she parsed through the emotions pushing her thoughts in a few different directions, finding the shape of the place where they all intersected.

The answer came to her suddenly, as clear and bright as the first star in the night sky.

Maggie raised a questioning brow. Erin tapped her glass against her sister's. "You're absolutely right." She grinned. "I should sleep with him."

Chapter 7

Brendan could swear the church basement smelled worse than usual, but he filled a mug with coffee and took his seat nonetheless.

He checked his watch, already impatient to get his weekly hour of grudging self-examination over with. At least there was no cell reception down here, so he'd have sixty minutes free from resisting the temptation to return Erin's call.

In fact, avoiding her was exactly why he'd opted to join the Monday-morning meeting instead of his usual Sunday-night one. He had a rest day with Skyline and he was ninety-nine percent sure there was no chance that Erin could be here. She was probably in her big, fancy office, staring out her big, fancy windows, scheming up ways to hold his newly revived career over his head until he did anything she wanted.

"Like this?" He drew lazy lines between her legs before slipping one finger inside and asking, "Or like this? Tell me what you want."

"Anything you're offering," she purred, writhing in the vast expanse of the hotel bed.

He slapped his hand over his eyes and then shoved it through his hair, willing his thoughts to go anywhere else. Yet his mind drifted back to that night in Vegas, the woman she'd been then, her body under and over and beside his.

Against his better judgment, he took out his phone and reread the text message she'd sent yesterday morning.

Hi. It's Erin. This is stupid. Can we talk?

He would've mercilessly deleted it if it weren't for the voicemail that followed when he refused to answer her call.

"Hi, Brendan." Damn, just the way she said his name was… "I'm sure you got my text, and I'm sure you're screening my call. I don't blame you. I saw the match last night and I know what's on the line for you now. Let's stop doing whatever we're doing and be friends again, at least."

He had no reason to believe this was anything other than a new twist in her self-advancing professional strategy. Yet something in the tone of her voice, its openness, its hesitation—no. He wasn't going there. She wanted to screw him over. He had to protect himself.

He took stock of the other participants filtering into the meeting. He didn't know any of them except Lenny, who nodded a greeting as he pulled up a folding chair. There were more attendants than he expected for nine o'clock on a Monday, but then again, few of them looked like they had jobs to go to. As he watched a man with few teeth pour coffee into a mug clutched in a shaking hand, he decided this meeting was definitely more depressing than the one on Sunday night. Another reason to resent Erin—she'd chased him out of his preferred Gamblers Anonymous meeting.

Lenny offered what appeared to be recognizing smiles to most of the people in the room, and shortly after nine o'clock he brought his hands together to signal that it was time to begin.

"Let's start with a recitation of our twelve steps." Lenny trotted out his well-used line at the same time as he opened his well-used pamphlet. Brendan swallowed a groan. He was so sick of this shit.

He muttered his way through all twelve steps and the introduction of a new attendee, who wasn't really new at all but had fallen off the wagon after two years bet-free. That story concluded, Lenny looked around the room, waiting for someone else to offer to share.

After a long, awkward minute of silence in which everyone studied the floor, he prompted, "Brendan. I know you, but I don't think anyone else here does. Would you like to share your story?"

I'd like to head butt that overgrown beard off your face. Brendan forced a smile, flattening his palms on his thighs. "Okay."

Eight sets of eyes turned on him, reflecting a combination of interest, relief, and sympathy.

He cleared his throat. "Hi, my name is Brendan, and I'm an obsessive gambler."

"Hi, Brendan." His name echoed around the room.

"I'm a professional athlete."

He paused, scanning the room for any sign of recognition.

Nothing.

Typical.

"I'm a professional athlete," he repeated. "And I—"

The clatter of high heels descending the stairwell made him stop. Attention in the room diverted to the door, which promptly opened.

Erin stood in the frame, firelight-red hair drifting in thick waves over the shoulders of a crisply ironed blouse.

Their eyes locked and held for a second. Then she smiled.

"Sorry," she chirped, dropping into a vacant chair in the middle of his line of sight.

Convenient.

She nodded for him to go on, which seemed to satisfy the curious stares of the other attendees. Once again he became the center of the room's focus.

"I, uh—" He stuttered, recollecting his thoughts, adjusting the narrative to fit the new, unwelcome addition to his audience. Although he studiously avoided looking at her he felt the pressure of her gaze, the weight of her attention.

"I used to bet on the sport I play. But not my team," he added hastily. "Not even the same league."

He glanced at Lenny, who'd heard this before and would know if he was lying. He exhaled, caught between two listeners to whom he wouldn't give the same account if he could help it.

Anxiety flared in his chest and he took a long, slow breath to beat it down, simultaneously trying to ignore the stock ticker of worst-case scenarios running at a breakneck pace behind his eyes.

He couldn't tell the story they each wanted to hear. Lenny expected self-flagellation and guilt, but anything other than a declaration of innocence would strengthen Erin's power over him. There was no way to appease them both. He was trapped.

He set his back teeth, talking himself down out of his fevered thoughts.

What did he do when he stood between the goalposts, waiting for a player to take a penalty kick? He planned as best he could. He read the player's posture, considered their penalty record, readied himself physically—but in the end he could only ever do one thing.

Pick a direction and dive.

He looked between Lenny and Erin. Then he made a choice.

"But I did bet on teams I used to play for. Players I used to play beside. Whether you have a position on gambling or not, I think almost anyone would agree that's a little immoral."

He was sure he sensed Lenny's tacit approval, right alongside Erin's arched brow.

He plowed ahead. "I never saw the problem with my betting. I was good at it. I won a lot of money. It was a stress reliever, a hobby to take my mind off whatever was happening in the rest of my life. Although, in retrospect, I must've known it wasn't the right thing to do because I kept it secret.

"Anyway, earlier this year my gambling became public in a way that was totally out of my control. My family found out, my friends found out, and worst of all, my boss found out. What I thought was a harmless extracurricular activity put my entire career into the firing line."

He stole a glance at Erin. She hadn't moved an inch, her face totally unreadable.

He exhaled as he neared the end of the story, bracing himself for what might result. Lenny had heard his practiced, slightly untruthful version before—he couldn't change it now—and Erin would instantly know he was lying.

He had everything to play for and no option left but the one right in front of him. Straightening in his seat, he looked her square in the eye.

"The day my manager told me I was suspended was my rock bottom," he lied, deploying the organization's preferred rhetoric. "I stepped away from my charts, my graphs, my notebooks full of player stats, and fixture schedules. I started attending meetings and never looked back. It's been five and a half months since my last bet."

Smiles adorned the faces around the circle—except for one. As Lenny thanked him for sharing, Erin's expression was impassive, offering neither accusation nor affirmation.

He crossed his arms over his chest, refusing to look away before she did. Everything was out there, now. She knew exactly what he was doing—and what he wasn't. She said she wanted to be friends. He had no choice but to hold her to it.

* * * *

To her credit, she waited until most of the meeting's attendants drifted outside to smoke before approaching him. He watched her with narrowed eyes, steadying himself as he rode a surge of irritation at her presence, her doggedness, her outright refusal to leave him the hell alone.

She held up her palms as she stopped in front of him. "I know. I'm the last person you want to see, especially here. But we should talk."

He said nothing. He had no words for her in that moment.

She glanced left, then right, almost certainly noticing Lenny's watchful attention from a few feet away.

"Let's get out of here," she suggested quietly. "I'll buy you breakfast. There must be a diner nearby."

He couldn't help himself. He smiled.

"A diner," he repeated. "You can take the girl out of New Jersey..."

She returned his smile, and it was the first of hers that he'd seen since Vegas that seemed genuine.

He couldn't trust her. But maybe he didn't have to fight with her, either.

He nodded to the door. "Come on. I know a place."

Fifteen minutes later they slid into opposite sides of a booth in a café.

"I'll have the egg-white omelet with asparagus and peppers. No muffin. And coffee, with skim milk on the side," Erin ordered.

Brendan didn't bother opening the menu. "Two eggs, scrambled, with cheddar cheese. Sausage, bacon, mushrooms, wheat toast. Black coffee. And a cinnamon roll."

Erin scowled as the waitress walked away. "That's just unfair."

"Be nice to me and I'll let you have a bite of my cinnamon roll."

"Speaking of." She folded her hands on the table. "I want to call a truce."

He regarded her steadily, considering his response as the waitress returned to place two mugs of coffee between them. He watched her stir milk into hers, then asked, "Why?"

"Because this is exhausting and stressful, and it doesn't need to be."

"I think it does unless your plan to sell me out in the year-end report has radically changed." He raised his mug, testing the temperature between his palms.

"It has."

He looked up with renewed interest, surprised by her response. "Say more."

She exhaled. "We're both in predicaments. I have certain things I want to achieve in my job, and I can't get the authorization or resources I need to do them until I deliver other things. Right now, I have to deliver you."

"I don't understand."

"I want to launch a campaign for the women's game," she explained. "Doing so requires a travel budget. I've been told I can't have this travel budget until I show results on the anti-gambling initiative."

He nodded, the pieces coming together. "And I'm all you've got."

"Exactly. On the flipside, you've just become the number-one goalkeeper for a team headed to the league final. You're about to be redeemed and leave the sport in a blaze of glory—if you don't get nailed in the year-end report, and if no one finds out about the pretty detailed odds-making activities going on in your basement."

He opened his mouth to protest and she held up a finger. "Correct me if I'm wrong, but you're also currently banned from fully partaking in one of your preferred stress relievers. Meanwhile you've got stressful times ahead."

He couldn't argue. He drummed his fingers on the mug, waiting for her to continue.

She grinned. "We can change it all."

Suspicion stirred in his gut, pinching his brows together. "Go on."

She leaned forward, lowering her voice. "Quid pro quo."

He eyed her carefully, trying to read any hints of deception or manipulation in her body language. Her expression seemed open, her tone sincere.

He took a long sip of coffee, then replaced his mug squarely on the table. "I'm listening."

She paused as the waitress arrived with their plates. He watched Erin warily as she thanked the server and took up her fork and knife, swallowing two bites before speaking.

"You scratch my back, I'll scratch yours," she explained. "You must know other gamblers in the league. Each piece of information you throw my way pulls the spotlight further away from you."

"What makes you think I know anything or anyone that could be useful?"

She rolled her eyes. "You do, though. Don't you?"

He did. Of course he did. He wasn't the only gambler in the league—not by a long shot. That didn't mean he was happy to sell people down the river to save himself, though.

"You're asking me to rat on players. I can't do that."

"Sure you can. Don't pretend you're friends with every single player in the league, or that they've all had your back as you've been vilified for the same thing they're doing. Anyway, you don't have to give me names. Leads would be enough. Point me in the right direction and I'll do my own digging."

He chewed thoughtfully on a slice of toast. She had a point. There were plenty of Judases in the game who'd gone from begging to learn his system to barely looking at him.

As far as having his back, no one had, not really. For the most part his Skyline teammates had the good grace not to mention it, and a couple of them—Pavel, most notably—had privately expressed supportive opinions that the punishment didn't fit the crime.

But everyone else? Could go fuck themselves.

Not that she needed to know that.

He whistled to suggest the enormity of what she was asking. "I don't know, Erin. I'm not sure what you're offering is enough to justify it."

"Don't worry, I'm not done." She stuck her fork across the table and snagged a piece of bacon. "Let's be honest. Neither of us is exactly a twelve-step success story."

He declined to respond, still guarded about implicating himself. She brushed off his silence with a dismissive hand.

"It's fine, you don't have to confirm or deny. Just hear me out. We both love to gamble. If you're anything like me, playing without real money on the table isn't enough. I tried downloading some phony slot-machine app where you don't bet actual cash, but I didn't make it more than a half a day before I deleted it and reloaded a real one. With no money, there are no stakes, and with no stakes, there's no rush, no release, no high. I believed you when you said you were working the odds but not betting, so tell me whether I'm right. Is it the same?"

Her words resonated so perfectly that he exhaled, dropping his defensive shields on a rush of air. "No. It's awful. I hate it."

"But you can't even attempt to put money down because if it somehow gets out, your career is well and truly over, and neither I nor anyone else in the sport can save it."

"Correct."

"This is where I come in." She winked, and God help him, his dick stirred in his jeans. "I'll be your proxy. I'll place the bets for you. I have so many credit cards on the go, no one will ever connect the dots. If along the way you decide to teach me some of your system, maybe even share the winnings, I certainly won't complain—and neither will my credit limit."

He sat back in the booth, regarding her steadily. It wasn't a bad idea. In fact it bordered on being a pretty good one.

"Let me get this straight," he said, punctuating his words with a piece of bacon. "I give you some leads on gambling in the league and you'll place my bets. I stay out of the year-end report and you make a little money from our winnings."

"You've got it," she confirmed. "And if you want, we can have sex, too."

He choked on the bacon. He coughed harshly and repeatedly, his eyes watering as he grabbed a glass of water, desperately trying to suck in air around the pork lodged in his throat.

"Oops, sorry." She shifted into his side of the booth, patting his back—and then dropping her hand to his thigh.

"Slow down," he commanded, and she reluctantly retrieved her hand and resumed her seat. "Where the hell did that come from?"

She shrugged, evidently completely unbothered by the bombshell that had nearly turned his breakfast into a lethal weapon. "You know I like to be direct. We had fun in Vegas. I thought maybe we could have fun here, too."

He held up his palms. "I'm flattered, I guess, but that's not how I play. Vegas was a one-off. I don't do the casual thing."

"That's fine," she replied, sounding like it genuinely was. "I'm not in the market for anything but the casual thing, so it probably wouldn't work. Just thought I'd put it out there."

"Okay, well, you can put it back in now."

"Don't worry, I won't solicit you again, especially not when you're eating." Her eyes gleamed playfully. "Does that mean you'll be wife-hunting once you get to Nebraska?"

He took a noncommittal bite of egg. "Maybe."

"I can see it already, the tall, blond Midwestern girl who will never understand the offside rule no matter how many times you explain it. She's probably a teacher, and her first name ends in 'i'. She wanted to marry a quarterback, but she'll settle for—"

"Settle?" he interrupted. "No one settles for a multiple clean-sheet record holder and Golden Glove recipient."

She shook her head, smiling fondly. "Brendan. How many people in Nebraska know what 'clean sheet' means? They'll think you ran a laundromat."

"You'd be surprised," he muttered, ignoring that she had a point. In high school he was nationally ranked, recruited to the best college soccer program in the country and awarded a full athletic scholarship. Yet the yearbook superlative for Most Likely to Play Professional Sports went to the mediocre quarterback, who followed up the team's sixth-place finish with immense weight gain, two years of community college and a drunk-driving charge Brendan's mother had cut out of the newspaper to show him.

But times changed. People, places, attitudes—it was all up in the air at any given moment.

Anyway, he owed it to his parents to come back. At least for a little while.

"Are we done?" he asked more briskly than he intended, trying to shake off the suddenly negative pivot of his thoughts.

"I don't know," Erin replied. "Are we?"

He stared unseeingly at his plate, listening for any internal alarm bells. It wasn't the most morally upright plan—trading information so he could place bets in contravention of the terms on which he'd been reinstated. In fact both of them would be in enormous trouble if their collusion ever became public.

But it meant he'd be able to bet again. Real money. Real odds, real results. The temptation was immense, especially considering the pressure he was about to face on the pitch over the next two months. In barely a week he'd gone from cold shadow to scorching spotlight, and if he was honest with himself, the mental release of working odds, placing bets and winning or losing was probably all that stood between him and a nervous breakdown.

High stakes. The highest.

He couldn't say no.

"We're good."

"Shake on it."

They clasped hands over the table. Hers was soft and small in his much-bigger one, her grip confident and firm. Suddenly he was back in that Vegas hotel room, her hand around another part of his body, moving with the same assuredness, the same strength yet underlined by an unexpected tenderness, a part of her she didn't want anyone to see...

"Pleasure doing business with you." Her comment jerked him out of his thoughts. She tossed her napkin on the table and stood up. "I have to get back to the office."

He waved her on. "Go. I'll get this."

"I should hope so. You've seen my credit card statement. You know I can't afford it."

He looked up just in time to catch her flirty wink before she sauntered out of the restaurant, flicking her hair over her shoulders. Two men in suits twisted in their seats to watch her leave, and he sighed as he signaled for the waitress to bring the check.

He'd made a deal with the devil. Now he had to work to keep his soul safe and his hands clean—and off of her.

Chapter 8

Erin shivered on Brendan's porch in the pre-dawn chill, waiting for him to answer the door. She glanced from side to side, doubtful any of his neighbors would recognize her but paranoid nonetheless.

Then again, it was Brendan who'd insisted they meet at his house to place their first round of bets, so he had to be reasonably confident they didn't run the risk of discovery.

Or stupid, she reasoned unhappily.

Her finger hovered over the bell, about to press it a second time when he opened the door.

Be cool, she coached herself, managing to keep her jaw from falling open as she took in his early-morning appearance. Finger-combed hair, white cotton T-shirt, slim-fitting gray joggers that weren't quite long enough. She fought the urge to fling her arms around his neck and kiss his stubbly, drowsy face.

"Nice of you to dress up for the occasion," she said tartly instead.

"The invitation didn't stipulate formal attire." His gaze swept her from head to toe.

"I don't own anything else," she fibbed. Truthfully she'd put an inordinate amount of thought into her jeans-and-dressy-top combination, particularly since he'd made it clear he wasn't interested in anything more than a business partnership. She was fine with that—she was, really—but it didn't hurt to let him know what he was missing.

He motioned her inside. "Coffee's brewed. I assume you remember the way to the kitchen."

"Hard to forget those granite countertops." She stepped over the threshold and followed him into the spotlessly clean kitchen. "I hope your neighbors aren't nosy. I can't think of any non-shady reasons I'd be on your doorstep at five o'clock on a Saturday morning."

"Unlikely any of them would notice, but I see your point. I'll give you a garage remote when you leave. Next time you can park inside and come straight in."

"Next time? Why can't we do this over the phone?" She propped one elbow against his expensive counter as he filled a mug with coffee and passed it over.

He shook his head disapprovingly, opening a bakery box and arranging a delicious-looking series of doughnuts on a large plate.

"Do you have any idea how many people would love to be here right now, and to see what I'm about to show you?"

"Ooh, pink frosting." She snatched up a doughnut and took a bite.

"I'm serious. I've been offered enormous sums of money to teach people my system. I was even approached by this day-trader guy in Brazil to fly down there to do a group lesson." He picked up his coffee, the plate, and headed to the door to the basement.

"I thought this was all super secret. How do these people know who you are?" She opened the door and held it while he descended the staircase with his hands full.

"Technically they don't know they're approaching Brendan Young, goalkeeper extraordinaire. There are some online forums where people trade tips. I was a frequent flier when I lived in England."

"Signed to one of the best clubs in the world and he spent his time trolling online message boards." She sighed.

"Visit Liverpool in November. You'll understand. Eventually I got nervous about being identified and stopped posting. Also I moved to Spain, and sunshine became a real thing again instead of an abstract concept."

"Nice work if you can get it. I still don't understand why I need to learn your system at all, though. Can't I just be your minion, carrying out your bidding?"

He took up a stool in front of the bar and motioned her to join him, setting down the doughnuts. He slid over a stack of two marble composition books, taking a tattered one off the top and passing a brand-new one to her.

"How do you think you got into all that debt?" he asked.

"By losing more than I won?"

He shook his head. "By being compulsive. Reckless. Disorganized."

"It's not possible to be strategic on a slot-machine app. That's the point."

"It is. I can't tell you how—not my game—but trust me, everything can be won and nothing is insurmountably random. With a little discipline and dedication, not to mention a way to keep the league from finding out, I promise you'll pay off that debt and generate some nice income, too."

She rolled her eyes. "You sound like an infomercial. No, I don't want to buy a timeshare on the Lake of the Ozarks, but thanks."

"I'm serious. Gambling is an art and a science. I can't just start texting you my bets. You have to understand the framework behind it, even if you decide never to try it yourself."

"Whatever. As long as doughnuts are involved, I'm in."

He passed her a pen and opened his notebook. She did the same.

"Step one. Comfortable surroundings, free of distraction." He gestured to the replica pub.

"I'm not writing that down."

"You shouldn't. That notebook is for your odds, fixtures, and bets. In fact, that's step two—make sure you have a tidy, well-organized central database. In my case"— he tapped the notebook—"I get through one of these every couple of months, but I save them all, ordered by season, so I can refer back to my previous wagers and whether or not they panned out."

"Step three. Doughnut." She helped herself to a blueberry one and lifted her coffee mug in salute.

"That's probably part of step one, but never mind. Step four... Or three... Forget the steps."

He waved one hand distractedly and shoved the other through his hair, and it hit her again, that almost irresistible tug of affection that had her gripping her pen to keep her hand from touching his shoulder.

An unbidden, unfamiliar, and unwelcome impulse, she frowned at the blank page in front of her in an effort to ignore it. She'd never been the gooey lovey type, never dreamed of a doting husband, got bored halfway through most of her dates and over the years had developed a preference for skipping straight to sex. Scratch the itch, enjoy the night, and move on.

Brendan stood out as a lifetime exception. He'd ingratiated himself early with his act of kindness toward a naïve freshman, and so maybe she'd been predisposed to think generously on everything he did thereafter, but he was special in other ways, too. In college she'd been drawn to his quiet intensity, the introversion that lay just beneath the surface of his otherwise affable, polite persona. He seemed to approach life with a gravity lacking in other guys, particularly other athletes. He studied hard, trained hard, fulfilled all the social expectations of a number-one-ranked soccer team yet always seemed slightly aloof. Like he'd rather be somewhere else, probably alone.

At first she'd trailed him like a typical fangirl, her heart leaping whenever she caught sight of him on campus yet never approaching him, deciding it wasn't the right moment or she wasn't wearing the right outfit. If she knew he'd be at a party she dressed to the nines, spending hours perfecting her hair and makeup and then posing prettily near him, laughing too loudly with her friends, anxiously glancing his way to see if he noticed.

If he did, he never said anything. He certainly never made a move.

By Thanksgiving she'd more or less given up, distracted by her studies and her sport. Over Christmas she went home to New Jersey and promptly lost her virginity to the brother of one of her high-school classmates, having decided it was a complicating burden she was tired of working around. She started her second semester with greater confidence and authenticity, and although she still had a flutter when she ran into Brendan, she invested far less energy into caring what he thought of her.

They didn't exactly become friends, but they became friendly. Instead of staring at him at parties, she talked to him. Instead of stalking him around campus, she waved and continued on her way.

The following year she was a sophomore and he was a senior, and their paths diverged more than ever as he attracted attention from scouts for several international teams. She still thought he was mega hot and certainly wouldn't have turned him down if he'd asked, but sex had fallen so far down her list of priorities she barely remembered how it worked. Meanwhile he was almost a celebrity, the constant subject of awed gossip amongst the players, already rising so far above the rest of them that he seemed untouchable.

The last time they spoke was that spring, at a lunch during families' weekend, when most of the players' parents and siblings visited campus for two days of events. She watched him move through the dining room, the tallest in a tall-person family. His dad and older brother were both big and heavyset, with football-player builds. His mom was slim and sharp-eyed, clearly the mobilizing force in the household. His younger brother, Liam—gregarious, playful, unself-conscious—instantly became the center of attention as he showed anyone who would look his head-to-toe Notre Dame outfit printed with his brother's name and number.

Seemingly by chance, their two families ended up at the same table, but as Brendan took the seat next to her she wondered if she'd been a safe option, offering no risk of teammates' jealous parents ruing his disproportionate success. The meal was short and only slightly awkward. Her parents were their usual charming, diplomatic selves, downplaying their affluence as her dad asked earnest questions about Keith Young's car dealership and her mother made appropriate noises during Marie's tale of fighting the public school system to offer Liam a more mainstream curriculum. Maggie and Aidan—the eldest brother—both looked like they'd rather be somewhere else but had the good sense not to say anything.

Brendan kept quiet beside her, and instinctively she didn't press him. Something told her he liked to disappear on occasion, to slip between everyone's lines of attention and withdraw into whatever was happening inside his handsome head.

Toward the end of lunch, he seemed to collect himself and turned to her. "Do you have plans for the summer?"

"I've got an internship in New York City, working in the sports department at a TV network," she replied proudly.

He smiled, rare and so fulfilling. "Nice."

"It's only three days a week, and it's not paid, but I figure that gives me time to train and maybe get a part-time job, too. Last summer I worked at my dad's law firm and the money was definitely helpful, but I didn't feel like I was moving my career forward, and you only really get three summers before..." She trailed off, deciding he probably wasn't that interested. "Anyway, what are you up to this summer?"

She regretted the question as soon as it was out of her mouth. She knew what he was doing. Everyone did.

But if he thought it was a stupid question he gave no sign. "Hanging out at home for a while. Then, in July, I'm moving to England."

"Awesome," she said softly, unsure how to follow it up. Luckily she didn't have to, as chairs started scraping the floor around the room. Another event started in five minutes.

Every occupant at their table stood, ready to go their separate ways. As the dads shook hands and the moms insisted it had been nice to meet each other, she turned to Brendan.

"So, good luck in—"

He cut her off with a sudden, tight hug, one of his hands cupping the nape of her neck beneath her ponytail. She closed her eyes against his firm chest, inhaling the scent she didn't know then she'd still remember when she sat next to him at a wedding more than ten years later.

His grip lingered, its pressure so much more than friendly, but she was young and confused and he was a shooting star bolting away from her and when he let go she didn't know what to think, let alone what to say. She stared at him dumbly, arms at her sides, bewildered and excited and suddenly on the verge of tears.

"Be good," he said simply, as remote and inscrutable as always. She nodded as though she had any idea what he meant, and then they both turned and walked out in separate directions.

Months ago, brimming with champagne and triumph at finally catching the biggest fish in her romantic sea, she'd alluded to that moment in one of their postcoital calms. He just shook his head, and although she wasn't sure whether he meant he didn't remember or he didn't want to talk about college, she decided not to push it. Like it or not, she treasured that hug for years and years. It would hurt too much to finally be told it never meant anything.

"Are you listening?"

She jerked back to the present, blueberry doughnut still clutched halfway to her mouth. "Not at all. Sorry. Start again."

"I said, the reason we're up so early is the time difference. England is five hours ahead of Atlanta. Most of the matches are in the afternoon, but today we have a midday kickoff because—"

"It's a big derby and they schedule those at noon so the fans don't have too much time to get wasted and punch each other," she supplied. "I may not have reached the dizzy heights you did, but I did play professionally. I know my sport. Try not to patronize me."

He held up a hand. "Fair point."

"Is there a reason we can't place bets on the English games the night before?"

"If absolutely necessary, we can. This week I'm playing on Sunday, but if I'd had a game this morning I would've put in the bets last night. Ideally, though, you want to bet as close to kickoff as possible, so you have the maximum amount of information. We won't really know which players are in, and in what formation until they walk onto the pitch."

She tilted her head thoughtfully. "I can see that in the tight matches, but what about when the number-one team is playing number twelve? Surely that's a safe choice, even if one or two players from the top team pick up unexpected injuries."

He patted her hand. "Oh, Erin. So much to learn."

She polished off her doughnut. "All right, then, Maestro. Go for it."

"Here's the thing. Anyone can pick Manchester United to beat Swansea City at Old Trafford. The bookmakers' odds will reflect that. The upsets are where you make the real money, and those can be predicted with detailed analysis and a whole lot of thought."

She wrinkled her nose. "Thought takes the fun out of gambling. I prefer the instinct-and-luck method."

"Most people do. That's why they end up in a church basement talking about their feelings instead of a nice, big house like this one."

She picked up her pen. "Where do we start?"

"The midday derby in London." He pointed to the relevant line on his whiteboard. "Those are the bookies' odds for a win, a loss, and a draw, plus whether both teams will score. You can get into really detailed bets, like who will score first, which striker will score and how many times, but for the most part I stick with the overall result. With so many matches, it's better to hedge across the whole league rather than put too big a wager on any one specific occurrence."

She squinted at the chart. "Where did you get those odds? Are those from a particular site?"

"Yeah. The slight downside to winning a lot is the bookies tend to shut your account or put a ceiling on your wagers, so you have to move from one to the other. These are from the one my account is still live on—but I guess now we can start over since we're using your details, not mine."

He turned to her, thoughtful. "You're sure no one can trace this? I get that no one has an eye out for you like they do for me, but are you absolutely certain—"

"Totally," she assured him. "First, I have about a million credit cards. Second, they're all under my initials—E. Bailey or E.P. Bailey. The likelihood of anyone linking that back to me is tiny."

"Okay. Okay," he repeated, sounding as if he was trying to convince himself. He looked up. "What's the 'P' for?"

"Patricia."

"Nice."

"I guess. What's your middle name?"

"David."

"That's a good name."

"Sure."

They looked at each other for a few seconds, the atmosphere softening along this random personal detour. She summoned her memory of the young man he'd been that spring afternoon, comparing the twenty-two-year-old at the table with the thirty-three-year-old in front of her, taking the time to measure the changes.

His hair was longer, cut better, no less thick or blond for the years in between. He had a strong jaw, a straight nose, green eyes darkened by the shifting shadows of what went on behind them. Lines spliced his forehead now, and although the other physical changes were surprisingly minimal, his expression was always underlined by a slight weariness that was hard to ignore. As though he'd grown used to disappointment, expected it, but felt its full weight nonetheless.

He returned her gaze for another second before dropping it to his notebook. She wondered if he'd attempted to make the same comparison she had, the present versus the past, and what he'd concluded about the woman she'd become.

"London derby," he announced, bringing them both back to the task at hand. "Historic rivals, managers are sworn enemies, both teams sitting near the top of the table. Each one wants the three points as much as they want to deny the other from getting them. So. Who will win?"

She tapped her chin, considering what she knew about each team, then pointed. "One-nil to them."

"Why?"

"They finished higher last season, and they bought that Congolese guy who's a goal machine."

He shook his head. "Here's what we do."

He turned to a blank page in his notebook and jotted down two sets of names on either side, representing the full squads of both teams.

"How do you remember all this?" she asked, impressed as he easily recalled more than twenty names with no Google in sight.

"I just do. Anyway." He pointed to the Congolese player's name. "Let's take your striker. He was a late purchase in the transfer window after this club supposedly outbid one up north. As a result he only landed in London at the beginning of August, so he's had relatively little time to train with the team. He's also never played in England before."

He looked at her expectantly, but she shrugged.

"You have to consider each player's mindset, not just their stats." He tapped his temple. "This guy doesn't know his teammates very well. His English probably isn't great, so he's feeling a little isolated in the dressing room and in a new country. He hasn't played for the club long enough to be truly invested in this derby, or to understand beyond an academic level what it means for the fans. I think the quality of play in this match and the intensity of the atmosphere is going to make him stumble. If he scores, it'll be a lucky header. He's not going to beat the keeper."

She frowned, simultaneously impressed and skeptical. "But that's all speculation. He's a professional. Maybe he can put aside all these emotional issues and just play."

"Maybe," he agreed. "That's why it's a gamble."

"It works for you, though. This system, this psychological approach."

He nodded. "Always has."

"Here goes nothing." In her own notebook, she wrote down the striker's name and added a hyphen and a zero afterward, indicating that he wouldn't score.

Brendan pointed to one of the winger's names. "Right, let's figure out whether this guy will score."

It took nearly an hour to go through each player and settle on a result, which would draw a decent but not enormous payout if it came good. Erin sat back and exhaled, picking up her coffee mug to discover it was empty.

"That took forever. How do you manage to make any money out of this? It must suck up all your time."

"It's quicker when I do it by myself, mostly because I read all the news in the week up to the game so by the time the team is announced I have a pretty good idea of the result to expect. Anyway, I enjoy it." He shrugged.

"No one could fault your attention to detail. Now let's put our money where our mouths are." She unlocked her phone screen. He scooted his stool closer to hers to get a look.

"I'm signed up on this site as E.P. Bailey, under a credit card with the same name," she explained, scrolling to the betting coupon for the match they'd just analyzed. "Here are the odds they're offering me. Happy with these?"

His gaze darted between his whiteboard and the screen of her phone. After a minute he nodded. "These are slightly better than what I was offered."

"Probably because it's a brand-new account. I'll shop around, though. We can spread today's results over a couple of sites, hopefully keep getting such competitive offers."

She tapped a few keys, hit "enter" and the bet was placed.

"Voila," she announced.

"Is that it?"

She looked up to find his expression slightly crestfallen. "What, did you want to hold hands or something?"

"No," he shot back so defensively she thought maybe that's exactly what he wanted. "I just thought the first transaction of our new enterprise might be a little more...ceremonial."

"I'll cue up the Notre Dame Victory March on my phone for the next one." She stood and stretched, and as she finished she was ninety-nine percent sure she caught Brendan glancing at her breasts.

She arched a brow. "Does this pub have a bathroom?"

He shook his head. "Upstairs."

She collected her mug and nodded to his. "Do you want a refill while I'm up there?"

"Yes, please. Be quick, though. We have two more matches today."

* * * *

"Mark him. He's wide open. Mark him, you idiot, he's...shit," Brendan swore at the screen as the team they'd picked to lose came close—too close—to scoring the first and only goal of the sixty-minute-old match.

Erin blew out her relief, rising to pace behind the sofa in Brendan's family room. She got the feeling he normally watched the games in his bedroom—he'd struggled to find the remote for this TV—but she appreciated his temporary relocation on her behalf.

She'd been at his house for hours, far longer than she intended. She'd had to cancel a lunch date and she'd eaten so many doughnuts and drank so much coffee she felt nauseous.

She didn't care. They won their London derby bet, splitting it to take a hundred dollars each. In only two hours she'd doubled her slots winning for the last week.

This match, though, was one of Brendan's meticulously predicted upsets. They stood to triple what they'd pulled in on the derby. Her doughnut-filled stomach was in knots.

Which is why, when he suddenly flicked to the other match on another channel, she screeched, "What the hell are you doing? Put it back!"

"Just checking. Still two-nil. We should be fine." He tapped the remote to return to the previous channel.

"Oh God. Set piece. I can't look. Tell me what happens." She slapped her hands over her eyes as their team—picked to win—arranged themselves to take a corner kick.

"The German's taking it. He's not going to—get over! Fucking move! Dammit!"

She dropped her hands in time to watch a spectacularly tragic missed opportunity, as one of the defenders jumped for a header that missed the winger's perfectly placed ball by a hairsbreadth.

"Morons," she hissed. "Where was that French guy? Why is he all the way over there?"

"Because he has the mental capacity of a goldfish," Brendan muttered gloomily. "Have you ever heard his post-match interviews?"

"Are they funny?"

"Let's say he's unlikely to find a second career as a motivational speaker." He glanced at her over his shoulder. "I played against him a couple of times. He was pretty young then, but his ego was already fully grown."

The reminder that she was watching the world's best soccer league with someone who'd once been a part of it stopped her pacing. An unsettling mixture of awe and empathy tightened her throat as she watched him lean forward on the couch, muttering instructions to players three thousand miles away.

By all accounts his career was enviable for their sport. He still played at thirty-three, and he'd reached international heights that maybe a handful in a generation of American players attained.

She carried some degree of jealousy for any reasonably successful male player, resenting that the road was so much longer and more lucratively paved for them than for any woman. She never gave much thought to the end, though, and how it felt when they got there. She had her post-playing plan in place from the beginning—she had no choice.

Brendan had a pretty soft landing, transferring to one of the best teams in the league in his home country. He should've ridden out his twilight period as a big fish in a small pond, waving to stadiums full of ecstatic fans, delivering spectacular saves and finally leaving the pitch with the reputation he'd earned over more than a decade.

For the first time, she realized just how painful that SportBetNet leak and the subsequent public shaming must've been for him. He'd been a star amongst soccer fans, but he'd never been a national headline until he was one of a handful of professional athletes discovered to be betting on their own sports.

That was the risk of flying so high. The fall back to earth could kill you.

She propped her hands on the back of the couch, her fingers an inch from his shoulder. She fought the sudden, inappropriate urge to touch him, to trail her hand down his back and soothe him.

You deserve more, she assured him silently. Don't worry. I'll make sure you get it.

"Look." He pointed to the screen. "Look at their number ten, arguing with the referee. I knew it." Brendan snapped his fingers as the famous goal-scorer was booked for dissent.

Erin rounded the sofa and dropped down beside him. "Oh my God. He never gets a yellow."

"He's had run-ins with this referee before, plus he'll be annoyed that the manager didn't start him. Watch, he'll go missing now. He can't handle being booked. Doesn't jive with his cover-model, golden-boy persona."

"He's the only one who's had a remotely on-target attempt. If he loses steam…"

"Then our boys win in a huge upset."

"Twenty minutes to go." She knotted her fingers together, nerves and exhilaration flipping her stomach.

He pivoted to look at her side-on. "I thought I would hate watching with someone else, but it's actually not bad."

She spread her palms. "Thanks?"

"I mean I'm enjoying your company. It's nice to have someone here who knows the sport, and who doesn't keep asking why one team got a corner and not the other or how many minutes are left."

"Is that a problem you've had in the past?"

"Not, like, a lot." He raised a shoulder, clearly regretting turning the conversation in this direction. "Just, you know, other women I've... When I've watched with..."

"Ex-girlfriends," she supplied bluntly. "Or hadn't they earned that title, even?"

"Not necessarily. Come on, ref, that's a high boot," he insisted, unsubtly trying to change the subject.

She rolled her eyes but didn't press him. What did she care how many women he'd been with? She wasn't interested in his ex-girlfriends.

Actually, yes she was.

"Have you had many female viewing companions in the past?" she asked.

"Not really."

"What number am I?"

He shot her a look that said he wasn't answering that.

"Tell me about the most recent one, then," she suggested, undeterred.

"That would be you."

She shook her head. "Today doesn't count. The last one before me."

His eyes found hers with such unwavering focus that for a moment her breath caught.

"I mean you're the last person I slept with," he told her softly.

"Oh. Okay." Well, that backfired. "Your last serious girlfriend, then. What was she like?"

"Why are you asking me this?" He turned back to the screen, his expressing growing irritable.

"You piqued my curiosity with your comment about soccer ignoramuses. Now give."

"I'll tell you about my last girlfriend if you tell me about your last boyfriend."

"Deal."

"Fine." He leaned back on the sofa, eyes never leaving the action on the TV. "Catalina, when I lived in Valencia. Spanish, from Madrid originally, but she'd lived in the UK for a while so she spoke English. That was important—my Spanish was good enough for everyday stuff but not really for a relationship. Anyway, she was an art director for an advertising agency. We lasted about ten months. She was always skeptical about dating a footballer. Didn't like photos of us popping up in the papers and was convinced I'd cheat on her eventually."

"Did you?"

"Of course not," he shot back, and she raised a hand in apology. "She got a job offer in Dubai and she went. *El fin*, as they say in Spain. Your turn."

"Okay. I've never had a boyfriend. Done."

He tore his gaze away from the screen long enough to give her a hard stare. "You're lying."

"God's honest truth. I think five dates is my record. I'm not really the committed type. Friends with benefits are more my sort of arrangement."

"You mentioned that," he said grimly. "Tell me about the five-dates guy then."

She tapped her chin, trying to remember him. "I was at one of the TV networks' studios in New York. It was the anniversary of some milestone in women's soccer, and they interviewed me about what it meant to me as a child and whether it influenced my career. The truth is I only ever watched the men's game, but I gave them a couple of good sound bites and they were happy. Meanwhile this guy was hanging around in the background. I thought he was a production assistant, but afterward we bumped into each other in the lobby and he introduced himself. Caleb, went by Cal. In-house counsel for the network."

"Cal," Brendan repeated derisively.

"Hey, he was the five-date record-setter. Don't knock him."

"And what was so amazing about Cal that he reached that pinnacle of achievements?"

"He happened to catch me in a moment of existential crisis, for one. My sister had just gotten engaged and I had about a month where I decided to get serious about settling down."

"But you moved on from that?"

"Completely. Anyway, to be fair to him, Cal was smart, funny, and successful. He had a gorgeous loft apartment in SoHo and wore the most beautiful bespoke suits I've ever seen. Also, he had an immense cock."

He slapped his hands over his ears. "Jesus, Erin. I don't want to know that."

"Yours is better," she offered conciliatorily.

"Stop. Just stop."

"Excuse me." She rolled her eyes. "I didn't realize one of us took his Catholic upbringing so seriously. But then I wouldn't have, given your performance at New Year's. All the champagne must've helped you overcome your prude side because anyone who can do what you did when we..."

She trailed off, his head slowly turning until their gazes locked.

She'd read plenty of novels and seen tons of movies in which characters connect through a single look, a momentarily shared glance. She'd even had friends swear the catalyst to their loving relationship had been eyes meeting across a crowded restaurant, or lecture hall, or strobe-lit nightclub.

She didn't believe a word of it.

Until now.

There was no love pulsating between them—not even a little, tiny, imaginary bit—but there was lust. Pounding, relentless, heart-quickening physical attraction. Instantly her nipples hardened to aching peaks, and the place between her thighs swelled and throbbed with unfulfilled desire.

She saw every inch of her reaction reflected in his face. His pupils dilated. The line of his jaw hardened. His chest moved more rapidly with the pace of his breath. When his tongue darted out to wet his lower lip she wanted to shove him back against the sofa, yank his joggers down his hips and find the hot, impatient flesh she knew was already steel-hard for her.

Maybe she should just do it. What could she lose? They'd had sex before—the best sex of her life. He said he wasn't interested in something casual, but one time didn't really qualify as something. A one-off. A Saturday treat. A nagging, insistent itch so deliciously scratched. She'd put her mouth on him, to celebrate their win, to thank him for taking so much time to show her how he bet, to satisfy the restless demand of her tongue to run up and down his shaft, to circle over his velvety tip, to bring him past the point of control and taste—

"And it's good! Finally a point on the board in the eighty-fifth minute!"

They both jerked their gazes toward the TV at the enthusiasm of the announcer's voice.

"They scored!" She was on her feet, gaping at the one-nil showing on the top left hand of the screen.

"I fucking knew it." He punched the air, jumping up off the couch and taking her by the shoulders. "Didn't I say they would score toward the end?"

"Hell yeah, you did." Her own hands dropped to his waist.

"Seven hundred dollars," he reminded her unnecessarily. "As long as they hold off the other team for five minutes, we will be seven hundred goddamn dollars to the good."

"They're going to do it," she promised. "I know they are. You're a genius."

"I know," he agreed. Then he leaned down and kissed her.

It was everything and nothing she wanted, too much and nowhere near enough. His mouth was hungry, urgent and she responded in kind, their tongues circling and bumping and stroking exactly as their bodies had done so many months earlier. She moaned at the contact, at the memory of how much further they'd gone, at the wet heat and singular taste of him.

He tightened his arms around her, pulling her flat against his chest, the warmth of him making her nipples taut and sore with need. She shoved one of her hands beneath the waistband of his cotton joggers and savored the contours of his lower back, his smooth, bare skin, the ridges of muscle beneath it.

He shifted his grip, urging her hips closer. She accommodated him gladly, redoubling her pressure on his mouth when she found the jutting length of his erection. She ground against him, even the suggestion of his arousal between all those layers of cloth enough to completely soak her panties.

Forget sex. Another two minutes and she might just dry hump her way to climax.

Some segmented, annoyingly practical part of her brain registered a whistle and then another. Her player's instinct took over at the familiar sound and despite her body screaming to the contrary, she broke the kiss to glance at the TV, prompting him to do the same.

"Full time," he said breathlessly.

She looked back at him. "We won."

He smiled, big and broad and eminently kissable. "We did."

She leaned in to resume what they'd started but he stepped all the way out of the embrace, definite and deliberate.

"We got carried away. We shouldn't do that again." He dropped back onto the couch and picked up the remote.

She propped a hand on her hip. "Why?"

He flicked to the other channel to check the score. They'd won there, too.

"You're beautiful, Erin. You know that. Beautiful and smart and so fucking sexy, I'm not surprised no man has ever been good enough to win a sixth date."

"Thanks," she preened, taking her seat beside him. "And those are reasons not to have sex because?"

"Because you're soccer."

She tilted her head quizzically. "No, I'm Erin. Nice to meet you."

"You're soccer," he repeated. "Everything about you is the game I love. You understand it, you played it, and you're one of the women's game's legends. It's your job, too, and will be for a long time. Probably forever."

"And?"

"Soccer and I are breaking up. We're getting divorced. We've been together for a long time—childhood sweethearts—and now she's moving out. We're divvying up our books, splitting the cutlery, packing our boxes, and selling the house."

She squinted at him, wondering if he really was as nuts as his whiteboard and notebooks implied. "What on earth are you talking about?"

"In six months I'll be in Nebraska. I'll be a retired pro—someone who used to be sort-of famous—and I'll be at the beginning of the next phase. The post-soccer phase. Also known as the rest of my life."

A pang of sadness for him poked at her heart, but she still didn't follow his reasoning. "Spell it out for me."

"Having sex with you would be like having sex with the woman I'm divorcing," he explained. "You're so deep in that world—the world I love and the world I'm leaving, whether I like it or not. I've spent the last six months emotionally distancing myself so it won't hurt quite so bad when I finally say goodbye. You and I—this—would only make it worse."

She frowned. "I think I understand, but I disagree. Strongly."

One side of his mouth quirked. "I thought you might."

"Yes, soccer is how we met, what we have most in common, as well as both of our current professions. But I am not a sport, Brendan. I am a woman. A woman you've slept with before. I am offering you no-strings, purely physical, mutually satisfying sex on tap. It doesn't have to interfere with your emotional breakup because emotion won't be involved. I've perfected the art of no-commitment intercourse. You'll pick it up in no time."

He took longer to respond this time, his gaze lingering on her face, and suddenly he was that twenty-two-year-old again, his inscrutable expression hiding a host of complicated mental machinations.

"I can't," he told her finally, and she knew from his tone there would be no further explanation.

"Whatever. Your loss," she decreed, rising again, this time to find her purse and make her way home. He nodded his agreement but as she crossed the room to retrieve her bag and dug around inside for her car keys, she couldn't help but think it was her loss.

Massively, overwhelmingly her loss.

Chapter 9

Skyline pressed Boston hard, all ten players over the midline, yet every one of Brendan's nerves seemed to whine with alertness. A high, tinny buzz like a hundred mosquitos drifted in and out of the space between his thoughts.

He squinted toward the other end of the pitch, shifting his weight from foot to foot. Only fifteen minutes left and the score was nil-nil. Not wildly unexpected against such a high-quality opponent—particularly because Roland used to be Boston's manager so a few of the players had axes to grind—but not the victory they were capable of, either.

Whether or not they scored was totally out of his hands. Whether or not they kept a clean sheet, however, fell squarely at his feet.

He leaned left, right, bouncing on the balls of his feet, his mental stock ticker running faster than ever. Despite the players' distance, every second he imagined another scenario, another angle from which Boston Liberty might try to score and moved in preparation, only to frantically reset his position to the center.

He glanced needlessly at the match clock. Fourteen minutes left. Exactly one minute since he'd last looked.

"Stop," he instructed himself quietly, standing motionless in the center of the goal. His anxiety on the pitch hadn't been this bad since the beginning of his career, and although he expected to be frazzled in his first match since last season, he didn't think it would be so extreme.

To be fair, he'd been better in the first half. His almost year-long absence from the pitch hadn't seemed to impact his concentration, his reaction times or his communication with the defensive players. He made two crucial saves to the cheers and applause of the away fans, and at halftime, Roland acknowledged his contribution in his dressing-room talk.

He began the second half with his characteristically efficient hyper-focus, but as the clock ticked it progressively moved from awareness to worry to anxiety to borderline panic. The physical exhaustion of playing a full ninety minutes for the first time in such a long time, plus the added pressure of knowing there was no one to sub him out if he made a catastrophic error or picked up an injury eroded his mental self-control. Over the second half, he spiraled from on-point and alert to agitated and scattered.

Stilling himself, he took several long, slow breaths, fighting to rein in his veering thoughts.

Visualize what you want and focus on it. The league trophy, glinting gold under bright lights. Renovating the house in Nebraska, knocking down walls, ripping up old carpet, days filled with useful exertion. A big, fat payout from the wagers he and Erin placed that weekend.

Erin. Blue eyes alight with mischief. Sensuous lips curving in satisfaction. Broad, muscular thighs, echoes of her time as a professional athlete. Soft breasts pressed against his chest, her warm fingers on his bare skin—

He shook his head, shutting down that line of thought and throwing all his energy into breathing slowly, watching carefully, blocking out everything except the match.

Boston was on the counterattack, passing the ball back into Skyline's half with their striker in possession. Brendan dug his cleats into the earth as the action shifted in his direction.

Instinctively he exhaled, pulling down the screen of cool-headed serenity he'd developed to keep his paranoid anxieties separate from the supercharged analytical machinations that created them. He had nothing to worry about. He was unbeatable. He was the best.

The affirmation tucked safely in his turbo-boosted brain, he narrowed his eyes at his own defenders as they sprinted to beat Boston back to their goal.

He widened his stance and slightly bent his knees, gloved hands raised in readiness. One of Skyline's center-backs, Paulo, got close enough to make eye contact. Brendan nodded to ease the concern in the Brazilian's expression.

I've got your back, his nod assured his teammate. Do what you need to do.

Paulo received his message loud and clear. The defender turned his back on the goal to mark an advancing Boston winger. It was a sensible decision—the winger was the most likely person for the striker to pass to, and by all accounts, he really should pass given no less than three Skyline players were vying for possession.

But Brendan read the striker's posture, his face, the momentary glance he tried to conceal by immediately looking the other way.

He shot. An audacious chance, backed up by serious technical skill as it arced over the heads of the Skyline players on a perfect trajectory toward the upper right-hand corner of the net. Clever, elegant, well executed, with potential not only to win the game but make the striker man of the match.

Except for the third-choice goalkeeper on the pitch.

Brendan's feet left the ground as he jumped to save the shot, batting the sixty-mile-an-hour ball away from the goal.

The away fans cheered the save and the Skyline players' postures registered visible relief, but a quick sweep of his opponents told Brendan they weren't safe yet. The ball was still too close to the goal for his liking.

Guedes—Paulo's counterpart—captured possession and passed to Oz, who passed to Paulo, who lost the ball in an interception. The Boston winger pivoted and booted the ball toward the goal in an accurate, powerful shot. Skyline's defenders were so spread out they couldn't do anything but watch it, faces stricken.

Brendan leaped sideways to intercept the shot, cupping his hands together in front of his chest. As soon as the ball thudded against his body he fell on it, trapping it underneath his ribs.

The force of the impact had knocked the air out of his lungs and he gave himself a second to recover, resting facedown, his forehead pressed into the grass. Slowly he made his way up, pleased to find his teammates had already started running back toward the midline. He gestured for them to keep going, assessing each one of their positions before placing the ball at his feet. He took a couple of steps backward to give himself a run-up, noted Oz was unmarked, and thwacked the ball in a long-range kick which the left-back controlled out of the sky with his head, his chest and finally his feet.

Oz negotiated the ball down the left channel, and Brendan checked the clock as his teammate made an aggressive run.

Nine minutes left.

He stepped to the edge of his area, watching Oz's unstoppable sprint. The left-back was hungry to score against his former club, and in the last thirty minutes, he'd channeled his first-half frustration into sheer determination.

He flexed his fingers, rolled his shoulders. At the other end of the pitch, Oz made laughingstocks of one of Boston's central defenders, popping the ball over his head and recovering it on his other side, then slamming it into the net.

Brendan smiled as his teammates celebrated. The away fans lost their minds and the scoreboard ticked up to one-nil. Boston wouldn't score in the next seven minutes—they were too tired, and now would be too demoralized, knowing their only hope was to equalize.

They would try, though. He reset his position between the goalposts, bending his ankles, exhaling the swell of anxiety that bubbled up in his mind, recapturing his all-over calm as Boston charged toward Skyline's half.

They would try. They would fail.

* * * *

Midfielder Brian Scholtz slapped his hands over his ears as Swedish techno music thumped through the dressing room.

"Do we really have to listen to this shit?"

"Goal-scorer's pick," Nico reminded him. "Terim got the winning point so Terim picks the music. When you score the winning point, we'll listen to whatever you want."

"Still, I'm not sure it needs to be so loud," Brian grumbled.

"Brian." Laurent shot him a withering look from across the dressing room. "You didn't even play. Stop being a dick."

Brendan exchanged an amused glance with Nico as the young midfielder backed down against Laurent's remark, delivered in his thick French accent.

"Here's the man of the hour," Nico enthused as Oz walked past them toward the showers. They both stood to embrace the left-back in turn.

"Fantastic shot," Brendan commended him, choosing his words carefully. Oz and Roland were thick as thieves, having played together in Boston and in Sweden before that. Although he trusted Oz as a teammate and they'd never been less than friendly, Brendan had no illusion that anything he did or said had potential to get back to Roland.

"Would've been a different story without your double save. It was a pleasure to have you behind us today. You really are a world-class keeper."

Oz stuck out his hand, and Brendan shook it gratefully. The young Swede wasn't a particularly forthcoming guy, and Brendan knew this was Oz's way of telling him the gambling scandal was behind them and that he had the left-back's support.

He smiled his appreciation at Oz's back as the defender proceeded toward the showers. His teammates' approval used to be the last thing he cared about. Now, at the end of his career, he treasured it.

"He's right," Nico agreed. "You saved our one-nil-scraping asses today. No one will forget it."

"Just doing my job." He slapped the winger on the back and sat down to finish untying his cleats. He stowed his boots in the cubby below the locker, stripped off his socks to toss into the laundry bin, and stuck his feet into his shower flip-flops. Then he reached up and pulled his jersey over his head, holding it at arm's length to read the name and number printed on the back.

Young. 1.

He'd come to Skyline as number one and kept the number after Roland arrived and he dropped to second and then third choice. At points over the last year, he'd felt like a fraud, tugging on a number-one shirt for training, knowing full well he wouldn't even be dressing for the next match, let alone playing in it. The badge of honor he'd spent so long earning became a scarlet letter, mocking his fall from grace, signifying everything he'd thrown away.

Pride swelled in his chest. He'd never take anything so important, so rare, or so hard-won for granted again.

He added the jersey to the laundry pile, then took off his shorts, his briefs, and wrapped the provided towel from Boston Liberty's sponsor around his waist.

He looked down. "Oh."

Nico glanced over and burst into hysterical laughter, pointing at the too-small towel's early finish at the top of his thighs.

"Guys, look at Young's towel," he called to the room at large, wiping tears from the corners of his eyes. "They gave him an extra small."

"To be fair, they don't make towels in giraffe size," Laurent joked.

"He asked for extra long, but then they called his ex-girlfriend," Oz hollered from the shower.

"Very funny." But Brendan grinned as he made his way to the showers, enjoying being a part of the team banter after so long on its fringes. He picked a stall and turned on the water, ducking under the showerhead. Then he balled up the offending towel and hurled it at Nico's head, hitting his mark with accuracy that would make any striker envious.

His good mood persisted as he dressed, boarded the bus with the rest of the Skyline players and took the short journey back to their hotel. He waited until he was safely in his room to read a text message from Erin, easing onto the edge of the bed.

They hadn't seen each other since the previous weekend's strategy session—as she had coined it—but they'd texted constantly, trading updates on odds and player stats and lobbing predictions about the results of the upcoming match schedule.

Hey, you! Watched the 1st half, great stuff! You look like you don't even know where the bench is let alone been on it most of the season. Best of luck in the 2nd 45 mins!

He smiled. He expected it to be one of her reminders to send her the finalized wagers to place early tomorrow morning.

He tapped out a reply. *Hope you enjoyed the 2nd half. Nice to get a clean sheet, important win for the team. Will send final picks tonight.*

He'd leaned over to plug his phone into its charger when it dinged. He raised it again and read her reply.

The humble Mr. Young not taking credit for his super speedy double save in the last 20 mins. Very well played sir, good to see you on the pitch where you belong.

He shook his head, endeared by her love of emojis as he put his phone down. She didn't quite get the complexities of his system yet, but he appreciated her enthusiasm. He also appreciated her irresponsibly vast array of credit cards, with which they were able to shop for odds and win tangible, exciting sums of money—money he didn't need financially but emotionally he was surprisingly dependent on.

Maybe the monetary wins were the validation he needed to prop up his often faltering ego, he considered, opening the menu for the hotel restaurant. Or maybe they made his endless charts and notebook scribblings real, in a way. Legitimizing his mental maneuverings in the real world instead of only in his head.

Either way, it worked. What should've been one of the most stressful weeks of his life as he prepared for today's match was relaxed and easy. Whenever his anxiety built he pulled out a notebook and reviewed that weekend's bets, finding calm in the systematic analysis and reassurance in the knowledge these hypotheses would be put to the real-life test and would live or die on Erin's credit cards.

He refocused on the menu, deciding to spend the evening in the restaurant with a celebratory steak and page after page of match analysis. He tucked his notebook under his arm and headed downstairs.

The restaurant hostess was still halfway through her greeting when his name rang across the crowded room. He turned in that direction to find a handful of his teammates seated around a table, gesturing for him to join them.

Dammit. He wasn't in the mood for socializing. His brain was tender after the exertion and fierce control required for the match and his grip on his anxiety felt tenuous, in the same way his hands shook and cramped at the end of a long set of weights repetitions. They'd seen him now, though, and there was no way he could politely move on to sit by himself in a dark corner. He'd have to stay for at least one drink, then make an excuse and find somewhere else to eat.

His body sagged with weariness but he forced a smile as he joined his teammates. Winger Rio Vidal stood and shifted his chair over, then grabbed another from a nearby table and stuffed it into the empty space.

Brendan thanked the Chilean as he took his seat. Between his iffy Spanish and Rio's iffy English the two of them had a surprisingly good rapport.

"This looks like a Midfielders Anonymous meeting. Are you sure I'm allowed to be here?" He looked around the table at Laurent, Nico, Rio, and Aaron Jackson, Laurent's American counterpart in central midfield.

"Just this once we'll make an exception. It's your lucky day, we haven't ordered yet. Do you want to see a menu?" Laurent asked.

"I had a look in the room. I just came down for a drink. I'm not hungry enough to eat yet."

"We'll wait," Nico offered. "We can have a few starters while you work up an appetite."

"No, really, I'm fine. I might go for a walk. See what's in the neighborhood."

Laurent shrugged off his excuse but Nico frowned. Brendan shoved his notebook farther down his lap, balancing it precariously on his knees and safely out of sight of his teammates.

"Wine?" Laurent asked as the waitress arrived with an expensive bottle of red. He'd planned to indulge in no more than a post-match beer, maybe two, but at this point, Brendan felt he had to go with the flow.

"Sure." He snagged a wineglass from another table and pushed it forward. Laurent expertly poured out the bottle between their five glasses and Brendan took a sip, supposing it would be bad manners to down it all in one, although it would get him out of there faster.

He managed to drag it out over forty minutes in the end. He bantered with the midfielders and returned the good-humored ribbing he received in equal measure. Time well spent, bonding with the teammates from whom he'd become alienated over the last season as they felt their way back to relying on each other.

By the time he took the final, draining sip from the glass his thoughts whirred and roared like a buzz saw about to cut through his skull.

"I'm off," he announced. "Time to leave you midfield dynamos to congratulate yourselves on your creative passes and clever maneuvers, conveniently forgetting that a defender scored our only goal today."

"Hilarious. What's that?" Nico pointed to his notebook as he stood up from the table.

Brendan deployed the answer he'd come up with midway through his glass of wine. "Secret goalkeeper stuff."

Nico looked like he was about to ask for more detail when Aaron jumped in.

"You know I love you, Young, but damn, goalkeepers are weird. Have you guys ever noticed that?"

The other midfielders nodded and Aaron continued, "Every goalkeeper I've ever played with has been totally offbeat. Good guys, but strange. I think you might be the most normal one I've met."

If only you knew. "I'll take that as a compliment. Anyway, enjoy your dinner, gentlemen. I'll see you tomorrow for the trip home."

He exchanged goodbyes with his teammates and then had to stop himself from running out of the restaurant, across the lobby and outside. When he finally made it through the hotel doors he leaned against the wall, taking deep breaths of humid air in an effort to calm his racing heart.

He had nothing to worry about, he informed himself. The notebook was so heavily coded he doubted anyone could make it out without any context, and certainly not after a couple seconds' glimpse. His teammates were his friends and allies, not his enemies.

Having rationalized his stock-ticker thoughts to a crawl instead of a sprint, he pushed off the wall and walked down the street, keeping his eyes open for a suitable venue for a beer, some dinner and a couple of hours of statistics.

He wandered for a while, enjoying the Friday-night bustle on the sidewalks as Bostonians enjoyed a warm, late-summer evening. Well-dressed couples held hands as they stepped inside expensive-looking restaurants, and he tried to imagine where he'd be this time next year. A hot, dry Nebraska summer was more or less guaranteed, but what about everything else?

By then maybe he'd have someone to take to nice restaurants. Whose hand he could hold on a Friday night. Who'd take an interest in his conjectures about the next day's soccer results. Who wouldn't mind the time he spent analyzing the sport he used to play, and who would appreciate his winnings, not judge him for playing for them.

Or maybe—more likely—he'd still be alone. Sitting in a bar with his notebooks and his beer, making bets on people who used to fear him, who wanted to face anyone but him for a penalty kick.

He circled back to a bar he'd seen right after leaving the hotel. Its low-key exterior flagged his interest when he first passed it, and in twenty minutes of walking, he hadn't found anywhere as attractively unassuming. He pushed open the door.

The situation inside was exactly as he'd glimpsed through the window. The décor sat somewhere between an Irish pub and a sports bar, with Guinness logos and Red Sox memorabilia vying for dominance. Men watching a baseball game lined the bar, but that was fine with him. He wanted one of the empty booths along the back wall instead.

He found enough space at the end of the bar to lean in and get the bartender's attention. She was surprisingly young and pretty to be working somewhere with such an old-man vibe. Maybe she dug old men.

"What can I get you?" She flashed him a warm, seemingly genuine smile. Or maybe she worked here because these oldies fell for her grin and tipped her better.

"Sam Adams draught." He pointed to a laminated piece of paper stuck under a bowl of nuts. "Is this the menu?"

She nodded. "I can recommend the burgers. We bring them in from the restaurant next door."

He accepted his beer and ordered a cheeseburger, then crossed to a corner booth. His notebook stuck to the surface of the table and the un-cushioned wooden bench dug into his tailbone.

Perfect.

Calmer than he'd been all day, he pulled out his notebook, flipped to his in-progress page and methodically worked through tomorrow's fixtures.

One cheeseburger, one beer, and an hour later, he sensed someone standing near the edge of his table.

"Another Sam Adams would be great, thanks," he murmured, barely looking up from his notebook. Only when someone slid into the other side of the booth did he manage to tear his gaze away from the page.

"What are you doing here?" he demanded.

"Nice to see you, too." Erin plucked one of the fries from the wax paper-lined basket and bit into it, then wrinkled her nose and put it back. "These are stone cold."

"I thought you were the bartender, coming to take this away."

"She's busy." Erin thumbed toward the bar, which was significantly more crowded than when he sat down. Still mostly old men, though, all glued to the TV.

"What's so exciting?"

"Some shitty sport with wooden sticks where no one kicks anything. Want to go somewhere else?"

He shut the notebook, sizing her up across the table. Her hair cascaded loosely over her shoulders, and she wore jeans and a V-neck T-shirt. Too casual to be here on business, but surely she would've told him if she'd come to watch his match.

Either way, she stood out in their dingy surroundings like a vase of bright red roses in the middle of a junkyard. He found himself breathing a bit easier, as though she'd brought a gust of fresh air with her from outside.

He fought to keep a stern expression. "Let's start with here, specifically your presence. I thought you were in Atlanta."

"You thought wrong."

"You didn't tell me you were going to be in Boston."

"You didn't ask."

He rolled his eyes. "Just tell me why you're here."

"I had a meeting this afternoon with Liberty Ladies, to discuss next season's marketing campaign. I didn't tell you because it was scheduled at short notice and I didn't want to distract you ahead of your match. Also, it wasn't your business."

"And this bar? This booth? How did you get here?"

"Coincidence…ish."

"Ish?" he repeated.

"I thought it might be nice to check in on you. Make sure you weren't beating yourself up over that mistake in the first half when the central midfielder's shot hit the post."

He bolted upright. "That wasn't a mistake. I saw that wasn't going in and I knew if I touched it there was as much chance of it becoming an own goal as—"

"I'm kidding. You played great. Anyway, I'm not here to offer performance feedback."

"Back to the central question, then. Why are you here?"

She raised a shoulder. "I spotted one of the other players leaving the restaurant and he said you'd gone for a walk. I saw this place, near the hotel, with all the Brendan Young hallmarks—dark, dingy, generally uninviting—and decided to look inside to see if you were here. If you weren't, I would've gone back to the hotel. But you are, and here I am."

He narrowed his eyes. "Not sure it was a great idea to ask my teammates where I was. Now they'll link the two of us."

"I thought of that, but it was the guy who doesn't speak English."

"Rio," Brendan supplied, relieved.

"I don't think he knew who I was. He started to sign a napkin for me. Anyway, we can safely assume there are no soccer fans amongst the loyal over there."

He glanced again at the crowd near the bar, then back at her. "Are you hungry?"

"Starving. Want another drink?"

He pushed his glass across the table. "Go for it."

"Oh, I will," she promised, winking as she gathered up the discarded burger basket and the empty glass.

He watched her sidle up to the group looking at the TV and navigate her way through a clump of men. He couldn't hear her from across the room, but he noted the amount of smiling, giggling and back-touching seemed unnecessary for placing an order from a female bartender. After a few minutes she came back with a beer in each hand, and instead of resuming her previous seat she motioned him closer to the wall so she could squeeze in beside him.

"How much do I owe you?" he asked, trying to ignore the fresh, summery whiff of jasmine that lit up his senses as her hip bumped his. He thought again of the creeping, twisting jasmine vine that climbed a trellis along the back of his house. According to his gardener, it was quite a mature plant, lovingly cultivated by the couple from whom he'd bought the house three years earlier. Its delicate flowers and sweet scent belied its strength and endurance, and every month it reached higher like it was intent on growing all the way to the roof.

"These were free," Erin explained. "Courtesy of my new friends, Richard and Larry."

As if on cue, two men turned around at the bar and waved. Erin waved back.

"I've seen women get free drinks before, but never extras for their male friends."

"I told them you play for Boston Liberty."

He laughed. Not the muted laugh he offered his bantering teammates, or the privately bemused chuckle when something randomly struck him as funny. A belly-deep, rib-vibrating, utterly spontaneous laugh that kept going until it brought tears to his eyes.

It took a minute or two to collect himself. He hadn't laughed like that in a while.

"I ordered nachos," she announced, pulling out her phone. "And while we wait for them, you're going to put away your notebook and lose some money."

He groaned as she tapped open a slot-machine app. "I hate this crap."

"You'll love it once you learn how to play it."

"I doubt that," he grumbled, but leaned over the screen anyway.

"Looks like I'm out of credit. We need to load that up first." She tapped through various options until her balance to play with was fifty dollars.

He whistled. "Are you sure you can afford to lose that?"

"Who says I'm going to lose it?" She bet one dollar on her first spin, pressed the button, lost.

"Ouch."

She brushed off his comment with a waved hand. "I'm still warming up. Let's amp up the action." She bet five dollars, pressed the button, and lost again.

A knot of discomfort fisted in his stomach as he looked at the depleting sum of credit at the top right-hand corner of the screen. "Let's call it quits. You can cash out the money you haven't bet, right?"

"Nope," she replied with a flourish, losing another five dollars.

"At least bet smaller sums. This is stupid."

"Chill. You're missing the point."

"If losing money on nothing is the point, I'm getting it."

She shook her head. "The point is it's random. Out of your hands. Pure luck."

"It's not luck, it's an algorithm developed to make sure the betting site never pays out more than it takes in."

She sighed. "You are so uptight. I know how slot machines work, online and in-person. You have to let go of the math and hope that you'll be the one who gets the big payout or any payout at all. Sometimes it happens, and that sometimes makes it exciting."

"It makes it stressful," he amended.

"Because sitting for hours poring over player stats and fixture records is like being on the beach? Here, try." She stuck her phone in his hand.

"I really don't—" She reached across him to press the button, the side of her breast brushing his arm. The air caught in his lungs as the faint contact sent a bolt of sensation rocketing up to his shoulder.

"You won a dollar! See, we're already on an upswing."

She pressed in more closely and he knew it was deliberate. He took a stalling drink of beer as his mental stock ticker whirred to life, analyzing the genuineness of her intentions, the long-term implications, the potential for someone to see them and get the wrong idea—or the right one.

"Your turn," she goaded, nudging him in the ribs.

"I won't gamble with your money."

"You already do. You tell me how to wager on soccer."

"I give you advice. You don't have to take it."

"I'd be a fool not to." Her hand slid along the wooden seat to bump into his leg. The stock ticker whirred a little bit faster.

He lowered his left hand to rest on top of hers. She looped her fingers through his.

"Go on," she urged. "Spin again."

He shook his head, paranoia ramping up with every passing second. He tried to glance past her to make sure they knew no one in the bar but when he turned his head she filled his vision, red hair and moist lips and that coy, tantalizing smile.

"We'll do it together." She positioned the phone on the table and guided his hand above it. Then she dropped their interlinked fingers to press the button.

Jackpot.

"Thirty dollars!" She dropped his hand to clap in excitement, bouncing on the seat. "That's incredible. Never mind your system, you have a gift."

He began to protest but she silenced him with her mouth, one hand moving to his neck, the other to his waist.

He sank into the kiss like submerging into a warm, Floridian ocean. The sounds of the bar became muffled, distant, distorted, and the stock ticker ground to a welcome halt.

He didn't care about consequences or possibilities. He wanted her. Now. Nothing else mattered.

He gripped the enticing curve of her waist, responding impatiently to the pressure of her lips. She didn't need much encouragement—instantly she cracked her jaw to give him access, meeting the thrusts of his tongue with eagerness and hunger.

His erection rose quickly and mercilessly, threatening the limits of his jeans as he shifted to hold more of her, to fill his palms with as much soft, sweet woman as possible.

She made him a glutton, he realized as he moved one hand to her neck, twining his fingers in her hair. Structure and systems and moderation dictated the rest of his life, but with her, he was a starving beggar unexpectedly admitted to a royal feast—no, he was a diabetic bingeing on jumbo-sized chocolate bars. He knew it would hurt later. He knew it might even kill him. Still, he couldn't stop, couldn't find satisfaction, couldn't ever get enough.

She tasted like beer, hoppy and summery and relaxing. Her body was a mix of soft and hard—lush breasts, generous hips, unyielding muscles in her legs and upper arms. Her jasmine scent curled around him like a vine, drawing him nearer.

"Nachos."

The clunk of porcelain on wood jerked them apart. The bartender scowled at him, shot Erin a look that said she'd better still get her tip, and stormed back across the room.

The stock ticker hummed in double time. The bartender would remember them now. Would she go to the tabloids? It wouldn't be difficult to figure out he was a Skyline player, not Liberty. Any reasonably intelligent sports correspondent would—

Erin trailed her fingertips down his side, releasing the line of tension tightening the space between his shoulders. His paranoia receded like low tide. Of course, the bartender wouldn't go to the tabloids, nor would she think about them for longer than it took him to leave a big tip.

Maybe Erin was right. He should chill.

She took a long draught of beer, then smiled at him over the rim of her glass, mischief gleaming in her eyes. "So you do know how."

"How to what?"

"Have fun."

"I have fun all the time. Vegas was fun."

"You were drunk."

"Is that what you tell yourself?"

The words slipped from his mouth with unexpectedly sharp edges, piercing the moment. His gaze dropped to his lap. Erin replaced her glass on the table, lining it up in the wet ring it had left when she picked it up.

He resisted the urge to withdraw from the ache that had started in the center of his chest at the mention of their night together. He knew this might happen and he kissed her anyway. He couldn't evade the consequences.

"We drank, but we weren't drunk," he spelled out. "Don't pretend that either of us had anything less than an absolutely clear idea of what we were doing. It's insulting."

"You know that's not what I meant." But her voice trailed off and her hands settled around the bottom of her glass, fingers tapping distractedly.

He wanted to touch her, but he didn't. He wanted to drape his arm over her shoulder, pull her against his side and assure her he wasn't offended.

Except for every time he touched her, another string of jasmine flowers looped around his waist and tightened, tying him to her in a way that made it harder and harder to pull away.

He needed room to move. To leave. And when the time came for him to tangle up in a web of strings, she wouldn't be on the other end of them.

He sensed her posture change. She tapped the side of the glass once more, then slipped around the edge of the table to sit across from him, not beside him.

When their eyes met again hers were cool and evaluating. He tightened his jaw. Had he made a mistake?

"This was fun, but it wasn't free." She tilted her head. "Our deal was that you would feed me some leads on gambling in the league. I have to update my boss on Monday. What am I going to tell him?"

He flexed his hands under the table. He knew this moment was on its way, but that didn't make its arrival any less disappointing.

"Tucson United," he told her quietly. "A couple of the guys have an online fantasy soccer team. They lose more than they win, but I'm guessing that doesn't matter."

"Not a bit. But thank you. I'll take it from here."

He pulled a twenty-dollar note from his wallet and tucked it under the plate of untouched nachos, then stuck his notebook under his arm and stood up.

"We shouldn't be seen together near the hotel. I'll send you the fixture choices tonight."

"I'll let you know when the money's down. See you in Atlanta." She plucked a tortilla chip from the top of the stack and bit into it delicately.

He stormed out of the bar, head down.

He knew the rules when he asked to be dealt in, and he knew the minimum bet. Stepping out of the league's spotlight while keeping his betting habit alive would cost him.

He clutched his notebook more tightly, already mentally composing an email to Erin with his picks, imagining her clicking to accept the bookie's odds.

Fuck it—it was worth it. He needed to bet more than he needed friends at Tucson United. And he'd pay a hell of a lot more than what they cost him to keep going.

Chapter 10

"Gorgeous. Good job, Paul." Erin nodded her approval of the diamond engagement ring as she released her friend's hand.

"I know, I'm so impressed." Molly smiled at the ring one more time before wrapping her hand around the stem of her wineglass.

"Have you set a date?"

Her former national-squad teammate shrugged. "We're not in a hurry. Paul's still negotiating his contract with Tucson. We don't want to book anywhere with a big deposit before we know what the bank accounts will be like."

"It doesn't all have to depend on his career," Erin reminded her. "You're doing amazing things with the women's team. You could get the manager's job in a year or two."

"Even if I did, we couldn't live on my salary alone."

"So demand a better salary."

Molly smiled affectionately. "That's what I love about you, Erin. You never let anyone tell you no."

"That's not entirely true," she muttered. Over the last week, a certain person had told her no repeatedly, despite being the only one whose yes seemed to matter more each day.

She hadn't spoken to Brendan, not in person anyway since he left her in the bar in Boston. They'd exchanged texts and emails, but her suggestion that they meet to start looking at the weekend matches was declined, as was her offer to stop by his house to show him the odds she'd been offered on a range of bookmakers' websites.

His distance shouldn't have been a black spot in an otherwise positive week. Randall was delighted with her lead on the Tucson United fantasy team—the "online syndicate," he called it—and happy to authorize a last-minute trip to Arizona. He was even happier when she called him from the Tucson manager's office to inform him the two players responsible had come forward immediately, were conciliatory and willing to undertake the compliance awareness training she recommended.

That dirty business dispensed, she'd spent hours with the staff and players from Tucson's women's team. Everyone loved the idea of the marketing campaign and jumped in with thoughts on how to implement it given the resources at their disposal, as well as to maximize its impact locally, like translating some of the materials into Spanish. She and Molly exchanged delighted looks throughout the afternoon, silently applauding themselves for helping the game to come so far from when they played professionally only a handful of years earlier.

Now a fun Saturday night in a trendy bar with one of her good friends stretched ahead of her, unpressured by work demands, yet she struggled to stay centered as her wildly impractical thoughts kept drifting to Brendan. Eccentric, peculiar Brendan, with his charts and his numbers and his codes. Weirdly comforting Brendan, with his soft voice and slow smile. Sexy, intriguing, irresistible Brendan, whose face and body and capable hands invaded her mind every night as she fell asleep.

Clever, calculating Brendan, who'd helped her win more money in three weeks than she had in three months.

She picked up her phone and unlocked the screen, opening the app she'd recently downloaded which posted live international soccer results. She'd had such a busy day she hadn't even thought about checking the bets she'd placed shortly before midnight.

She scanned the league table and the score breakdowns. There were still a few matches to be played on Sunday, but of the six they'd wagered on he'd correctly called the result on four.

Two hundred and fifty dollars on those bets alone, with four more results due tomorrow.

"Erin?"

Molly's voice snapped her back to the present as she stuffed her phone into her bag. "Sorry. What did you say?"

Molly nodded to the bartender, who repeated what Erin suspected he'd already asked multiple times. "Would you like another glass of wine?"

"Yes, please. Another for each of us."

Molly shot her a probing look as the bartender refilled their glasses, but waited until he moved away to ask, "Are you okay? You seem distracted."

"I am distracted. I need to have sex, Mols."

"Gotcha." She glanced around the room. "I see the problem. Zero eligibles. But we can move on after this. There's a place—"

Erin shook her head. "I need to have sex with someone in particular."

Molly's attention sharpened. "He wasn't interested?"

"Yes and no. I think he'd be willing but only if it was in the context of something serious."

"Like long-term serious?"

"Medium-term, at least," she replied, leaving out the crucial detail that in more than the medium term they'd be living a thousand miles apart.

"Here's a radical suggestion. Go for it."

"No way. You know me. I don't do relationships." Erin waved her forefinger in the negative.

Molly sighed. "Should I bother giving you my opinion, or are you going to dismiss me on the basis I'm probably high on wedding fumes?"

Ouch. That's exactly what I was about to do. "I want your opinion."

"It won't be a surprise. I think you should give commitment a try. You might discover that you're more ready for it than you realize."

"I sure as hell don't feel ready." She circled her glass on the bar, watching the white wine swirl counterclockwise.

"I didn't feel ready when I met Paul, either. I'd just started my assistant manager job with Tucson and I was so focused on getting it right, meeting everyone at the club, finding an apartment, the whole transition from player to coaching staff, apparently, he attempted to flirt with me for months before I noticed."

Erin arched a brow. "I find that hard to believe. Paul is dangerously charming."

"I'm telling you, I was that preoccupied, I had no idea. Anyway, when we finally got on the same page, he was ready to get serious a lot earlier than I was. Eventually, I decided to give him a chance, and here we are." She wiggled her newly bejeweled finger.

"That's the 'what,' not the 'why.' You went for a guy who was crazy about you, who you were reasonably crazy about in return, having never been as anti-commitment as I am. Different scenario. Why should I change the way I've been running my life for years given I'm still perfectly happy?"

She lifted a shoulder. "Why do anything?"

"That's a non-answer."

"Let's turn it around. Maybe it's not about you. Maybe it's about this guy and the significance of the fact that he likes you enough to want something more than casual sex."

Erin rolled her eyes. "He's not the first one to say it. It doesn't make him special."

"But is he the first one to make it a condition?"

She had to think about that. With some astonishment, she replied, "Yes."

"And is he also the first one you've liked enough to consider it?"

"I'm not considering it."

"We're discussing it now," Molly countered. "That's considering."

She exhaled her defeat. "Okay, yes. He's the first. But I'm not open to the relationship thing. I'm thinking more along the lines of a premium version of friends with benefits."

Her friend's gaze was skeptical as she took a sip of wine. "Do I even want to know?"

"So friends with benefits aren't usually really friends, right? They're amicable hookups. Friendly, not friends. In my premium version"—she drew her hands across the space like she was unveiling a marquee—"we are real, honest-to-God friends. We hang out, we spend time together, we go out for drinks, and then we have sex."

"Erin, that's a relationship."

"No, because there's no emotional attachment beyond the friend level. The friend part stays over here, and the sex part stays over here." She held her two fists apart.

Molly's expression wasn't convinced. "Have you presented this to the man in question?"

"I wanted your input first. What do you think?"

Her friend took her time in answering, running her fingers up and down the stem of her glass. Erin tried to defuse the moment with a goofy smile but Molly was impenetrable, as thoughtful and incisive as she had been as a masterful central midfielder.

"What?" Erin asked finally, unable to stand another second of silence.

"It's not like you to need advice or permission for anything. You don't consult—you decide what you want and go for it. You always have. I think you might really care about this guy," Molly concluded.

Automatically Erin opened her mouth to disagree—then closed it again. Molly had a point. She'd never struggled to brush off a guy as much as she was struggling to brush off Brendan. But did she care about him?

"Maybe I care about his feelings, a little bit," she conceded.

Molly's responding smile was irritatingly knowing.

"Don't you dare," Erin warned. "And we're done talking about my love life. Soccer, weddings, and gossip only from now on."

"Cheers to that." They clinked their glasses together.

"That reminds me." She signaled to the bartender. "Would you mind changing the TV channel? There should be a soccer game on one of the sports channels. Eugene Pines at Atlanta Skyline."

* * * *

"Try me. Just try me." Brendan narrowed his eyes at Eugene's striker, Adam Francis, as he started toward Skyline's half. He'd played against the Englishman years ago—they'd been on opposite sides in a hotly contested local rivalry.

They hadn't liked each other then, and they didn't like each other now. Adam was an egotistical, melodramatic player who loved nothing more than throwing himself down in the penalty area if one of his opponents so much as breathed on him. He and Brendan had faced off over tenuously awarded penalties more than once.

In their training sessions leading up to the match, Brendan warned his defenders that Adam would try to provoke them. They'd heeded his advice meticulously in the first half, stopping Adam with precise, clean tackles. Clearly frustrated with the nil-nil score at halftime, though, the striker started the second forty-five minutes with double the belligerence he'd shown earlier, arguing with the referee and calling for fouls every time anyone got near him.

His tactics were pathetic, but Brendan knew from experience they were effective. The linesmen already looked nervous, probably second-guessing some of their calls given Adam's vehement responses. His defenders were getting worn down, too. Oz was on international duty and in his place was the second-choice left-back, an up-and-coming young American called Gabe Garcia. Gabe was quick and skillful, but he didn't have Oz's emotional self-control, and Brendan could see that Adam's antics were beginning to wear him down. It was only a matter of time before things got ugly.

Near the center line, Kojo stole possession from Adam and passed to Laurent, who passed to Nico, who drove the ball back up toward Eugene's goal. Brendan kept his attention sharp for a possible counterattack. He felt confident, in control of his mind, ready for anything.

He felt like the seasoned pro he was.

At the other end of the pitch, both teams clustered around Eugene's goal. Skyline pressed them back, harder and harder, as their defenders thickened in the space between the two posts.

Rio found the ball on the wing and punted a high pass to Skyline's striker, Deon Ellis, who headed it toward the goal.

One of Eugene's center-backs and their goalkeeper jumped at the same time to clear it. The center-back realized his mistake too late, and he accidentally knocked the ball into the net.

Own goal.

The Skyline players cheered as the score ticked up to one-nil. It wasn't the most elegant way to win, but a victory was a victory. Now they had to hold on to it for—he checked the clock—half an hour. Difficult, but doable.

Eugene took a while to recover from the error. Their shell-shocked defense and scattered forwards nearly gave Skyline a second goal as Laurent found a shot, but the keeper saved it comfortably.

Eugene seemed to pull themselves together and reconsolidated their efforts to equalize the score. Brendan's focus sharpened as Adam recaptured possession and pushed into Skyline's half.

"Stay cool," he called to his defenders, who stuck their thumbs up to show they'd heard without turning to look at him.

Kojo caught Adam in his run down the right-hand channel, neatly tackling him to pass the ball to Nico. The maneuver was clinical but Adam hurled himself on the ground, holding his ankle and rolling back and forth.

A few of the Skyline players threw up their hands in exasperation, but Brendan watched Adam carefully. Goalkeepers had the broadest views of the pitch, and it was his responsibility to notice as much as he could and communicate to the other players. He was Skyline's anchor, keeping the big ship safely moored no matter how hard the wind blew.

As Adam insisted on the medic, Brendan noted the heaving shoulders and sweat-soaked jerseys of the Pines players. They were tired, and evidently not as match-fit as Skyline. Adam was deliberately wasting time to give them a rest.

On the sideline, Roland noticed it too and began shouting his dissatisfaction at the referee. It wasn't like the Swede, and Brendan shook his head ruefully. The ref was already under pressure from Eugene's pushy striker and Skyline's irritated players. He didn't need a manager in his ear too.

"Be calm," he encouraged the defenders. "Tight and clean. No mistakes."

Kojo nodded. The Brazilians stuck up their thumbs. Gabe tossed a halfhearted smile over his shoulder, but his agitation was clear in his posture.

"Garcia." Brendan summoned the left-back's attention, then lowered his hands in a simmer-down gesture. The young player nodded, visibly calming himself, but Brendan knew his self-control could be the weak link in their chain.

Unsurprisingly Adam was fine to continue, and play resumed with the Pines palpably refreshed from the break. Brendan drummed his heels against the ground as they pressed Skyline backward into their half. They wanted to score, and they wouldn't stop trying until they did.

He exhaled, loosening his shoulders and centering his thoughts. Let Eugene test him. Let Adam take him one-on-one. They wouldn't beat him. He was unstoppable.

Sunset-red hair, mischievous blue eyes, skin as pale and soft as a pink rose petal...

He flinched at the intruding image of Erin. Where the hell did that come from? And why on earth—

"Shit."

Adam passed to one of Eugene's midfielders who took an ambitious shot on goal from his position far outside the area. Brendan instantly knew it would go wide but chased its direction anyway, mindful of the other players and their potential to knock it in. Thankfully none of the others were far enough forward and Skyline took a throw-in, but as they jogged back up the pitch his heart thudded hard in his chest.

"Focus," he chanted under his breath. He hadn't seen Erin in a week and he thought she was well out of his mind. Okay, maybe he'd given her— and more accurately what he would like to do with her—the odd thought now and again. Particularly late at night, in bed. And once or twice in the morning. And in the shower after training the other day, and—

"Enough," he muttered. Eugene was wheeling in his direction with Adam leading the charge. Time to get his head in the game and keep it there.

Adam passed to a winger, who passed to a central midfielder. Brendan read Adam's plan long before he could implement it, and when he ran across the goal to execute a quick turnaround shot Brendan was ready for him. He caught the ball in two hands, then motioned for the Skyline players to fall back in order to gain ground on the goal kick.

Adam growled in frustration, unwisely remaining near the goal while his teammates tracked back in preparation to defend Skyline's possession. "You're wasting time."

"That's funny, coming from you."

Adam spat on the grass. "Your high and mighty act doesn't work anymore, Young. You're a disgrace. Did you put a bet on this match? You should have. A thousand dollars that I'll score against you."

Brendan let Adam's words sink in, knowing that resisting would only waste energy and destabilize his concentration. Instead, he absorbed them, registered them, filed them for review later. He took a couple of steps backward to give himself a run-up, then looked Adam level in the face.

"Fuck off."

Adam's eyes flashed with anger as he jumped forward in a clumsy attempt to capture the ball, but he was too slow. Brendan walloped it in one long, powerful kick that sent it halfway up the field to Deon, who controlled it out of the air and passed to Laurent.

Brendan watched Adam scramble back up the pitch, forcing himself to breathe slowly in an effort to pour cold water over the striker's stinging words.

Adam wanted to get him riled up. Brendan wouldn't give him the satisfaction.

The two teams grappled near the center line for a few minutes, then as the Pines made an attack on Skyline's half Gabe caught one of their wingers in a late challenge. The winger's dramatics on the pitch were unnecessary, but the foul awarded by the referee was unfortunately totally fair. Gabe punched a fist into his open palm, and Brendan wished he was near enough to remind the hotheaded young player to keep his cool.

Eugene took their free kick near the center line and hustled play into Skyline's half. Brendan focused intently as both teams came nearer, blocking out everything except anticipating the future position of the ball at any second. Instinctively he scanned players' faces, took in the angles of their feet, caught their exchanged glances, making and adjusting and readjusting what felt like millions of decisions per minute.

A Pines winger shot, Guedes blocked it. Adam picked up the loose ball. Gabe stuck to Adam's side, trying to pluck the ball from between his feet. Brendan watched as they stepped over the line into the penalty area. Gabe extended his hand across the striker's chest to keep his own balance. Adam flung himself over Gabe's arm in a dramatic somersault, landing on his back and slamming his fists into the grass in exaggerated outrage.

Brendan ran his gloved hand over his face as the referee blew his whistle. He knew what the decision would be, but that didn't make him any less angry when the ref announced it.

Penalty.

He kept his fury and frustration entirely inside as Gabe looked at him with a stricken expression.

"I didn't touch him," the left-back told him urgently, and Brendan waved him off.

"Don't worry. I've got it."

A few feet away Guedes had gotten into a confrontation with one of Eugene's midfielders, and Kojo and Paulo inserted themselves between the two to prevent a full-blown fight. The referee spoke sternly to all of them, the two managers gestured angrily from the sideline, and the whole stadium seemed to seethe with acrimony.

Adam placed the ball in position for the penalty kick, calmly waiting for the commotion to die down so he could take his shot.

They watched each other carefully, two pillars of absolute stillness in a noisy group of het-up men. Brendan shut the door on everything he felt about Adam and concentrated on technical data. The stock ticker sped with intricately remembered stats about which direction Adam had picked in his last ten penalty kicks, only three of which had been during his tenure in the Championship League, however, they made up an overall pattern that included his international appearances.

To the numbers, Brendan added his personal experience, although it was many years ago now and Adam had undoubtedly evolved. He cataloged minute details about the way Adam prepared, the way he stepped up to the ball, the way he breathed as he drew back his leg to shoot.

Time. Adam needed time. If he had no time he'd be inaccurate. He'd screw up.

Brendan smiled at Adam as the referee motioned for the other players to back up. "Ready?"

The striker's answering smirk was tight. Nervous. "To make a fool of you? Always."

Brendan clapped his gloved hands together and raised his arms, filling as much of the goal with his body as he could. He had a plan, and it was risky. If it worked he'd be a hero. If he didn't, well, he supposed he'd be no worse off than he'd been a month ago.

Brendan nodded to the referee, who blew the whistle to signal for Adam to take his shot. The striker gathered himself, rolled his neck—and Brendan feinted a lunge off the goal line. The rules forbade him from actually leaving the line but the movement was enough to trigger Adam's instinct, which was to kick the ball before it could be taken from him.

The striker took his shot, opting to send it straight down the middle. Suspecting that he might, Brendan hadn't lunged left or right and instead jumped to clear the ball.

He didn't need to. It hit the bar on the upper edge of the goal and bounced uselessly over the top of the net.

Adam dropped his arms to his sides, staring in disbelief. The Skyline fans exploded into cheering, and what felt like their validation of his risky maneuver yanked off the lid of the cauldron where he'd been storing all his bitterness and resentment and raging distaste for Adam Francis. It bubbled over in a steaming flood of emotion and before he could stop himself he stepped up to the despondent striker and stood as close as possible without touching him, using his two extra inches of height to every fraction of intimidating advantage.

"Now who's a disgrace?" he demanded, and in answer the striker bumped his chest, pushing in even closer.

"You're only on the pitch because two better keepers are injured. You're third-rate. You always will be," Adam sneered.

Brendan shook off Adam's comments. When he retired from the game and walked off the pitch for the last time, everyone would know how good he was. He'd hold his head high and leave the sport a champion. Erin would help him do it. She'd promised. He trusted her.

Brendan drew back his arms to shove the striker out of his face but someone caught one of them. Levelheaded Kojo shook his head as the referee jogged up to give them both a verbal warning, and they begrudgingly shook hands so the match could continue.

"This isn't over," Adam warned under his breath, but Brendan rolled his eyes. Skyline had already played the Pines away. The two of them would never meet on the pitch again. This was over.

The matched finished one-nil, with Eugene's own goal the only one achieved in the ninety-minute slog. The opposing teams exchanged reluctant handshakes as they trudged off the pitch and into the tunnel.

Brendan lingered on the pitch to applaud the away fans, who burst into the chorus of the old Rod Stewart song, "Forever Young"—the song originally coined for him by the English crowds.

Out of the corner of his eye, he saw Roland waiting for him at the mouth of the tunnel, and he clapped the fans a little longer. At least they were thankful for his penalty save if his manager wasn't.

Finally, he pulled himself away and walked down the tunnel to leave the pitch. Roland waited for him at the place where the tunnel branched off into dressing rooms, offices, and underground parking.

Brendan held up his hands in apology as he approached his manager. "I know, I lost my composure, and I'm sorry. It won't happen again."

"It better not," Roland told him tersely. "Great save on the penalty. Risky tactic but it paid out. Nicely played."

Brendan opened his mouth to argue, then realized his manager had given him a compliment. "Thanks," he replied, blinking in astonishment.

"Good work." Roland slapped him on the back and Brendan continued to the dressing room in a daze. Roland's comment was the most gushing praise he'd ever offered his third-choice goalkeeper. Brendan committed every word to memory, just in case he needed to dig it out for an ego boost someday.

Buoyed by the manager's feedback, Brendan walked into the dressing room and after exchanging a few high-fives and encouraging words with his teammates, he opened his locker and picked up his phone.

He shouldn't text Erin. He was barely managing to stay on the right side of the line with her, keeping things friendly and nothing more, but he was on a high and he wanted to hear from her. He wanted her to agree with his manager that he'd had a good performance.

Although if she hadn't watched it he'd be disappointed. Not that he expected her to watch his games, of course—why should she?

But if she didn't, he didn't want to know. He liked imagining her eyes on the scoreboard, her attention on his decisions. Even his parents had stopped watching him play every week—too many games to keep track of, apparently—so if he couldn't imagine her caring, he was playing for no one except the anonymous fans.

Which was still a privilege, he reminded himself, deciding not to be so melodramatic.

If she watched, she watched. If she didn't, she didn't. It meant nothing either way.

He'd send her a quick text. Just a one-liner suggesting she check out the penalty online. She probably hadn't watched, so he was simply flagging the moment for her interest. She'd know who Adam was so there was more to it than his save. As a woman who knew soccer, she might— His phone flashed with a new message notification. He tapped to open it, expecting a misspelled but enthusiastic message from his younger brother, the only remaining soccer fan in the family.

Instead, his mental stock ticker ground to a halt as a saw the sender, and a single word throbbed behind his eyes.

Erin.

Ballsy move on that penalty but not surprised it worked out. Starting to think you're legit psychic.

Don't respond, his occasionally sensible brain demanded, but his gut-listening thumb was already tapping the keys.

Just another day at the office.

His arm was halfway inside his locker to replace the phone when it chimed again. Against his better judgment, he glanced at it, even though most of his teammates were already in the shower and he lagged behind.

I'm in Tucson, flying back to ATL tomorrow. Let's get together on Wednesday before you travel for Friday's game.

No emojis. No x's or o's in her sign-off. No question mark, either. As usual, with Erin, it was a command, not an invitation.

He typed his response, then deleted it with a smile and stowed his phone. No need to respond too hastily. Let her wonder for a while.

Chapter 11

"Hey." Erin poked Brendan in the arm with her pen.

"Sorry, did you say something?"

"I said I'm sick of your handwritten method. I'm going to start doing my charts on my tablet. I downloaded this app. You enter your fixtures in this side and then—are you listening?"

"I'm listening. An app." He blinked. "Wait, what does it do?"

She squinted at him. "Are you okay? You've barely said anything all evening."

"I'm fine." But it was clearly untrue.

She had three days of increasingly flirty text messages on her phone as they'd planned this evening's stats session. She read each one at least five times, wondering what had changed, and whether he was now open to something casual, had moved beyond the notion that a finite fling would make it harder for him to leave, or if he thought he could convince her to commit, even if only for a few months.

His flirtatious tone totally jarred with everything he'd said before and since that night in Boston. None of it made sense.

Then again, neither did her feelings for him. She'd turned over her conversation with Molly in her head a million times since leaving Tucson and she was no closer to figuring out what she wanted.

Actually, that wasn't accurate. She wanted to sleep with Brendan. Whether she wanted anything more—or would be able to bring herself to offer anything more—remained in doubt.

Not because she didn't like him. On the contrary, maybe she liked him too much. She'd spent most of her adult life steering clear of relationships because the expectation of returning someone else's emotional attachment felt like a hassle and a burden, a taxing distraction she preferred to avoid. For the first time, though, she worried it might be her own emotional attachment that became inconvenient.

She had to face facts. Her career was flying and Brendan was leaving. Physical satisfaction was all she could afford to give him. Anything more would be foolish.

Maybe he was thinking the same thing. He seemed preoccupied, distant, a little worried. Her multiple attempts to cajole him into enjoying their betting analysis had failed, and she began to wonder if they should call the whole thing off.

She reached across the bar in his basement pub, removed his pen from his hand, and shut his notebook.

"Quit sulking and tell me what's wrong."

"Nothing."

She shook her head.

He sighed, relenting. "One of the guys I know at Tucson United called me this morning. He wanted me to hear about the fantasy-league bust from him before it made its way down the grapevine."

"Did he connect us in any way?" she asked urgently.

"No, thank God. Not even close. He called to warn me about you. Said the league is on the warpath."

"But he must know you haven't been betting, right? Until recently you weren't. He would have no way of knowing that changed."

"He wouldn't, but his call made me think that maybe a lot of players suspect I've secretly kept up the gambling all season. I know I stopped, but it feels like there's been a rumor that I didn't." He looked at her, worry etched in his brow. "Do you think that's why the league is so intent on making an example out of me? Maybe this whisper ran all the way up to the top."

She considered it, briefly replaying her last conversation with Randall. Brendan's name hadn't come up once.

"I don't think so," she concluded. "The league's spotlight on you is dimming."

His posture eased slightly, but concern still darkened his eyes. "Still, I didn't like learning that everyone believes I've been violating the terms of my reinstatement for months. Especially now that I am."

"Players talk. Ignore them. We're being careful. We'll be fine."

He straightened in his seat, rubbing his hand over his eyes. "I'm really feeling the pressure on the pitch these days. Maybe I've lost my edge."

"Don't be ridiculous," she scoffed. "You were untouchable on Saturday. Well, except for—"

"When I nearly punched Adam Francis in the face."

"You should've. He was asking for it."

"And get a red card with a three-match ban? Who would Skyline get to take my place? A seventeen-year-old from the academy?"

"I was kidding," she assured him, taken aback by his bristly response. "Is that what's bothering you? That there's no one behind you to step in?"

He nodded slowly. "Maybe. Yes. It's not the level of competition in the matches that's stressing me as much as knowing I'm the last line of defense. I can't make any mistakes and I sure as hell can't get injured. That's a big ask at this point in my career." He sighed. "I'm getting too old for this."

"No one would know from watching you. But I guess that doesn't change the way it feels from your side."

He started to shake his head, then fixed his eyes on her. "Know what helps?"

"What?"

"This." He gestured to include the whiteboard and their matching marble notebooks.

"Makes sense. All the keepers I've known spend a lot of time in their own heads. I can see how focusing on something external could be an outlet so you can stay sharp on the pitch."

"That's part of it. The bigger part for me is the money. The actual betting. Laying a wager and seeing whether or not it comes good."

She arched a brow, intrigued. "How does that make a difference?"

"It makes it real. Important. Even if I lose it's okay because it matters. It's such a cliché, but it makes me feel...alive." He waved a hand. "Never mind, it's cheesy."

"I get it." She laughed, delighted that he'd articulated something she'd struggled to articulate to herself for years. "I totally get it. Like sometimes life feels flat, even when it's stressful—especially when it's stressful. The bad things that could happen—losing my job, not being able to pay rent, moving in with my parents—seem so conceptual that I can't worry about them. Same with good stuff—I just can't get it up, emotionally. But the highs and lows of pressing that slot-machine button are real. The money's real, the pain is real, and so is the joy." She wrinkled her nose. "I hate it, in a way. I was genuinely more excited about our first round of wins than I was about my sister's wedding."

"Does it make you feel like a bad person?"

"All the time."

"Me too," he admitted. "Not enough to stop, though."

"I'm not sure anything will make me stop."

He pivoted on his stool, reaching for the single bottle of beer he'd been nursing for over an hour. "When did you start?"

"My first job after retiring from the pro game. I went to a conference in Atlantic City and joined in with a couple of people who wanted to play the slots. I always associated slots with sad, lonely oldies chain-smoking and losing quarters. But as soon as I tried them, I was hooked. I lost so much money that night, I only ate frozen vegetables and bagels for the rest of the month." She bit her lower lip. "I've never told anyone that."

He smiled encouragingly. "I'm not exactly in a position to judge."

She exhaled, compelled to unload more, knowing he was the only person in her life who could possibly understand. "I downloaded a couple of slot-machine apps and started playing them. Everything I won I spent on designer clothes, believing that you should dress for the job you want. I'm sorry to say it worked. It helped that I was smart and worked hard, but you can never underestimate the power of a fresh manicure and a tight skirt in the sports industry. The more money I earned, the more I bet, the more I lost—the more I needed to try again. So here I am." She spread her hands. "Thirty-one years old, successful sportswoman who's transitioned to a huge job at league corporate, and I'm in so much credit-card debt I'll probably have to work until I'm two hundred to make a dent in it."

"No, you won't. I'll make sure of that." He tapped the cover of his notebook.

"Gambling to recover gambling debt. If poor Lenny at those meetings had any idea what we were up to..." But she smiled. Screwed up as it was, Brendan's willingness to help her was the sweetest thing anyone had done for her in a long time.

"I'm sure he has some idea, but he can't say anything. That's how the whole thing works. You have to take accountability."

"I'm accountable. I just don't want to quit."

His smile turned melancholy. "Me neither."

"Anyway." She cleared her throat. She'd intended to cheer him up and she'd gone down a long road of confession instead. "My point, somewhere way back in this conversation, was that you should know that no matter what's happening in your head, your last couple of performances on the pitch have been top notch. No one would know that you've been out all season, or that you're even half as stressed as you say you are."

She put her hand on his knee, immediately questioned whether it was a good idea, opted to leave it there. "You're a world-class player, Brendan. One of the best. Everyone will remember that. Nothing else."

For a few moments he was silent, inscrutable green eyes locked with hers, expression so unreadable it was no wonder the league's best strikers struggled to get past him.

Then he grinned, big and broad and so warm she felt its heat tingle from her toes to her cheeks.

"Thank you. That means a lot coming from one of the best strikers I've seen play."

"Please." She snatched her hand back, rolling her eyes. "You don't have to pretend you watched women's soccer."

"I watched you."

Her eyes widened at his suddenly serious tone, humor vanishing from his face. For a second he was the twenty-two-year-old who'd hugged her in that long-ago dining room, so strange and so alluring, the mystery she'd never managed to solve.

"Did you bet on me?" The words were breathy. Her breasts rose and fell with the heightened pace of her lungs, her nipples tightening. The idea of him watching her from the towering heights of his career in Europe, coding her name in his notebook, spending all that time considering her stats, trying to get into her head—something about it was so deeply erotic she pressed her crossed legs together, applying pressure to her hungry core.

He responded with an enigmatic smile as he stood up, stretching his arms over his head.

"I need a break. And I have an idea."

She hoped the idea involved the bedroom. Or the kitchen table. Even the floor. "Which is?"

"I'll show you."

She followed him upstairs, her enthusiasm fading as they passed a series of what she felt were eligible surfaces. Eventually, they made their way to the backyard, now only dimly lit by the ambient glow of the streetlights and the neighboring houses.

She easily made out what he gestured to in the semi-darkness. A soccer goal, complete with a bright white net.

"I'm wearing flip-flops," she informed him, already reading the intention in his smile.

"I have a couple of youth-size cleats in the shed, for my nephews. This whole setup is for them, actually."

"I didn't know Aidan had kids."

"You met Aidan?"

She nodded. "At that same Family Day when I met Liam and your parents."

He shoved his hands in his pockets. "He has two boys. Jordan and Tucker, ten and eight. He works in my dad's dealership now so I don't see too much of them, but they came out for a visit in June. I spent a small fortune getting this ready, only to be told about their plans to become star quarterbacks."

"Ew." Erin wrinkled her nose. "There's still time. Hopefully one of them will come around. And although I'm flattered you think I'll fit into a ten-year-old's shoes, there's an ugly truth you should know about me, and about most women my height. Dainty of foot we are not."

"At least try them on."

She did her best to look annoyed.

"Humor me," he requested, momentarily disappearing into the shed at the back of the yard. He reappeared carrying two pairs of brand-new, professional-quality cleats from his own sponsor. He handed them over, and she noted each boy's name printed on the relevant pair.

"Wow, these are really nice. They didn't want to take them home?"

He shook his head. "I don't think either of them even wore them."

"Let's see if I can get them on." She drew a circle in the air. "Turn around."

He obliged, and she slipped a foot into one shoe in each size. She grimaced when Jordan's larger shoes were a near-perfect fit, then sat down to tie them.

"Can I look?"

"I guess so."

He did and smiled even more broadly when he saw her tying the laces. "Those look like Tucker's."

"Damn right they do, and you better not check to make sure." She stood up tentatively, testing the cleats in the grass. Brendan returned to the shed, this time emerging with a soccer ball and a pair of goalkeeper's gloves.

"Oh, hell no." She shook her head. "That goal is youth size. You can barely stand up in it. No way is that fair."

"Penalties are all about beating the keeper. The size of the goal shouldn't make a difference."

He rolled the ball toward her. She stopped it with her foot.

"I'm out of shape," she protested.

He leveled an appraising gaze as he took his position between the posts. "You look good to me."

She couldn't help fluffing her hair, enjoying his scrutiny. "You're a match-fit professional. I'm retired. I'm also not wearing any socks."

He tightened the straps on his gloves. "I'm hearing a lot of excuses. If you think you can't beat me, just say so."

"Get on your line."

She smiled inwardly as she dribbled the ball to what she estimated was an equivalent penalty distance. Brendan thought he was pushing her competitive buttons, and to some extent he was. Greater than her need to beat him, though, was pure hunger for testing herself against a world-class keeper.

During her professional career, she'd frequently refused to participate in men versus women exhibition events, viewing them as degrading and making a spectacle of the women's game she was trying to get people to take seriously. Secretly she would've loved to take on some of the male players and see whether she could compete with them.

A post-retirement penalty shootout in the dark in a suburban backyard wearing kids' shoes wasn't exactly what she had in mind, but she'd take it.

She flexed her ankles and pulled each knee up to her stomach to stretch her hamstrings, fully aware she was giving Brendan a view of her pink-and-white polka dot panties beneath her sundress. She watched his jaw slacken as she bent over to touch her toes, the dress's thin-strapped bodice barely holding her breasts in place.

Hey, tactics were tactics.

He visibly gathered himself, widening his stance and holding out his arms. She toed the ball up to her knee, then back to her foot, then positioned it in front of the goal.

The small goal exaggerated Brendan's size and wingspan, but she could see how he intimidated strikers even in a full-size net. Long-limbed, so tall he seemed to loom over the line, and an expression so intense it felt like he was reading your intentions before you knew what they were.

Which he probably was.

She squared her shoulders, determined to outwit him. "How many shots do I get?"

"As many as you want."

"I'll beat you in five."

"No, you won't."

She knew gamesmanship when she saw it. "Okay. Three."

"I won't make it easy for you."

"You better not."

He bent his knees and slapped his hands together. "Enough chat. Let's do this."

She took two steps back to give herself a run-up. She hadn't memorized his stats but she vaguely recalled a couple of instances in which he dove left. She feinted left, then booted the ball in the right-hand side of the net.

He read her like a book. He leaped right and knocked the ball out of the way, falling on the grass.

"Dammit," she muttered as he brushed off his shorts and reset his position. She jogged to recover the ball, then walked it back to her spot.

"Well, that's disappointing," he remarked. "Here I thought it was a big misconception that women suck at soccer."

"You'll have to try harder to wind me up," she tossed back, although in truth his words sent irritation prickling along the back of her neck. "What do you say to the stars when they face you down?"

"Profanity about their mothers, mostly," he replied mildly.

She cracked a smile, then forced it off her face as she focused on the challenge. She couldn't beat him on speed or power—she was a woman, like it or not—so she'd have to outthink him.

Big ask against one of the cleverest goalkeepers in the world. But then she was one of the women's games best strikers, so why not?

She quickly ran through her mental list of the greatest penalties of all time. She landed on a recent one, scored by Skyline's own Rio Vidal to win the South American Cup for Chile. It had been a cheeky end to a hard-fought contest and required balls twelve times as big as the one at her feet.

Yeah, she'd try that one.

"Come on, striker," he called. "I haven't got all night."

She didn't bother wasting energy on a response. She took several long steps backward, ran at the ball with increasing pace and energy—and then chipped it in a gentle arc toward the net.

It was an audacious, genius way to take a penalty. Most keepers would've jumped left or right or even center so long before such a soft shot reached them that they had no chance of saving it.

Instead, Brendan dropped to his haunches and comfortably caught the ball, then tossed it back to her before she could get an expletive out of her mouth.

"Do you want to tell me again that you're not wearing socks? I'm sure that's to blame."

She couldn't help but return his smile. She bet he had no idea that he was far sexier than he was intimidating. Of course, she was pissed he saved that last penalty—one she thought was unstoppable—but at the same time his precision, his foresight, his unparalleled ability to anticipate her every move was straight-up hot.

For a few seconds, she simply stared at him. She wasn't trying to psych him out—she doubted anything could—but she wanted to savor this unlikely moment in her life.

When they walked in different directions on Family Day all those years ago, she figured that would be the last time she saw him. She thought the same when the door clicked shut behind her in the hotel in Vegas. Even the other night in Boston, when he'd left the bar with his shoulders set and his expression cold, she wondered whether it might be the end of this brief whatever-it-was.

She never imagined he'd crack open the door of his impenetrable exterior enough to let her slip inside. To confide in her the way he had tonight. To listen so openly and nonjudgmentally in return. To show her the respect of saving both her attempts, treating her as an equal, holding her to the same standard he'd hold one of his male teammates.

Too bad she wasn't the relationship type. Otherwise, he'd be a pretty good candidate.

He raised one gloved hand to cover an exaggerated yawn. "Are you still there? It's getting so dark I can barely tell. Any chance we can wrap this up before dawn?"

"Don't worry," she assured him. "We'll be done in a second."

As he spread his arms for the third time, she decided the best way to keep him from reading her intentions was not to have any. No hesitation, no overthinking.

She drew back her leg, muscle memory shaping her body into position for one of the fiercely accurate, incredibly fast shots that made her one of the most feared strikers in the women's game.

She cleared her mind and closed her eyes. Then she swung her leg forward to kick, relishing the familiar pressure against her toe, the fulfilling thump as her foot sent the ball flying through the air.

She opened her eyes just in time to see the net shudder as the ball found the back of it. Her shot hit dead center. Straight down the middle.

Brendan was on the ground. He'd dived left.

She beat him.

She whooped her delight, punching her fists in the air. Brendan rolled over onto his back and pressed his hands over his eyes.

"Beat you in three," she taunted as she skipped over, dropping to her knees beside him and prying his hands from his face. "And don't you dare say you let me win."

"I didn't. You got me on that last one. That's not something a lot of strikers can claim."

She straddled his waist and pinned his arms to the ground on either side of his head. "Now I intend to claim my reward."

She leaned down to kiss him, her better judgment overwhelmed by the scents of the freshly cut lawn, and the jasmine climbing a trellis on the back of the house, and the hint of citrus and smoke that was utterly, uniquely his.

He shifted beneath her and she held his wrists more tightly, pressing her calves against his thighs, not ready to let him go. He spread his still-gloved palms in surrender, matching the pressure of her mouth and the eager movements of her tongue.

He didn't kiss her like a man who was afraid of getting his heart broken, or who couldn't settle for anything less than commitment. His lips said he wanted her, and the hungry rumble in his throat said he didn't care what it took to get her.

Maybe she could have her cake and eat it after all.

"I like you like this," she murmured against his temple. "Powerless. Defenseless. Mine to have my way with."

He said nothing, but his wide eyes as she scooted higher up his chest told her he was enjoying this too. She pulled open the Velcro straps around his wrists, tugged his arms straight and positioned his hands on either side of the goal post. Then she reattached the straps to each other, left to right and right to left, effectively tying him to the post.

She glanced at the upstairs windows of the houses next door. "Do you have nosy neighbors?"

He shook his head. "Family with three little kids on one side. They're too busy to care. An old lady in the other house, but if she sees anything she's too Southern to mention it."

"I hope she enjoys the show." She shoved his T-shirt up beneath his arms and ran her hands down his long, lean, finely chiseled torso. Unlike most soccer players he didn't wax, and hair the same ash-blond as his head filled the space between his pecs, then narrowed into a line that ran down the middle of his stomach. His lanky build disguised a weights-honed body, and she traced the contours of his six-pack with her thumbs.

She slid down to straddle his rock-hard thighs, then took her time unbuttoning his shorts, skimming her fingertips over his exposed skin.

"I have an idea I'd like to share with you." She toyed with his zipper and then began tugging it open slowly, so slowly that her fingers itched with impatience.

"Okay," he said hoarsely, slightly raising his head to watch her progress.

His zipper finally all the way down, she reached inside and gripped him through his cotton boxers, squirming with pleasure at the hard heft of him in her palm.

"I know you're not in the market for something casual, and I'm not interested in a relationship. But I think there may be a middle ground." She squeezed him gently.

He dropped his head back on the grass with a soft groan she interpreted as his signal for her to go on. She bit her lower lip briefly, trying to quell her matching, lusty moan.

She failed and echoed his sound of desire as she repositioned herself on his thighs so she brushed her clit through her panties every time she drew her fingers down his length.

"Think of a friends-with-benefits scenario, but better," she explained, reaching through the opening in the front of his boxers to hold him, skin-on-skin. "We hang out. We do our stats thing. Maybe I'll even make you dinner."

With her free hand, she shoved the gusset of her panties aside and rocked her bare slit against him. "We're friends. Friends who fuck."

He shut his eyes and arched his hips, grimacing as she moved over him. She let her head fall back, enjoying the illicit friction, the lack of anything separating them except will power.

It would be so easy to lower herself onto him right now. Totally irresponsible, both emotionally and in terms of contraception, which is why the mere thought of it ramped up her heartbeat and stiffened her nipples to the point of aching.

She pushed up onto her knees and teased his tip against her core, running it up and down, circling it over her clit. He moved beneath her and bent his knees to keep her from sliding back down his legs, trapping her in temptation. He could easily pull free from the Velcro straps but he didn't, opting to play her game, to let her take control. If she parted her thighs wider and took him inside her now, he wouldn't stop her.

Maybe that's exactly what he wanted. All the pleasure, none of the accountability, and afterward he'd repeat his line about needing more than sex and send her on her way.

Sorry, handsome. That's not how this works.

Reluctantly she shifted her panties back into place and released his erection, then shuffled up his body, widening her squat to fit over his ribs. His gaze fixed on her questioningly.

She slipped one of the straps of her sundress over her arm, then followed it with the strap of her bra. She reached inside as if to release her breast, but instead, she stroked her nipple, ensuring Brendan's only view was of the suggestive motions of her fingers.

He licked his lips, eyes following every move.

"So what do you think? It wouldn't be much different than tonight. I come over here, or you come to my place. We talk, we have a drink, we look at the fixtures."

She leaned in closer, exposing another half-inch of her breast as she dropped her voice to a throaty whisper. "Then we kiss, and you touch me, and I taste you, and you slide that big cock of yours in and out of me until neither of us remembers who we are."

She felt his breathing quicken, the rise and fall of his chest rapid between her legs. He swallowed hard. His eyes never left hers, unblinking, shimmering with hot desire.

A second later the sound of uncoupling Velcro was like an unexpectedly cold blast from a shower that had run out of hot water. She plopped ungracefully onto the grass as he twisted his way out from under her, stripping off the gloves and stuffing himself back into his shorts.

She tried not to pout as she yanked the straps back up her shoulder and straightened the bodice of her dress. "I take it you're rejecting my suggestion."

"Maybe. I don't know." He ran his hand through his hair. "Is it always this hard to say no to you?"

"Most people quit trying pretty early on."

"I can see why."

"Don't feel bad. You may become the only man to see my boobs and subsequently turn me down."

"It's not easy. They're spectacular."

"Then say yes," she urged, resting her hand on his leg. "You can't jump into a relationship with anyone here anyway, not when you're leaving in a couple of months. Why not enjoy yourself in the meantime?"

"You're so sure it'll be that simple, all cut and dried and we both walk away no worse for wear. What if it isn't? Have you considered that you might develop feelings for me, or is that too absurd to contemplate?"

She rolled her eyes. "Oh my God, men and their feelings. Don't take it so personally. It's not about whether I like you—obviously, I do. And as for your *feelings*, I'm not interested, not with you or anyone else. As long as we go into this with open eyes, knowing we're good friends but nothing more, we'll be fine on the other side. Nothing lost, but a hell of a lot gained."

She pulled her knees to her chest and began unlacing the cleats, making no effort to block his view of her still-damp crotch. "Friendly friends who fuck. That's my offer. Take it or leave it."

He was quiet for a minute, thoughtfully picking blades of grass off his shorts. When he finally spoke his voice was hushed, his tone so confiding that she snapped to attention.

"I'm worried you'll be wrong," he told her softly. "I'm worried it'll hurt."

"It won't," she replied hastily. Too hastily. She realized after the words were out of her mouth that she might not believe them.

If she was honest with herself, she was worried too. Never in her life had any other man penetrated her no-strings armor like Brendan had, from the day he shoved that bottle of water in her hand to seriously considering unprotected sex with him only minutes earlier.

Not only had he threatened her long-untouched defenses, he did it without even trying. If anything, she was the one pushing him and not the other way around. What would happen if he became a full-fledged fuck buddy?

But she'd made her offer and she couldn't—no, didn't want to withdraw it now. If their arrangement started to get emotional—and that was a big if—she'd deal with it.

No point in denying herself what she wanted on the slim chance it became complicated.

"I have to think about it," he concluded, pushing to his feet. He offered her a hand and she took it, levering herself upright.

"There's not much to think about. You're leaving to find your Midwestern dream girl. I'm not interested in anything except my career and the occasional externally assisted orgasm. It's just sex, Brendan. I promise."

"I know you do." He nodded toward the back door into the house. "I'll walk you out."

Silently she followed him across the jasmine-scented back porch, through the kitchen and into the garage, where he held her door open as she settled into the driver's seat of the gleaming white sports car for which she barely managed to make the monthly payments.

"I need time to get it right in my mind," he said suddenly, stalling her hand mid-turn in the ignition. "I have to consider all the angles, all the possibilities. I don't want to do something I'll regret."

"Don't make me wait too long or the offer will expire." She forced a confident smile, trying to ignore the unease stirring in her gut.

"I won't." He straightened and pressed the remote to open the garage door. "Let me know you're home safe."

"I will."

He shut her door and stepped back, raising a hand in farewell. She returned the gesture, then shifted into reverse and backed out of the driveway. The quiet residential street was empty, and in seconds she was out of sight of the house and speeding her way home.

The engine purred. Her thoughts spun. Her underwear stuck damply between her legs.

She spent the entire drive wondering whether she was making the biggest mistake of her life.

Chapter 12

"Brendan." Iveta Kovar smiled warmly as she opened the door of Pavel's sprawling house in Buckhead, then opened her arms for a hug. "It's good to see you."

He pulled in the former model for a quick embrace, then raised the expensive bottle of Scotch he'd brought. "I'm sorry I didn't come sooner. I'm hoping he'll forgive me once he sees this."

She shook her head, motioning for him to step inside. "There's nothing to forgive. Pavel didn't want any visitors at the hospital. Now that he's home he's agreed to see a few people. Your name was at the top of his list."

"Good to know he's feeling well enough to velvet-rope his sickbed." He stopped Iveta's brisk progress through the entrance hall with a hand on her arm. "How is he?"

"He'll be fine," she assured him, her stiff smile undermining her positive tone. "It was a serious skull fracture, but he got the surgery he needed right away and the doctor says he's extremely lucky. He'll be out for three months but should be able to start training just in time for the new season."

"That's great," he told her sincerely. "How are you and Adela holding up?"

She hesitated, eventually letting the smile drop from her face. "It's been hard, Brendan. We almost lost him."

"I know." He put his arm around her as her chin started to quiver. "But he's a hardheaded son of a bitch and he'll be absolutely fine."

She nodded weakly, regaining her composure. "I'll take you upstairs. He's waiting for you."

He followed her up the grand, curving staircase to the thickly carpeted upper floor. He'd been to Pavel's house before, but only when his teammate had thrown parties. Compared to those raucous, crowded visits the house seemed cavernous and eerily quiet. Their footsteps were inaudible as she led him down the hallway and tapped lightly on a door at the end.

He braced himself as she pushed it open. He'd developed a strong stomach after a decade of witnessing hideous injuries on the pitch but he prepared himself nonetheless, schooling his expression to stay relaxed and friendly.

As soon as he stepped through the doorway he realized there was no need. Pavel didn't look bad at all.

Fully dressed and seated in a chair in his masculine, oak-paneled study, Skyline's first-choice goalkeeper looked more like he'd had a bad fall than life-threatening brain surgery. Fading rings of bruises surrounded his eyes and a square of gauze was stuck against a patch of shaved hair, but otherwise, he seemed fine. He even smiled as he spotted the bottle of Scotch.

"Wow, it's the man who put Adam Francis off his penalty. I'm honored." Pavel motioned for Brendan to take the chair opposite him as Iveta slipped out of the room and shut the door.

"Don't be. I hope you're allowed to drink this." He plunked the bottle on the desk and took a seat.

"Not for another month at least. Can you believe that? I tried to tell the doctor that beer is like Czech milk, but he insisted."

"Check his medical credentials. Doesn't sound like he knows what he's doing."

Pavel grinned. "You've been in fine form on the pitch. How does it feel to finally start every match?"

"Well, given the circumstances..." Brendan shrugged, uncomfortable, but Pavel waved off his awkwardness.

"Don't. We both know we should've been competing to start all this time, and it was only a personality clash keeping you on the bench. I'm happy knowing you're standing between the posts in my place."

"I'm enjoying it," Brendan admitted. "We're a lock for the final. Even if we don't win, it would be a nice way to leave the game."

"Still intent on retiring?"

"My contract's up in December. Roland won't renew it. I doubt anyone else is interested in a thirty-three-year-old goalkeeper with a gambling problem." He raised a shoulder, resigned. "It's time. I'm ready."

"I'll miss you. Maybe not in the gym, though. I'll finally stop hearing, 'just one more rep.'"

"Very funny. Don't call me when you're too fat to dive for the ball. I won't answer."

They let the joke settle and dissipate between them, giving themselves time to make a comfortable transition to the seriousness of the situation. When the moment felt right Brendan asked, "How are you?"

Pavel shrugged, stretching his legs in front of him. "Physically, I'm all right. I get headaches sometimes, severe enough to put me in bed the whole day, but they're getting better. The swelling's going down, the bruising is less sore. I should be back in training in another couple of months."

"That's good," Brendan replied earnestly. "And emotionally?"

His teammate exhaled. "I don't remember a lot of what happened. One minute this midfielder was running at me, the next it was four days later and I was in intensive care. It took a long time for the reality of the situation to sink in."

Pavel shook his head slightly, glancing off to the side. "As players, we worry so much about injuries. We worry about whether they'll end our careers, or even interrupt them long enough to make us lose our spot in the lineup. But we never think they could be life-threatening."

"Never," Brendan echoed in agreement.

"I've been thinking about what's really important. My career, yes. The money, sure. But family must always come first. On some level, I always knew that, but it wasn't the same. Having Iveta by my side through this whole thing—knowing she'll still be there for me long after I become a forgotten piece of soccer history—it puts things in perspective."

Suddenly Pavel picked up his head and looked him square in the eye. "You need to get married."

Brendan blinked. "What?"

"I'm serious." Pavel leaned forward, propping his elbows on his knees. "You've been alone the whole time I've known you, and I've never understood why."

They stared at each other in silence for a few moments before Brendan realized Pavel was waiting for an answer.

"I haven't exactly made my love life a priority," he offered, thinking of the handful of brief but committed relationships that punctuated his adulthood. "I guess I assumed it would work itself out. Anyway, now it's too late to meet anyone in Atlanta. Maybe I'll give it more attention once I'm settled in Nebraska."

"You should," Pavel urged. "When she shows up—and you'll know when she does, I promise—don't doubt and don't hesitate. Just grab her. You can work out the details later."

Erin's image flashed in his mind.

Of course it did—she was the only woman he'd been intimate with in the last year, and they'd almost had sex on his lawn the night before. That didn't mean she was "the one." Far from it. He'd known her for years. If she was his soul mate, surely he would've figured it out before now.

He remembered the first time he saw her, a whirlwind of red hair and designer jeans and loudly articulated if slightly slurred opinions. It wasn't the first time he intervened to help a girl who'd had too much to drink, but it was the first time he had the urge to do more than offer some water and advice and move on.

They didn't spend long together—ten, fifteen minutes maybe—but it was enough for him to learn a lot about her. He leaned against the outside of the house as she told him all about her private girls' high school, the years she spent as the only girl on a boys' traveling soccer team, her plan to lobby the Athletics Department to better partner with the Career Center to make sure female athletes had an early understanding of the sports-related professions open to them.

He found her bemusing, intriguing and decidedly attractive. And so he decided to wrap up their conversation, opting not to ask for her number and leaving the party shortly after guiding her back inside.

At that point, his perspective was totally different to Erin's. His parents weren't wealthy. His younger brother's extra medical and social interventions strained their already tight finances, and his full-ride scholarship was the only thing putting him on the path to a professional soccer career. Otherwise he'd be at the University of Nebraska, living at home, working part-time in his dad's car dealership.

Erin could afford to get distracted by parties and dating. He couldn't. So he refused to acknowledge her blatant crush on him and was slightly relieved when her interest seemed to wane.

Sure, he noticed how hot she looked the few times they were together at parties, and he noticed that she looked sexy even when she was just slumming around campus in a hoodie. Of course he noticed her on the pitch—it was impossible not to. But that's all he did—noticed her—until he graduated and their lives diverged.

He thought about her sometimes, especially during that first couple of lonely years in Liverpool. He kept tabs on her pro career, clicked through her photos on social media, even put a bet on her a couple of times. But he thought of her in the same mildly wondering way he thought about all of his former classmates—not like she was the one who got away.

That proved it, then. Pavel said he'd know when he met her. He'd met and reconnected with Erin multiple times in more than ten years and he'd never had a lightning bolt of certainty. Not even close.

An electric shock, maybe. A tiny zap of awareness. An unshakeable pull to know her, to be beside her. But that didn't mean—

"Brendan?"

"Sorry. Got caught up in something for a second."

His teammate stared at him, then broke into a broad grin. "You've met her already. You know who she is. You were thinking about her."

Brendan shook his head emphatically. "No. Definitely not. I was thinking about someone else."

"Sure," Pavel replied, making no effort to hide his skepticism. "Anyway, try to make time for that part of your life. You don't want to be alone forever."

Brendan winced inwardly at Pavel's last two words. "Point taken. So, you've been watching the games?"

"Here and there, when I can concentrate long enough. How are things in the dressing room?"

"Same. Have you heard about this crazy shit with Oz?"

Pavel nodded. "This hate crime stuff. Insane. How's he doing?"

"Surprisingly well. But then, that's Oz."

"The iceman," Pavel agreed. "And Kojo? The Brazilians? All good?"

"All good," Brendan confirmed. "Anxious to hear how you are, though. I imagine my phone will be full of inquiring texts this evening."

"I guess I should probably start allowing more visitors. It's only recently that I can count on being well enough to sit up and talk for a couple of hours. Early on, there were days when I was so exhausted I couldn't get out of bed."

"Don't rush into seeing people before you're ready. The guys will understand."

Pavel nodded thoughtfully, then his attention sharpened. "Guess which one of our teammates hasn't been in touch at all? No well wishes after the accident, no texts to ask how I'm doing—nothing."

"I'm surprised there's anyone who would do that. Guedes, maybe? And only because he doesn't speak English and I could see him accidentally sending Portuglish texts with lots of emojis to the wrong number."

Pavel laughed, shaking his head. "No, even Guedes managed to send his version of a get-well note. Brian, on the other hand, hasn't said a word."

Brendan frowned at Pavel's revelation about the American winger, Brian Scholtz. Brian was having a tough season. He'd deservedly lost his first-team spot to Rio, his contract expired at the end of the year, and there hadn't been any rumors of other clubs keen to sign him. Roland was the type of manager who cared about dressing-room harmony, so snubbing a seriously injured goalkeeper wasn't the most strategic route to a new contract.

"Maybe he lost your number," he offered.

"I doubt it."

"Do you want me to speak to him?"

"No," Pavel replied so insistently that Brendan's gaze shot up. "Don't have anything to do with him if you can help it."

Brendan arched a brow, inviting his teammate to elaborate.

Pavel looked away, then back, his expression stiff. "Look, I know firsthand that goalkeepers are weird. We're part of a team, but we're apart from our teammates most of the time. We train separately, and we stand at one end of the pitch while they run all over it. I know we all have our idiosyncrasies, the quirks we use to channel our energy and make us successful."

"Like your drum kit."

"Like your notebooks."

Brendan froze, his hands knotted together in his lap.

Pavel leaned forward and patted his knee. "Don't worry, I had no idea what they meant until everything came out. Even then it took me a while to put the pieces together. I doubt anyone else even notices them."

"They're just stats. I like working the odds. It's relaxing. Helps me focus. Doesn't mean I'm actually betting on anything."

Pavel held up his hands. "It's none of my business. You know my position on the gambling thing. You were stupid to do it, but putting you on the bench for the rest of the season was overkill."

"Roland's been looking for an excuse to sideline me since he joined."

"And you gave him one," Pavel reminded him. "Don't give him another."

Panic flared in Brendan's chest. Pavel couldn't possibly know what he was doing with Erin—could he? His Czech counterpart could read any striker in the league, so maybe it wasn't a leap to think he could read his teammate's guilty conscience, too.

He feigned innocence, praying Pavel bought it. "I don't understand."

"Brian. I'm pretty sure he's up to something, and it isn't something good."

Relief softened his spine. "Like what?"

"I can't prove it, but I'm ninety percent sure he's betting on the Championship League. He never really got over Rio taking his spot, and when Rio came back from injury and was still light-years better than him, I think Brian gave up. Suddenly he stopped complaining when we had to watch footage of upcoming opponents and took a serious interest, even though he was unlikely to get off the bench. He started asking me questions, too, about other matches—did I think so-and-so was likely to score against whoever, and what did I think of the keeper at wherever FC. I didn't give it much thought at first, figuring he thought I had a broad view of the game as a goalkeeper, but after a while I realized he was asking far more about other teams' fixtures than our own. Then he bought a new car. Not a particularly smart thing to do when you're about to be out of contract."

"Maybe he's just not very smart."

"He isn't," Pavel agreed. "The question is whether he's not smart and betting on the league."

Brendan leaned back in his chair and folded his arms, pausing to absorb this information. It was exactly the sort of lead Erin wanted—and exactly what he couldn't deliver. He'd never been Brian's biggest fan, but he couldn't stab him in the back.

Could he?

"It would be a big deal if you're right," he said carefully. "I never bet on my own league and look at the trouble I got into."

"I know, which is why I would never go to Roland with this. I'm only telling you so you can protect yourself. I don't think he's dumb enough to try to involve you—but then again, maybe he is."

"I'll steer clear. Thanks for the heads-up."

Pavel looked like he wanted to say something else, but a knock on the door silenced him.

Iveta leaned into the room, smiling apologetically. "Sorry to interrupt. Are you both sober?"

"Unfortunately, yes." Brendan returned her smile, reading the signal in her expression that it was time for him to go.

He stood up from his chair. "That's enough soccer gossip for one afternoon. I'm sure you have something more important to do, like exaggerating your achievements in your memoir."

Pavel's smile weakened and Brendan instantly regretted his poor attempt at a joke. Maybe his teammate had trouble writing after his injury. Maybe the mention of a career-bookending milestone like a memoir was too sharp a reminder of how close he'd been to never playing again.

Hell, even at this point the notion that he'd play again was only theoretical. Anything could happen in the course of his recovery. He might very well have finished his last match on a stretcher.

Brendan cleared his throat awkwardly, not bothering to wave Pavel back down as his teammate stood to shake his hand.

"It's good to see you." Pavel's grip was firm, even if his expression had lost some of its humor.

"I hope I'll be allowed to come back."

"The sooner, the better." Pavel slapped Brendan's shoulder as he turned toward the door. "Good luck this weekend."

"Thanks. I need it."

"No, you don't."

For a few seconds, they stood in silence, sharing a knowing glance. One keeper scraping to recover his reputation in what little time he had left, the other's meteoric rise momentarily halted by what could've been a catastrophic injury. Two men used to being the anchor on the pitch, their good performances would be forgotten, their mistakes left to haunt them in the fans' memories for years. Goalkeeping was a thankless, difficult, essential art, and in that moment their unspoken understanding made them closer than any brothers.

"I'll call you," Brendan promised, forcing himself to take a step back.

Pavel just nodded, raising a palm in farewell.

* * * *

"The Tucson players are apologetic, and I think the message in the example is the need for awareness of the ethics framework. They both insisted they didn't realize a fantasy team violated the code, and the manager said the same thing totally independently."

Erin took a breath before continuing, preparing for the trickiest part of this conversation with Randall. She'd practiced to get the exact tone of this suggestion right—not too flippant, not too determined, nothing to raise suspicion. Brendan's reputation weighed heavily on her shoulders as she'd taken the long walk to his office for this meeting. For his sake, even more than her own, she couldn't screw this up.

"No other incidents have surfaced at this point, and I know the design team wants to start on the year-end report. I think we should structure it half and half, using the Tucson players as a cautionary story and Brendan Young as a redemptive one. Throughout his career Brendan has done a lot of advocacy for athletes with intellectual disabilities, and I thought we could highlight—"

"Do you watch many Championship League games, Erin?" Randall tilted his head inquiringly.

"Of course. As many as I can."

"Who do you think will be in the league final?"

She considered for a second. "Atlanta, Miami, maybe Charlotte."

"Agreed. So those are the clubs we need to feature in the year-end report."

Her effort to quickly think up a justification for disagreement must've looked worried, because he added, "Don't worry, you've already got something from one of them. If there's definitely no activity in either of the others, we'll go with what we have on Brendan Young."

He smiled, suggesting he genuinely thought this statement would reassure her. It did exactly the opposite.

She came to this meeting armed and ready to divert attention away from Brendan. Now he was back on center stage.

"Can I ask why we'd want to publicize negative stories on the two most successful teams? In my opinion," she added before he could answer, "it makes us look like we haven't done our job if gambling is happening at the most elite levels in an already elite league. Some of the smaller, newer clubs can be excused for having green players who don't know the rules, but if there's gambling amongst the big stars, the responsibility falls to us."

Erin held her breath as he gazed out the window thoughtfully.

"That's a good point," he replied finally.

She exhaled.

"I was so focused on the scale of the bust itself—the magnitude of the crime we successfully uncovered—that I didn't think about how it could be viewed in reverse. That if it was so big we should've seen it earlier. Nonetheless I still think we need something more significant than those guys at Tucson."

Erin bit her lower lip, pretending to think. In fact she was quietly panicking, already knowing the answer and praying Randall didn't arrive at it as well.

He snapped his fingers. "Brendan Young's gambling was uncovered only a month into the season. Technically we didn't figure it out ourselves, but the suggestion is we didn't have time. Plus he's leaving Skyline so it doesn't tarnish the club's achievements at all."

Well, shit. He nailed it.

"I totally agree," she lied, recrossing her legs in the uncomfortable chair in his office. "And I think you'll like what I've discussed with Brendan. As I mentioned earlier, he's given a lot of his time to organizations who work with—"

He wrinkled his nose. "I understand that he's back on the pitch, but it's not because of anything he did, and making out like he's some kind of hero risen from the ashes does a disservice to Skyline's main goalkeeper. If anyone should be made into a proud example, it's that guy."

"Interesting," she said slowly, buying time, wracking her brain for a new angle to offer him. "What if we switch focus completely? Instead of revisiting the gambling scandal at all, maybe we should profile Pavel Kovar and restate the league's commitment to fair play and punishment for dangerous tackles. It's more compliance than ethics, but still important."

"Maybe." Randall swiveled back and forth in his chair, drumming his fingers on his desktop as he gazed into the distance. Erin kept her smile steady and natural, every atom focused on selling him on this new direction.

Shifting the focus away from Brendan would solve so many problems. She wouldn't have to push him for insider information and burn with guilt every time. She wouldn't worry that the spotlight on him became bright enough to expose what the two of them were doing. She wouldn't feel responsible for his legacy, for protecting and preserving everything he'd worked so hard to achieve.

She would sleep with him, as many times as he let her, and she would be so happy, and then he would leave and she would be just as happy without him. She was sure of it.

Randall returned his gaze to her, completely unaware that what he was about to say would make her life ten thousand times better or ten thousand times more stressful.

Make it better, she urged on the off-chance she possessed a psychic influencing power she wasn't aware of. *Do what I say. Forget Brendan so I can have sex with him.*

"Let's stick with the Brendan Young idea," he concluded, jamming a painfully sharp pin into the overfull balloon of her optimism. "It's a big, splashy, juicy story, and might dig us out of some of the negative-press hole we fell into when it came out. Unless you find something better at Miami or Charlotte—or Atlanta, I suppose—I think this is our best bet."

Her smile grew brittle. "Absolutely."

"And don't lean too heavily on this heroism angle. I'm glad he did whatever he did for charity, but let's be honest, all of the players have a cause they give time to on the side. He behaved badly and he's been rehabilitated—that's it."

"Got it. We'll minimize the mention of the disability advocacy."

"Perfect." Randall pressed his hands together, signaling the end of their meeting. "Anything else you want to talk about?"

She shook her head. "Just to thank you again for authorizing this weekend's travel. I know the women's team in—"

"Fantastic, then I'll see you on Monday. We'll discuss your next travel request then."

"Thanks," she said sweetly, then rose from her chair and walked out of his office. She closed the door gently, forced neutrality into her expression and took a deliberately unhurried pace back to her office, even stopping to chat to one of the executive assistants. Eventually she took her place behind her own desk.

She picked up her cell phone and scrolled through her messages unseeingly.

Anger. Frustration. Anxiety. Stress. She'd left the meeting with the exact opposite of the outcome she wanted—she should feel all of the above at this point. Where were they?

Nowhere. She was numb. Randall could walk through the door and fire her and she wouldn't feel a thing.

She put down her phone and closed her eyes, taking a deep breath and counting to ten.

Her fingertips itched.

She wished she'd paid more attention in those Gamblers Anonymous meetings. The couple of times she went in New York she'd turned up in moments of delirious desperation, and at the two meetings she attended in Atlanta she'd been focused on Brendan. What was the technique the other attendees used to stave off the temptation to gamble? Rationalization. Had someone said that or was she making it up?

Either way, worth a try. She pushed the phone a little further away, slid a Post-It pad into its place and jotted down what she'd won in a couple of weeks with Brendan versus what she'd lost playing the app on her phone last month. The difference was a joke—the first number was five times the second.

She shoved the Post-It aside and turned toward her work computer, clicking to open a message from Prinisha.

The email blurred in her vision. She still wasn't stressed, wasn't worried about the year-end report. She couldn't think about anything except pressing the spin button on the app.

She picked up her phone, but with the sole intention of texting Brendan. She navigated to their intermittent text conversation, read their last exchange—a coded reference to the bets she would place for them while he was traveling with Skyline that weekend.

She tapped to enlarge the photo that appeared with every one of his messages. She looked at it a lot, mostly because it amused her that he'd chosen it for his profile picture. Probably taken by Skyline's team photographer, in the image Brendan stood with his arms crossed, wearing his training kit and a big, broad, mid-laugh grin.

There was something endearing about the idea of Brendan spotting this photo, downloading it from wherever and uploading it to his contact card. He'd clearly chosen it for the happy-go-lucky, cheerful version of himself it portrayed.

Her heart squeezed as she imagined him tapping the photo to upload it, opting into a different man than the one she knew. Content. Unworried. Free from the burdens he carried as a professional athlete, free from the attention and expectations and obligations. Free to be who he wanted. Free to find the woman who would love whoever he became.

She swallowed an unhelpful lump in her throat and swiped to close their conversation. She wouldn't text Brendan. She had nothing to say to him.

She ignored the guilt already blossoming in her stomach as she opened the slot-machine app. As if on autopilot her finger moved to top up her credit, and before she'd fully registered what she was doing she'd spun and lost ten dollars.

Fuck it, she decided miserably, increasing her wager. Damage is done. Might as well keep going.

She spun and lost and spun and lost and topped up her credit and spun and lost and spun and won three dollars and spun and lost and repeated the process over and over and over until she was so deep in her head she barely saw the results of each spin. Her thumb tapped to spin again and again while her thoughts swam with flashes of her meeting with Randall.

She hadn't done enough. She was back where she started, except now she cared about Brendan. Now she couldn't let this happen to him. Now she had to save him.

But she had to save her job, too. And her reputation. And her future.

She spun again and again, tapping the button as soon as it lit up to show it was ready. She had no idea how much she'd lost—probably everything she'd won with Brendan—and she didn't care. She was beginning to see through the fog, and the welcome sting of stress pricked her skin. As she spun numbness gradually gave way to concern, then worry, then full-on terror.

She inhaled sharply, relishing the flood of adrenaline accompanying the crushing weight of panic that thudded onto her shoulders and banished the last wisps of her detachment. Her heart rate peaked and then subsided, and she shivered as fear's cold fingertips danced up and down her spine.

Although stress made her head throb and her lungs tighten, she felt better. She felt, an improvement over emotional paralysis. She exhaled, stronger and steadier and sharper, ready to channel her stress into productivity.

She glanced down at the almost-forgotten phone in her hand.

Two hundred dollars gone in less than five minutes.

She put the phone aside, disgusted, noting the sweaty thumbprint marring the screen. She had a lot to figure out. Time to get to work.

Chapter 13

"Thanks, man." The taxi driver accepted Brendan's generous tip. "Are you gonna need a ride back later?"

"I'm not sure," Brendan said honestly. He'd told himself he would take a taxi to Erin's apartment this Sunday evening so his conspicuous yellow Aston Martin wasn't parked for her neighbors to see. As for the duration and intent of his stay, well…

"Here's my number in case you need a lift." The driver passed a card around the headrest of his seat.

Brendan tucked his notebook under his arm and climbed out of the shabby sedan, then looked up at the high-rise building in the heart of downtown Atlanta where Erin lived.

Ostensibly he was here to work on their bets for the midweek fixtures. In reality, he'd decided to accept her offer. Friends with benefits. No-strings sex. Whatever catchphrase she wanted to use to sum up two people colluding in an illicit gambling scheme who also slept together.

He cringed as he approached the front door. Not exactly romantic. But where had years of half-hearted attempts at romance gotten him? Here, apparently—ready to accept whatever crumbs Erin offered him, resigned to never getting the whole cake.

Not that he could blame anyone but himself. While his teammates spent their downtime in clubs or bars or otherwise sexually leveraging their fame and fortune, he buried his head in stats and betting coupons. When he finally looked up he was over thirty, single, and on the brink of retirement.

He squared his shoulders, returning the concierge's greeting. He was walking into a potential sex situation with the hottest woman he'd ever met like he was on his way to the gallows. So what if she didn't want a relationship? Even if he wanted to date her—which, okay, he did—it wouldn't go anywhere. His time in Atlanta got shorter every day. Pavel told him not to hesitate when he found a good woman, and Erin couldn't have been clearer about her interest and expectations. There were probably hundreds of men who'd give their right arms to be in his shoes. Time to quit moping and enjoy himself for once.

"I'm going to number eighteen-zero-six. It's Brendan."

The concierge nodded, picked up the phone and announced his visit. Then he hung up and nodded toward the elevators. "Eighteenth floor. Miss Bailey is expecting you."

He bet she was. He rode up through the sleek building, noting the signs for the in-house gym, pool deck and game room beside buttons in the elevator. This place wasn't his style at all—too big, too impersonal. And it must be costing her a fortune.

Erin was waiting for him in the hallway when he stepped out of the elevator, leaning out of her open door wearing heels and a tight black dress. Her hair fell in waves over her shoulders and she smiled, beckoning.

"You're early."

"Meeting was short. Low attendance this week, for some reason."

"How's Lenny and the crew?" She motioned him inside.

"Fine." He stopped as she shut the door behind them, taking in the spectacular view of downtown from the floor-to-ceiling windows that ran along one wall. The apartment itself was well decorated but small, with an open-plan living area. A long, black sofa sat at one end of the room in front of a TV on a black console. The other end housed the kitchen, where a marble-topped island vaguely demarcated the prep space from a dining area. A square table with two chairs had been laid with plates and silverware and a vase of fresh flowers. The lights were low and a bottle of red wine was open on the counter, next to a lit candle.

He turned to her quizzically. "Are you expecting someone?"

"Actually, I am. I have a date."

"Oh. Okay." His thoughts stumbled, mental gears grinding as he rewound his plan and revised his expectations. He leaned against the island and opened his notebook, dizzy from the shift in circumstances. "We can make this quick. I've already had a look at—"

"Brendan."

Erin's hands were on her hips, her expression stern. "Don't be deliberately obtuse."

He blinked. "What?"

"You're my date, idiot." She rolled her eyes, coy demeanor evaporating as she clomped across the hardwood floors to where he stood. She leaned over and shut his notebook, shooting him a pointed look.

He took in the lone candle, the wine, the napkins artfully folded on top of the dinner plates. Her fancy shoes. Her perfectly tailored dress.

The irritation narrowing her eyes.

He sure could fall for her if he wasn't careful.

"If I'd known I would've worn something a little classier." He raised his palms in a gesture of helplessness, glancing down at his jeans and beer logo T-shirt.

She grinned. "I like the casual look. I almost never get to wear heels, so I thought I'd take advantage while I could."

"How tall are you in those?"

"Six-foot-two."

"Still two inches shorter than me."

"Exactly. See?" She stepped in close, the tips of her breasts a breath away from brushing his chest. The scent of jasmine lit up his senses.

"I see. I like your dress, too. Real pretty."

"It's my seduction special. Is it working?" She turned a slow circle, giving him plenty of time to examine the way it hugged every contour, accentuated every swell.

He swallowed. "Yeah. It works."

"Good. I thought you might need some convincing."

"About that, I've been thinking—"

She shook her head. "First things first. Wine?"

He watched her pour herself a glass of the merlot, knowing full well he should decline. He had a full day of training tomorrow and the league final was around the corner. He was still shaking off the dust from all those months on the bench, and physically he wasn't quite where he wanted to be. He should knock off the booze until the season was over. He should get up early tomorrow and go for a run, too. He shouldn't stay up late. He shouldn't get distracted.

He probably shouldn't be here at all.

"Just half a glass," he acceded.

She ignored him, filling it to the brim and sliding it across the counter. They clinked their glasses together and then simultaneously took their first sips, eyes meeting over the rims.

Erin put her glass down first. "You said you've been thinking. About my offer?"

He nodded, placing his glass beside hers.

"And?"

"I'm worried."

"About?"

He looked away, his line of vision landing on a pricey box of chocolates wrapped with a bow on top of the microwave. The angle of its placement suggested Erin had tossed it there, a gift too meaningless to bother putting into a cupboard, let alone opening.

Had another man given it to her? He imagined a model-perfect guy in a suit turning up at the door he'd just walked through, hopeful, slightly desperate, his romantic gesture waved off as Erin explained it had been a one-time thing, it couldn't lead to anything more, and she appreciated his discretion.

Where had he heard those words before? Oh, right. Straight from her mouth on the same afternoon Roland informed him he was suspended for three months.

When he looked back she was still waiting for his answer.

"Obviously I like you," he admitted. "Otherwise I wouldn't be here, wouldn't even contemplate this. But we've been down this road before, you and I. That phone call in February—it hurt. You kicked me when I was down."

Her gaze dropped to the counter as she fiddled with the stem of her wineglass. "I was in negotiations with the league to take the new job and I panicked, worried that night in Vegas would come back on me somehow. That's not an excuse, though. It was a shitty way to behave, especially since we've known each other for so long. I'm sorry."

He shifted his weight, surprised. He'd expected her to roll her eyes or say something flippant that would make it easy for him to walk away. He never thought she would apologize.

"I like you too," she ventured, her gaze finding his again. "I've liked you since I met you. If I'd known that sleeping with you in Vegas was going to mess things up, I wouldn't have done it. If this is going to mess things up"—she gestured between them—"then let's forget about it. I can do sex without commitment—I always have—but I know that's new for you. I want us to be friends, and if the 'with benefits' element is going to derail that, I'd rather leave it than lose everything."

There it was—she'd given him an out. He should take it. Tell her they should keep things friendly, nothing more. Partners in bets but not in bed. Say goodbye in a couple of months with their friendship—and his heart—intact.

"I have a condition," he told her instead.

"Tell me."

"It has to be just me, no one else, for as long as we do this. I can't be with you knowing you're with other guys on other nights."

"I'll agree to that."

"Good. Any terms on your side?"

She shook her head. "Nothing I haven't already told you. We can be friends, we can have sex, but don't ask me for anything more."

"I won't," he said firmly, making the promise to her and to himself. He could do this. It would be worth it. He would be fine.

"Great." She raised her glass in a toast and he did the same. "When do we start?"

"I don't know." He glanced around the room, suddenly embarrassed, and his gaze snagged on the table. "You put plates out. Did you make dinner?"

"No, I just thought they made the table look nice. Why, are you hungry?"

"Not really."

"Me neither."

For a few moments they stared at each other, silent, the space between them growing tighter and heavier with each passing second. Eventually he asked, "Now what?"

"Now you take me to bed."

Before he could register her statement she replaced the glass on the counter and slightly shimmied her shoulders. The movement accentuated the heft of her breasts, and he knew it was rehearsed. Such a well-worn, practiced come-hither gesture he bet she didn't even realize she did it. It was part of her veneer—her personal brand. Erin the superstar athlete. Erin the high-flying executive. Erin the no-strings sexual dynamo, here today, gone tomorrow.

She closed the space between them and linked her arms behind his neck, but he stiffened. She sensed it and pulled back, and as her eyes searched his he saw it—the flash of uncertainty. The long-ago softness she worked so hard to pretend she'd outgrown.

"One more condition," he told her.

"What is it?" she asked, not impatiently.

"I want the Erin I met her first month in college."

He drew breath to go on but her shaking head interrupted him. "If you have some porno fantasy of a quivering, eighteen-year-old virgin we can call this off right now because that's the opposite of—"

"Stop." He silenced her with hands on her waist. "I want the Erin who trusted me. Who told me the biggest secret of her life, confident I would never share it with anyone. Who's walking into this with her arms wide open, because she knows she's safe with me—just like she was at that party."

She opened her mouth, the objection already half-spelled in the shape of her lips, then snapped it shut. A series of emotions chased across her face so quickly he only caught a few of them—disagreement, refusal, distress and outright panic—and he couldn't make out the winner as her expression resettled coolly.

For five heartbeats he held his breath, schooling his features not to give any indication of how much he wanted this. They stood inches apart but the distance between them was vast, maybe insurmountable. Maybe they were about to wrench apart irreparably.

Or maybe they were about to fill the aching void that had yawned between them all these long, lonely years.

She slid one palm along the back of his shoulders, drawing nearer.

"Okay," she whispered, the word as intimate as a confession. "You've got me."

He cupped her cheeks and kissed her, choosing to believe what she said and hurling himself headlong into this...whatever it was. Tryst. Affair. Arrangement. Whatever you called a situation where nothing was held back but nothing was given or kept, either.

Her red-wine taste raised memories of Vegas, of decadence and reckless indulgence. As much as he thought he read her promised trust in the softness of her posture and the gentle parting of her lips, for a second he stopped himself, his mouth pausing on hers.

No strings. Two words resonating in his mind with the dull thud of a dealer knocking card decks against the table.

He'd always been a cautious gambler. Obsessive, calculating, risk-averse. This might be the first bet he couldn't afford to lose.

Erin leaned back in his grip and looked up at him, her voice soft as she asked, "What?"

"Nothing," he said firmly, lowering his hands to her arms. He jerked her against his chest and brought their lips together again, lapping up her taste, luxuriating in the heat he found inside her mouth.

Too late for second-guessing. The cards were dealt, the chips were stacked. He was all in.

* * * *

Erin's heart had hiccups.

The first few times she ignored the twitching inside her ribs, too focused on Brendan's kiss. But as the erratic, fluttery beats became more frequent and intrusive, some self-preserving chunk of her mind detached to examine the situation. An irregular heart rate, tightness in her lungs, a slight but unpleasant tilt in her stomach.

Maybe it was something she ate. Early signs of food poisoning, even? Hopefully not—that would certainly spoil the evening. It was probably overexcitement. Or exhaustion from too much work and too much travel.

Or maybe she was having her first-ever panic attack.

No, there was something distantly familiar here, dimly remembered from many years ago. Unsteadiness in her fingertips, dryness in her throat.

She was nervous.

Brendan's palms sliding down to her waist told her she shouldn't be, as did his lazy thumbs lingering against the sides of her breasts. Not to mention they'd done this before. He'd seen every inch of her in Vegas, more than once lights off and on.

But while her mind rattled off these logical arguments, her heart knew better, and again hiccuped its anxiety.

In Vegas she'd been triumphant, her already dominant sexual style heightened by champagne and adrenaline and an overpowering sense of conquest. She'd caught the one who got away and spent all night having her way with him.

She reached for the sexual confidence which usually surfaced automatically but came up short. She rooted deeper, digging for the arrogance and self-satisfying impulses that normally spurred these encounters. The feverish drive for completion. The urgency to get what she wanted and slip away unhindered, a thief without remorse.

Except for this time she was complicit. Brendan was her co-conspirator, not her target. She already trusted him with her future, recommitting herself every time they placed a bet, and she'd shared her body with him on New Year's Eve. There was no reason to be fearful of the trust he asked for now.

Yet her heart hiccuped again.

Stop. Mentally she gripped her own shoulders and gave herself an almighty shake. Yes, Brendan was different from the men she normally slept with. They were friends—he wasn't disposable. That didn't mean anything else had to be different. Not the sex, not the post-sex expectations, and certainly not her personal performance.

Unless this was her one chance to make it different. To experience more than self-fulfillment. To allow intimacy. To give as well as take. To find someone who—

"Let's go," she said aloud, more to herself than to Brendan. She jerked out of his grasp and away from that momentary wobble, dragging on sexual bravado like a pair of jeans she hadn't worn in a long time. Tighter and less comfortable than she remembered, but she trusted it'd feel right in a few minutes.

She took Brendan's hand and pulled him toward the bedroom, barely looking at him as she charged across her apartment. She'd prepared the bedroom to be sex ready, as she often did before dates. Changed the sheets, shoved framed photographs into drawers, hid anything too personal, including perfume. Sterilized it so the man of the hour wouldn't see anything she hadn't carefully choreographed.

She practically shoved him inside and shut the door, yanked the curtains across the window, then hastily set about lighting the series of candles she kept arranged around the room for exactly this purpose. Candlelight was second only to alcohol when it came to dulling potentially mood-killing imperfections.

She tossed the spent match in a wicker trash bin, then leaned over where Brendan sat on the end of the bed to switch off the overhead light.

He switched it back on.

"I want to see you."

"Suit yourself." She shrugged with a nonchalance she didn't feel. "Just thought I'd create a little romantic atmosphere."

"But this is lust, not romance. Right?"

"Right," she agreed, hoping he hadn't heard the slight tremor in her voice. He held out his hand. "Come here."

She dropped onto his lap, tired of her internal back-and-forth. She'd wanted him for so long. Now he was here, ready, willing, and she was wasting all of her energy on stupid insecurities.

This was only lust like he said. Pure pleasure. About time she started enjoying it.

"Don't stress," he urged, arranging her legs on either side of his hips, her skirt sliding high on her thighs in the process.

"I'm not stressing."

"Don't lie to me, either."

"Stop talking and take off your clothes."

She slid off his lap, kicked off her heels and drew her legs up beneath her. His eyes widened but he obeyed and pulled his T-shirt over his head, leaving his hair mussed in its wake.

"Stand up," she instructed, relaxing into the familiarity of control. "Take off your jeans."

She admired the nearly six and a half feet of him as he straightened. He stepped on the heel of one sneaker to pry it off, then the other, never dropping eye contact—until he realized he had to reach down and tug off his socks. She muted her smile as he contorted, his lanky frame bent in half, all efforts at sexiness momentarily abandoned for the sake of logistics. When he stood again she made sure her expression gave no sign of how utterly adorable that had been.

He recovered quickly, undoing his belt and dropping it on the floor, the metal buckle clattering against the hardwood. The muscles in his forearms flexed as he lowered his zipper and let the waistband hang loose, briefly framing the ridges of muscle above his hips, the flat plane of his lower abdomen. Then he shoved his jeans to the floor and stepped out of them, kicking them against the wall.

She crossed her arms over taut nipples as she appraised him, smiling her approval. Long, long legs, from the elegant arches of his feet to the thick muscles of his thighs. Chiseled arms and broad shoulders, the delicious taper of all that width into a narrow waist. Pale hair standing out against tanned skin, fading evidence of a summer spent outdoors.

She imagined him lounging shirtless in his backyard, squinting at his notebooks through dark sunglasses. Tossing the books aside and moving restlessly around the perimeter, checking the gardener's handiwork. Taking a soccer ball from the shed and toeing it to his knees, to his head, back to his knees, counting the keep-ups until his sun-warmed skin was spotted with beads of sweat, moisture collecting on his forehead, between his pecs, in the hollow of his lower back.

For a second she closed her eyes, and in her mind her tongue swept the damp skin on his chest, the tip of her nose preceding its lazy trail. He would taste like salt. Sun. Heat. And beneath it, just Brendan. A flavor all his own.

She opened her eyes, licked her lips. Ready to make him sweat.

Finally she let her gaze drift below his waist. She was used to scanning designer labels on men's briefs, but Brendan wore plaid cotton boxers. She bet he bought them in packs of five for twenty dollars, tossed them in the car with blank notebooks and that cheap ground coffee he drank, then drove everything home in his Aston Martin.

Fuck, he was weird.

And unbelievably sexy.

She crooked a finger to summon him closer to the bed. When he came within reach she stuck that same finger in the waistband of his boxers, pulling it away from his body to assess what was beneath.

She couldn't stop her smile. He was all she remembered— maybe even more.

"These shorts don't fit you right," she murmured, brushing her fingertips over his skin, tracing the slight indentations made by the elastic. "You should buy some that do."

"I like these."

"I like this." She closed her hand around his length so suddenly that he flinched, giving her exactly the reaction she wanted. He was hot and hard in her fist and she tugged him mercilessly, tightening her grip at his base, then shimmying it up over his tip.

She watched his jaw tighten, saw him close his eyes for a split second before swearing under his breath and closing his hand on her wrist, stopping her mid-pull.

"Slow down," he said hoarsely. "You're not even undressed yet."

"Fix that." She released him abruptly and stretched out on the bed on her stomach, lowering her chin to folded hands.

The mattress shifted as Brendan eased down beside her. She closed her eyes, focusing on his proximity, the woodsy scent that drifted with it.

For a moment he simply sat, still and quiet. She wondered where he would touch her first, each part of her body livening as she visualized his hands there. Her shoulders, maybe. Her waist. The curve of her ass. The tender skin on the insides of her thighs, or the expectant, swollen flesh just beyond.

She heard the zipper on the back of her dress before she felt it, so light and careful were his fingers. The pressure of the tight garment eased and a slight draft moved over her exposed skin before his palm warmed it, flattening beneath the splayed halves of fabric.

She fidgeted pleasantly as he spread his fingers across her back. She was a tall, curvy woman with a robust figure, but Brendan's big hand made her feel dainty and petite, like the five-foot-nothing, perky-breasted women she'd always envied. Soon he had both hands on her shoulders, and she wriggled to help him pull the dress over her arms, then her hips, resettling on her stomach as it hit the floor.

He inched closer, his thigh pressing against hers. With her face on her hands she could just see his bare legs out of her peripheral vision as he undid the clasp on her bra. His fingers smoothed the red marks the straps had left on her skin.

"This bra doesn't fit you right," he murmured playfully. "You should buy a new one."

She laughed bitterly. "That's a slightly more complicated purchase than your boxers."

He hummed thoughtfully, kneading his knuckles over her back. The motion was relaxing—too relaxing. Need thrummed harder and harder at her core, and impatience prompted her to push up to a sitting position.

His expression registered surprise in her sudden movement but she ignored it, tossing her bra to the floor and scooting into his lap.

His brow furrowed as he steadied her with hands on her hips. "Sorry, was that not—"

"It was fine," she told him briskly, guiding his palms to cup her breasts. "But this is what I want."

He paused, his hands hovering over her breasts, awkward and uncertain. She pressed them into place and reached between them to grip him through his boxers, pleased with the wet spot that appeared on the cotton when she rubbed it over his crown.

"What are you in the mood for?" she asked, dropping her voice to a husky purr.

"I—I don't know," he stammered, thumbs moving unevenly over her nipples. "What do you want?"

She didn't have to think about her stock answer. She leaned in close and whispered beside his ear, "Make me come. Use your mouth."

His erection throbbed in her hand, and an answering jolt pounded in her sternum, quickening her heart rate.

"Whatever you say," he replied smoothly, then put his finger under her chin and brought their lips together.

Exasperation flashed automatically. She tried to avoid kissing after the first few minutes—it slowed everything down and, depending on the guy's skill, had the potential to completely kill her buzz. She supposed she had to go with it for a minute or two, though, if Brendan seemed into it.

She pushed her focus to the present, the physical, shelving the impulse to escalate their foreplay as quickly as possible. As he parted his lips she concentrated on his mouth, that lingering trace of red wine, the sultry, decisive sweep of his tongue over hers. She let herself sink into the kiss in the same way she had earlier, exhaling the anticipatory tension from her muscles, inhaling the scent of his aftershave as the tip of her nose brushed his cheek.

She abandoned her ruthless pursuit of his groin and draped her arms over his shoulders, widening her focus to include the lazy, almost distracted movement of his hand over her breast. His thumb toyed with her nipple, circling it, brushing its taut peak. Then he closed his hand over the fullness of her breast, hefting it, the slightest sound in his throat indicating how much he enjoyed its weight. Something about that idle attention sent a sharp, insistent pang of arousal arrowing through her body and settling so hotly between her legs that she moaned, the sound so unbidden and startling her eyes popped open, suddenly self-conscious.

Another hiccup, only this time he seemed to register her tension. He eased back to look at her, sweeping his thumb over her cheek.

"What's wrong?"

"Nothing," she said automatically, then sighed at the chiding skepticism in his eyes. "Maybe I'm a little nervous."

Incredulity drew his brows together. "Why? No strings, remember?"

"I know. And I know we've done this before, too. I'm not sure what's bothering me."

"This is supposed to be fun, and if it's not, we should wait. We don't have to rush into anything tonight."

His gentle, understanding tone made her heart clench, and then something clicked. Brendan wasn't just another guy who needed to be told what to do to get her off and then shoved out the door. He wasn't a selfish, self-centered one-night stand. He wouldn't leave her unsatisfied.

She had to trust him.

"Don't move," she instructed, then stood up from the bed. She blew out the candles, then opened the drawer in her bedside table and hauled out the cosmetics she'd stuffed inside, returning them to their typically haphazard arrangement. She crossed to the closet and opened the door, standing back as a wave of clothes and bags poured onto the floor. She made a vague attempt to kick the mess into a pile before turning to scan the bedroom, trying to pinpoint what still didn't feel right.

The sheets, she realized and motioned Brendan to the end of the bed while she untucked the flat sheet, threw back the duvet and tossed two ornamental pillows to the floor.

"Much better," she declared, meeting Brendan's bewildered expression with a broad smile.

"This is how it really looks," she explained, sinking down beside him. "I promised to be honest and trust you. To give you the real me. Here I am."

One side of his mouth quirked. "I think there's more to you than piles of clothes and an unmade bed."

"I'm serious. No man has ever seen my bedroom like this. Whenever I sleep with someone, I try to keep it tidy. So it never gets too intimate, and stays—"

"Transactional?"

Her attention sharpened at the word. "Exactly."

"I know."

"Vegas?"

He nodded.

"But you're here now."

"You kept me at arm's length, but that doesn't mean I didn't enjoy it. Or want to be with you again. Or hope you might let me get a little closer next time."

She held up her palms. "You can't get any closer than this."

He tilted his head, his coy smile saying, Try me. He leaned around her to pluck something off the bedside table. When he resettled she saw that he'd picked up a pack of makeup removing wipes.

"Oh, come on," she protested, but he'd already tugged out a wipe.

"Close your eyes."

She sighed exaggeratedly in response but did as he asked, folding her hands in her lap.

She was at his mercy, she realized with a mix of fear and excitement. Sightless, half-naked, the messy trappings of her messy life strewn around the room for his perusal. She couldn't remember the last time she'd been so exposed. Even the night she'd lost her virginity had been planned in advance, arming herself with condoms and practically throwing herself at her friend's notoriously slutty brother at a party, gritting her teeth through his grunting and later driving herself home, relieved to have what she considered a stupid milestone out of the way. She thought she'd taken a big step when she agreed to spend a single night at five-dates-Cal's apartment, but she spent the preceding days reading articles on how to style your hair before bed so it looked good first thing in the morning and arrived with more luggage than she'd bring on a week-long business trip.

No, she decided as she heard Brendan shift closer. She'd never, ever been this vulnerable.

She fought to be calm and relaxed, but she flinched at the first touch of the damp cloth. Brendan put a hand on her forearm, and its weight and heat were a welcome, anchoring contrast to the cool material sweeping over her cheeks, along her forehead, over her eyes.

"There you are," he said quietly, and she opened her eyes to find his approving smile.

"You haven't run screaming. That's a good start." She attempted a humorous grin, but he was having none of it.

"Lie down," he instructed.

She flopped back against the pillow, marveling at her newfound ability to surrender. If any other man had said that she would've bristled, wrestled for control of the situation, maybe kicked him out altogether. But as Brendan eased her panties over her hips and onto the floor, she felt totally safe. No need to resist, no impulse to take what she wanted. He'd give it to her eventually—she knew he would.

He splayed one of his big palms on her stomach and she luxuriated in her nudity, stretching her arms and arching her back, wanton and confident despite the harsh lighting and lack of makeup. Her nipples stiffened anew under his gaze, her thighs instinctively pressed together in a futile attempt to relieve the pressure building at their apex.

There's nothing left to hide from him, she realized with a jolt, her eyes lifting to meet his. He'd seen it all. The gambling. The debt. The selfish woman in Vegas who lapped up his body and then tossed him like a broken champagne flute.

Yet here he is. A different kind of heat suffused her body as he parted her knees and spread her wide, one that burned behind her eyes and into her throat, aching through her lungs and balling in her heart.

He was such a good, good man. Whoever he found in Nebraska better deserve him, because she sure as hell didn't.

The thought of some anonymous future woman putting her hands on him sent an irrational pang of jealousy slicing through her stomach. She pushed it aside, concentrating on his fingers running up the insides of her thighs, registering the way he was repositioning himself between her legs.

"Don't let me be selfish," she told him huskily, clamping a stilling hand on his wrist. "Make sure I give you what you want, too."

"This is what I want," he replied, then ran his tongue along her swollen, aching slit.

The noise that wrenched from her throat at that first touch must've been the sound of her brain vacating her skull because at that point any semblance of coherent thought gave way to pure, primal, all-consuming sensation. She writhed as he pinned her thighs against the bed, dragging the flat of his tongue up and down her core, then teased her clit with its tip. Her eyes squeezed shut and her breasts heaved as he tormented and tantalized, slowing exactly when she needed him to speed up, repeatedly bringing her to the edge of climax and then yanking her back. Her stomach muscles became sore from trying to evade his touch when it was too much and encourage it when it wasn't enough, and she shoved a restless, frantic hand through her hair as sweat broke out on her forehead.

When he slid his forearms further beneath her thighs and traced focused, unrelenting circles around her clit, she knew she had to pull herself together. It took every ounce of her will to drag herself out from under the heavy, inviting tide of her impending orgasm and push up to her elbows.

She threaded her fingers through Brendan's hair and pulled—hard—to bring his gaze to hers.

His eyes were bright but dazed, like green glass weathered by the ocean, and it took him a second to blink to awareness. "What?"

"Not like this." She planted her foot on his shoulder and pushed him away. "Condoms under the bed."

He stared at her. She poked through her sluggish thoughts, trying to figure out what she could've said wrong. Finally she came up with, "Are you not ready?"

"I'm ready," he said roughly, standing and stripping off his boxers to show her the evidence. "I was just thinking about why you'd keep condoms under the bed instead of the drawer."

"You're lucky I find that bizarro brain of yours so attractive because that is a weird thing to say given the circumstances."

"You never told me you found my brain attractive," he responded teasingly, dropping to the floor to fish under the bed.

"Of course I do. The crazy stats, the obsessive analysis, the annoyingly spot-on non-sequiturs… What's not to—"

She literally bit her tongue to stop the word from leaving her mouth. She didn't love him. She wouldn't love him. She wasn't sure she had the capacity to love anyone, ever.

Sex without commitment. No strings. Friends with—

"Found them." He returned to the bed.

"Let me do the honors." She pinched the top and slowly rolled the latex over his shaft, marveling at how small her hands looked as she circled it with thumb and forefinger.

"Do you want to be on top?" he asked.

She shook her head. "No."

"Are you sure? I don't mind. In Vegas you said—"

"I know what I said." Well, she didn't remember the exact words, but she could assume it was a variation on her standard line. I only come when I'm on top. Translation: I come a lot faster when I'm on top, and I want to make sure you don't leave me hanging.

She eased onto her back and opened her legs to him. He could take as long as he liked.

Brendan stretched out above her, supporting his weight on his elbows. She swept the fingers of one hand through his hair and planted her other hand on his taut ass, pressing him lower. She felt the heat and hardness of him jutting against her abdomen, the latex slick against her skin.

He traced the line of her cheekbone with his thumb. She felt his fingertips tracing the edge of her fresh bikini wax, then one finger slipping lower, testing her slickness, venturing inside.

She moaned her objection, pushing his hand away. "Not nearly enough."

"Then what do you want?"

"You know." She shifted impatiently beneath him.

"Tell me."

She crossed her wrists above her head, giving him the sultry, pleasure-drunk smile he was angling for. "You. I want you, in me. Now."

He obliged with a groan, positioning himself at her opening, then pushing inside in a single, unhesitating stroke.

She swore hotly at the delicious pressure, the simultaneous fulfillment of his body and her heightened need for more. She hooked her ankles together behind his back as he began a smooth rhythm. He stubbornly ignored her hands kneading his hips to move faster, and after a few seconds of frustration she breathed out and closed her eyes, reminding herself yet again to trust him, to relax and let her arousal move at its own pace.

Despite Brendan's calm, unhurried ministrations, that pace turned out to be pretty damn fast. She fidgeted beneath him, feverish with swelling desire, each thrust briefly satisfying and then increasing her body's demands.

She was on the verge of telling him to hurry the hell up when it happened. Her orgasm blindsided her, descending unannounced, as fierce and sudden and drenching as a summer-afternoon thunderstorm. She gasped from the shock of it, dug her fingers into Brendan's arms, arched her back as her jaw fell open and every muscle in her body clenched.

Scorching pulses of pleasure throbbed from her core through her abdomen, thundering through her heart, lodging in her chest. More than once she thought her climax was subsiding only to have it rear up with renewed insistence, thumping harder, suffusing every nerve.

"Fuck," she exhaled, rediscovering her voice as the pulsing finally dissipated.

"We are." Brendan smiled wryly. As she got to grips with the situation she realized he'd paused to study her, the tension in his face showing the effort of his self-restraint.

"You good?" he asked.

"Good? Try amazing. I've never come for that long."

His smile spread into a grin. "At your service."

They shared a happy gaze for another second, then she shifted her hips to encourage him to move.

"No one told you to stop."

She caught a gleam in his green eyes before he ducked his head, glancing between them at the place where they came together as he resumed the rhythm.

She relaxed against the pillow, her muscles loose and melty, her core still so sensitive with the aftershocks of her orgasm that Brendan's thrusts were welcome, each one sending a reminding shiver of pleasure down her legs.

Typically this was the point at which she lost all patience and found herself mentally composing emails, rearranging her to-do list, and getting more and more eager to wrap things up. At a certain point she would do or say whatever was necessary to get her partner off and send him out the door, but not tonight.

Instead of feeling trapped or uncomfortable, she actually enjoyed the weight of Brendan's body above her. Instead of closing her eyes and letting her mind wander she drank in the view of his face, what she could see of his chest, the muscles standing out in his arms. Instead of willing him to finish she savored him, lifting her hips to meet his strokes, arching her back to sip at his lower lip.

"You are so sexy, Brendan Young," she purred, running her hands along his ribs, smoothing them over his narrow haunches.

He grunted in response, increasing the pace. She murmured encouragement, tightening her crossed ankles to urge him deeper. Soon his thrusts became sloppy, quick and harried, and the sound of flesh slapping against flesh competed with their heavy exhalations. She relished the slick sensation of his erection sliding in and out, harder and harder. When he pushed inside and stayed, stiffening, she wrapped her arms around his neck and pulled him close. He pressed his cheek against her temple as he came, the shuddering jerks of his climax accompanied by a breathy, sighing moan that pulled hard at her heart.

She'd never been so pleased to see a man come, or so sorry he'd finished.

Brendan dropped lower against the bed and she felt his racing heart as their chests pressed together. Too soon he withdrew, and she turned on her side to watch his fumbling, clumsy movements as he took off the condom, tied the end and dropped it in the trash bin across the room.

When he turned she smiled an invitation, scooting over so he could join her on the bed. He stretched out and so did she, delighting yet again in how diminutive her body seemed beside his.

"Happy?" she asked.

He crossed one arm behind his head. "Very."

"Me too." She sighed contentedly.

"Do friends with benefits spoon after sex? Or should I get dressed?"

"Spooning definitely allowed." She rolled over at the same time he did, curling her back against his stomach as his arm came around her waist.

"Not a bad way to spend a Sunday night," he remarked.

She closed her eyes drowsily. "Stay for dinner. I'll grill chicken and vegetables. Or we'll get something delivered. Watch the match highlights from the weekend. Use up another condom to celebrate our winnings."

He chuckled into her hair. "What time do you have to leave for work in the morning?"

"Early," she groaned, mildly astonished that she was actually entertaining the possibility of asking him to spend the night—and equally disappointed that a breakfast meeting made it too unwise to consider. "I have coffee with a potential new hire at seven. Then I have my weekly meeting with the CFO. He's still harping on about making you the focus of an ethics insert in the year-end report."

Brendan stiffened behind her.

"I thought the Tucson thing got me off the hook," he said coolly, but the rigidity in his posture belied his casual tone.

She rolled over to face him. "I thought so, too, but he wants something bigger. Preferably involving one of the teams in the league final."

"But that narrows it down to Miami or Charlotte, most likely."

"Or Atlanta," she supplied grimly.

His expression darkened and so did the mood. She pushed her mouth into what she hoped was a reassuring smile. "I'll figure something out. We still have time."

"What we have is an agreement," he told her, sitting up and perching on the edge of the bed. "I help you settle your debt, you keep my name out of the report."

"I'm working on it," she said tartly, eyeing her robe across the room but deciding she had no reason to be embarrassed. She turned onto her back, refusing to shift from her reclined position. She hadn't done anything wrong. In fact she was doing everything she could to do right by him.

He shook his head slightly, then fished his boxers from the floor and stepped into them.

Tell him to stay, some part of her begged in desperation. Tell him you're doing your best and that you'll keep up your end of the bargain if it kills you. Tell him this was the closest you've ever felt to anyone you've slept with. Tell him he's different. Important. The first man you could maybe—

"No way," she muttered under her breath, drawing Brendan's attention. She schooled her features into neutrality as though she hadn't spoken, and he pulled his T-shirt over his head.

She said nothing as he resumed his seat on the edge of the bed to tie his shoes. Let him be mad at her. Let him storm out like a toddler having a tantrum. She didn't care.

Liar.

He finished and planted both feet on the floor, but he didn't get up. He sat for another couple of seconds, patient, contemplative. When he finally twisted to look at her she could tell he didn't want to say what he was about to say.

"I heard a rumor. A player who might be betting on the league."

"From which club?"

His pained hesitation gave her the answer, and she raised a hand to stop him having to say it aloud. "I get it. Don't say anything else."

He nodded, maybe a little gratefully, but mostly his expression was resigned.

She bit her lower lip, wanting so badly to take him in her arms and comfort him, acknowledge how hard it must be for him to tell her this, assure him everything would be fine. But that's what a wife would do, or a girlfriend, or a long-term lover.

They were just friends who had sex.

"Thank you," she told him instead. "I'll take it from here."

He stood, cleared his throat. "Despite…that…I had fun. Let's do it again soon."

"We will. Definitely."

He shoved his hands in his pockets, the atmosphere growing more awkward by the second. "I'm going to head home."

He put his hand on the doorknob and something propelled her to sit up. "Brendan, wait, I—"

He looked over his shoulder, brows lifted as he waited for her to speak, but the words had gummed up in her throat, thick and stuck and immoveable.

I want you to know this wasn't about our agreement. I wasn't trying to seduce you into ratting on your teammates. This was the most honest, open, sincere sexual experience I've ever had.

"I'll call you once I know my schedule for the week. We can pick a night to look at the odds and…whatever else."

"I'll speak to you tomorrow." He opened the door.

She nodded. "Bye."

He ducked his head in farewell and left the room. She heard his footsteps echo across the open-plan apartment, followed by the dull thud of the front door closing.

Then she flopped backward on her bed, her body still glowing from his touch, her heart already aching from his absence.

Chapter 14

"Who are you bringing to Family Day, Terim?" Aaron lobbed the question across the corridor as they walked through the training complex from the pitch to the locker room.

Brendan looked up just in time to catch the Swede's evasive glance. "Friend of mine's niece. A little girl named Dallas. How about you, Young?"

"Kid from the Down syndrome sports program. She won the keep-up competition." He smiled fondly, remembering the event back in... Actually it was only at the end of July. Not even two months earlier.

Yet life seemed completely different. Then he was doomed to the bench, going through the motions of day-to-day life, spending his nights with his head buried in his notebooks.

Now he was Skyline's starting goalkeeper. He was betting for real again and seeing his odds play out calmed his mental state more than six months of Gamblers Anonymous meetings had. Sitting in the league's crosshairs still worried him, but he believed Erin when she said she would fix it.

Erin.

He sighed contentedly as he tuned out his teammates' banter. Sunday night had exceeded his most optimistic fantasies of this friends-with-benefits scenario, to the point he'd had to leave before his emotional defenses became as soft as his sex-spent cock. Only once he got home did he worry that Erin might misread his departure as a storm-out. Given the openness and trust she'd shown him, that was the last signal he wanted to send, and he was halfway through his third version of a long-winded text explaining that he wasn't ready for no-strings post-sex cuddling when his phone had pinged with a text from Erin herself.

Or more accurately, a sext.

Should've made you stay. Thinking about round 1 has got me needing round 2.

He blinked at the message, then flicked back to his own and reread it. Overlong, wordy, explaining something he hadn't done but thought she might think he did.

He exhaled in disgust as he deleted it. No wonder he was such a hit with the ladies.

He stared at the blank message screen, briefly considered Googling "how to sext" for ideas, then stopped himself with a sharp mental slap.

One of the blissful elements of his evening with Erin was the submission to instinct. No overthinking. No analysis and reanalysis. Just touch, taste and all-consuming sensation.

He set his jaw and typed, then pressed send before he could change his mind.

Didn't realize the benefits part of 'friends w/' included round 2. Good to know for next time.

She fired back, *When is next time?*

He raised his brows. Guess she had a good time, too.

Got training this week, home match on Saturday. Thurs night?

Your place or mine?

Mine, he decided.

A short pause, then, *In my calendar. Had to put it in code b/c my PA has access. Cocktails w/ Brenda, 6 PM. Because your cock tells a hell of a tale. :)*

Brenda? he replied.

Code, she reminded him. *Anyway what do you have to say for leaving me high and dry like this? Just me & my right hand here all alone, not sure what to do w/out you.*

I think you know what to do. He moved to put down his phone, thinking they were finished, when it pinged again.

Tell me what to do.

He swallowed. Sat down on the edge of his bed. Braced his elbows on his knees.

Tease your clit, just a little.

Mm. Not as good as you but I'll take it. And?

His breathing quickened, already hard as he imagined her sprawled naked on her bed, hand between her thighs. He couldn't quite believe he was doing this—as a lover he'd always been more Harlequin than *Playboy*—but Erin had a way of pushing him past limits he hadn't realized existed. He shifted on the bed so he could type with one hand, using the other to unzip his fly.

Test yourself with 1 finger. Tell me how wet you are.

Mmmm. Very wet. Very slick. Still hot from your—

"Brendan, hi."

He stopped short, managing to drag himself out of his foggy line of recollection just in time to stop from colliding with—

"Erin," he remarked, briefly wondering if she was real or his fantasy had been so vivid he'd conjured her into three dimensions. "What are you doing here?"

"I had a meeting with Roland," she said, widening her eyes in warning as the manager stepped into the corridor behind her. Belatedly Brendan realized they stood a few feet from the manager's office.

"Brendan. I'd like to see you, please." Roland's tone was flat, implicitly telling his teammates to keep walking and stop nosily craning their necks.

"It was nice to see you again," Erin told him crisply.

He nodded, keeping his tone level and polite, schooling his features to show none of the excitement he felt at seeing her even in these dangerous circumstances. "You too. I hope you're settling into life in Atlanta."

Her smile was bright and professional. "Absolutely. Best of luck with the rest of the season."

They shared a fleeting, conspiratorial glance before she proceeded down the corridor.

He followed Roland into his immaculate office and sat down, feeling exceptionally unkempt in his grass-stained training kit, his mind lurching like a drunk on a sailboat as he assessed the situation from every angle, worked the odds, examined the probabilities.

Best-case scenario, he's decided I'm a hero and wants to extend my contract.

Worst, he's found out about our syndicate and I'm fired.

He held his breath as Roland folded his hands on the desk.

"You know Erin Bailey," he stated neutrally.

"We went to college together," Brendan explained, careful not to volunteer any more information than he had to.

Roland inclined his head, giving nothing away. Too bad he'd come into managing after only a brief career as a defensive midfielder because he could out-poker-face some of the best strikers in the league.

"Did you know Miss Bailey works for the league?"

Brendan nodded. "Ethics Director."

"Unfortunately her visit today wasn't a courtesy call. She's received an anonymous tip that one of my players is betting on the CSL."

Brendan said nothing, ignoring the panic beginning to stir in his gut. If Roland wanted to accuse him, he could go right ahead. He hadn't done anything wrong.

Okay, he had done—and continued to do—plenty wrong. But he hadn't bet on his own league. That was a line he'd never cross.

They regarded each other in silence. Brendan forced his breaths to slow, reminding himself that Erin was in his corner. She wouldn't say anything to Roland to jeopardize his career. They were in this together.

He resisted the urge to twitch his mouth in a half-smile. How times had changed.

Finally Roland leaned back in his chair and crossed his arms. "You've had an outstanding run since Pavel was injured. I'd hate to lose you at this point in the season, and that's why I need you to be completely honest with me."

He arched a brow, daring his manager to ask the question.

Roland's voice was hard as flint. "Are you betting on the league?"

"No," Brendan replied firmly, secretly grateful Roland had qualified the question with on the league.

Roland narrowed his eyes. Brendan held his gaze unwaveringly, refusing to fill the silence with anything but that single word.

"Fine." Roland dropped his palms to the desk. "I won't ask you again. But Erin Bailey might. She's opening a formal investigation, and she has my full support. I won't stand for ethics violations of any kind on this squad."

It was more of a thinly veiled threat than a statement, and Brendan simply smiled. "I'm happy to cooperate. It'll be nice to catch up after so long."

"I'll let you know when she wants to speak to you." Roland picked up a piece of paper from a pile, signaling the end of their conversation.

Brendan didn't bother with even a cursory parting statement. He just stood and left the room.

If Roland thought he could find a reason to freeze him out of the league final he had another think coming. He deserved his spot. No way in hell would he let go of it now.

* * * *

"Hello." Brendan grinned as he opened the door from the garage to the kitchen to find Erin framed in the dim light, red hair tumbling over her shoulders, a virginally white dress hugging the body he'd dreamed about for the last three days.

"Hello, yourself." She pushed up to her toes and brushed a kiss over his lips. He grabbed her wrist to keep her in place, lapped at her lower lip, stole a taste of her tongue. She hummed her approval and pressed in closer, but he used his grip on her arm to hold her back.

"Work, then pleasure."

"Boring," she whined but preceded him through the door to the pub.

"How was training today?" she asked over her shoulder, picking her way down the stairs in her high heels.

"Standard." Her ass looked sinful in that dress. In every dress. Was there a special store that made clothes that tight, or—

"No one mentioned anything about the investigation?"

Mention of the dark cloud hanging over him and Roland killed his boner faster than a cold shower in January. "No. But I'm not sure anyone knows about it except me."

"They will tomorrow. My assistant's sending out the interview schedule first thing in the morning." She took a seat at one of the barstools, slung her bag onto the one beside it, then pulled out her iPad. "I guess it's inevitable that some people will assume it's about you. Hopefully they won't let it affect the team dynamics."

He moved behind the bar to pour her gin and tonic, then emptied a beer bottle into a pint glass for himself.

"We have a rest day tomorrow, ahead of the early match on Saturday." He eased onto the stool beside her and opened his notebook. "If anyone wants to confront me about it, they can call. Otherwise they'll have to set their suspicions aside until after the game."

"Do you think anyone will be rude about it? Cheers, by the way." She tapped her glass against his.

"Cheers." He took a sip, then raised a shoulder as he put down the pint. "I doubt it. They're not a sanctimonious crowd. The only one I can see being difficult is the guilty party."

"What about Roland?" she prompted. "Was he difficult?"

"No more than usual. Anyway, let's get to work." Brendan picked up his pen, shoving aside images of his manager's brooding stare, his furrowed brow, his even greater reluctance to offer any praise to his goalkeeper.

She let the topic drop as she tapped the screen to life, but her sidelong glances told him she was still thinking about it.

He reached over and lowered the tablet, touching her cheek so she looked at him head-on.

"I'll be fine," he promised. "I don't need Roland to be nice to me, or anyone else for that matter. What I do need is for you to make a big bust and get my head off the chopping block."

"I know. And I will. It just makes me sad to think of people making assumptions about you that aren't true."

"Aren't they?" He gestured to the setup in front of them, sweeping his arm to include the whiteboard, his stats-clogged notebooks, her own spreadsheet.

She shook her head. "Definitely not. Betting on a league you haven't played in for years is completely different to betting on the one paying you every week."

"It's not great, though, is it." He sighed, smoothing his hand over a page made bumpy by the density and pressure of his handwriting.

"Moral or not, it's profitable," she said resolutely.

He nodded, glancing between the whiteboard and his notebook as he tried to find his focus, to summon the sense of relaxation that normally accompanied these stats sessions.

The last couple of days he'd found himself reluctant to open his notebooks, and he wasn't sure why. Part of him was grateful, hoping this was a natural easing of his obsession, that it showed the potential for finding a mental release valve in something other than a morally dubious, time- and money-consuming hobby.

The other part of him was quietly terrified that it meant the stats would stop working. That he wouldn't be able to reach for his notebooks when he needed to silence his clanging brain. That there would be no outlet for his anxiety and the erratic heartbeats, short breaths, and tickertape thoughts would become the status quo.

No, he assured himself, forcing his attention onto Erin's analysis of the first match on their list. He'd find another way. Something else to be his conduit out of mental chaos and pin him to earth.

He just had no idea what.

"I know their lineup looks stronger," Erin said. "But they had a big European match last night and I think the players will be tired. It'd be a huge upset, but I think they might draw."

Brendan frowned at the predicted team sheet Erin had pulled up on her iPad. "I'm not sure. I haven't thought about this one yet. We can go with your bet, though, if you think it's sound."

She bit her lower lip. "It's a big call. Maybe you should look at it when you get a chance and decide whether or not I'm on the right track."

"I can, but you're getting awfully good at this yourself. In a couple of months you'll be making all these decisions on your own. Time to start taking off the training wheels and sending you for some test runs, Bailey."

"Don't say that. I don't want to think about you leaving and taking that superstar cock of yours with you." She puffed her lips in a mock pout.

"I can't leave it here. Although it might finally get this house sale moving if it was included in the purchase price."

"Still no offers?"

"Nope. The realtor wants me to paint the second bedroom lilac. Says the whole place is too masculine." He exhaled his disgust.

"It's a sign. The universe is telling you to stay in Atlanta and serve as my private sex slave."

He laughed, but his groin twitched. He looked her up and down again, his eyes leveling on her breasts, the way they brushed the tops of her hands as she leaned over her folded forearms.

"Tempting," he admitted. "Not sure it would cover the mortgage repayments, though."

"I only pay in blowjobs, so unless the bank is willing to accept those…" She shrugged.

"I doubt it. Moving on." He cleared his throat and tried to focus on his notebook rather than the full-force erection demanding to be released from his jeans and stuffed between Erin's legs.

It was her turn to laugh, a sunny, arresting sound. "Brendan Young, you are positively blushing. Did I scandalize you with the b-word?"

"No," he protested, but she tilted her head knowingly.

"This is why I love sleeping with Catholic men. The overdeveloped sense of shame makes even the ordinary seem so much more taboo and delicious." She ran her hand up his thigh. "I'll give you one now if you want."

"No." *Yes.*

"I don't mind. It would be my pleasure," she purred.

"No," he repeated, summoning the strength to remove her hand from his leg. "Stats first."

"Your self-control is admirable and extremely boring." She sighed her defeat, sulkily propping her chin on her hand. "Next match on the list should be easy. Top-flight club at home against one already battling to stay out of relegation. The odds won't be worth much on this one."

He flipped two pages backward in his notebook to see if he could fill the blank he was drawing. Nothing—he hadn't started his analysis on this one either.

"I haven't worked this one. Let's park it for now. What's next?"

She gestured to the half-empty whiteboard. "You've hardly thought about any of these. I know it's only Thursday, but usually you've got at least an educated guess for every result. What's up?"

"I don't know," he told her honestly, sitting back on the stool. "Normally I can't stop thinking about the odds. I check them first thing in the morning, last thing before I go to bed. I dream about them. But this week I just couldn't get interested."

"That's weird," she agreed. "Do you know what's weirder?"

"What?"

"I had the exact same issue this week. The difference is I'm actively trying to give up my stupid slot-machine habit, with mixed results. The last couple of days, though, I haven't even opened the app on my phone. Haven't even thought about opening it."

"Interesting." He crossed his arms. "What did you think about instead?"

She looked at him squarely. "You."

"Very funny." He ducked his head, trying to conceal what he was sure must be bald recognition in his face.

Because he'd been doing exactly the same thing since he left her apartment on Sunday night.

For years his tendency to reach for his notebooks in response to stress had been automatic, almost unconscious. He'd pay an unexpectedly high credit card bill and before the glimmer of guilt or regret could take hold he was already opening to the current page and fumbling for a pen. Each notebook was an escape route out of worry, fear, irritation, or sadness, ten times as effective as any of the psychiatric medicines he tried in high school and a hundred times faster.

On Monday morning, though, he'd opened his notebooks more out of obligation than need. On Tuesday evening, after his confrontation with Roland, he'd settled into the chair in his bedroom with a notebook only to leave it open and untouched as he stared into space, his thoughts drifting to Erin. Her body. Her smile. Her laugh.

He told himself it was the newness of their arrangement. He was scratching a physical itch he'd ignored for a long time, and that could drive any man to distraction. This fixation with Erin would fade over time. It had to. It was already September. By Christmas he'd be nearly a thousand miles away in Nebraska.

"I'm serious," Erin insisted, drawing him out of his reverie as her hand found its way back onto his thigh. "It's like you're my new drug of choice."

"Same," he admitted, slowly raising his gaze to meet hers. "That's why I haven't looked at the matches yet."

They regarded each other in silence. He wondered if she was also thinking about their no-strings agreement. Or if her heart rebelled as fiercely on that point as his.

"Friend with benefits," he said aloud, as much for himself as for her. "I don't speak from experience, but I'm guessing that doesn't include sex as a replacement addiction."

"Definitely not," she replied, seeming to find the same resolve he had. "Doesn't mean we can't enjoy the diversion while it lasts, though."

He shut the notebook and swiveled on the stool, pressing his hand over hers. "We're not getting anywhere on these. Maybe we should get the diversion out of the way. Come back to the odds with clear heads."

"Best plan I've heard in weeks. One point of business first, though."

"Shoot."

"I've gotten approval to travel to Topeka next weekend to meet with the ladies' team. I'll be there for Skyline's away fixture on Friday night."

He smiled. His Friday night in Kansas just got more interesting. "I'll be on the same floor as all the other players, but I'm sure I can sneak into your room. Actually, if you book a different hotel, I can—"

"We'll deal with the logistics later. First I need to explain why I timed the trip this way." She grinned. "I have an ulterior motive."

"Don't you always?"

"I'm more like sixty-five percent hidden agenda, thirty-five percent open confrontation. Anyway, this falls into the former category. A little bird in the Skyline press office told me you're driving home to Lincoln on Saturday for an event."

"I usually do when we're away at Topeka. It's not a long drive to Lincoln, so I spend a night or two and fly home from there."

"And the event? The publicist told me it's similar to what you do here in Atlanta, promoting sports for people with intellectual disabilities."

"The organization I fund here in Atlanta is an offshoot of the one in Nebraska. When I first started playing professionally I set up a foundation in my brother's name and hired someone in Nebraska to disburse the money to worthy programs. He had so much trouble finding any, he suggested we start one." He smiled fondly, remembering the work that had gone into creating Young Legends. "Now it's a fully-fledged nonprofit. We have a couple of people who do the advocacy side, talking to legislators, partnering with parents and school districts to improve services. On the other we do all-abilities sports teams, targeted at a post-school age bracket, which is when the extracurricular programming tends to run out. Soccer in the fall, basketball in the winter, softball in the spring. I've got a whole staff running it now, but I like to turn up in person when I can. See the players, meet their parents. Keep my hand in."

"That's awesome, Brendan," she told him earnestly as he raised his beer glass to take a sip. "And that's why I'm going with you."

"You're what?" He put the glass down so hard some of the beer sloshed over the rim. He grabbed one of the towels he used to wipe down the bar and slapped it over the puddle, glancing at Erin over his shoulder. "Explain."

"This annual report thing rocks two ways. We both know I have to nail someone doing something worse than you did. The flip side is to make you look like a saint, and stuff your section full of uplifting content."

"Like the thing next weekend," he supplied.

"You've got it. The press office gave me a name of a photographer in Des Moines, and he's available to be in Lincoln on Saturday. While I'm out there I can get some quotes from whoever you've got running the nonprofit, maybe even some parents or players. It's perfect for what we need, especially as it has the hometown, end-of-career angle. You just have to say yes."

He arched a brow. "Since when? If it's what you want to do, you'll do it."

"Not when it's this personal. Not now that we're... You know."

He didn't know. In fact he was increasingly unsure of what they were, but he knew exactly what they were supposed to be. And it left no room for sentimentality.

"People will see us together," he pointed out. "You don't think that'll be a problem?"

"Not as long as you can keep your hands off me. Which will be difficult, I know." She winked teasingly. "Otherwise no one will suspect anything. The possibility of my dating someone is so improbable—especially a player—I doubt anyone would even think of it."

"Let's do it," he decided. "We can drive up together on Saturday morning."

She clapped her hands together in delight. "Road trip!"

"It's only a three-hour drive," he told her dryly, but her excitement was contagious and he couldn't help smiling.

"Good to know. I'll curate the playlist accordingly."

"No way. I'm driving, I pick the music."

Mischief sparkled in her eyes. "Let's play for it. Winner owns the stereo."

"Winner of?"

"The game I just made up." She reached back and slowly unzipped her dress. "We take turns. Whoever comes faster loses."

"You're on," he declared, already reaching for her.

Chapter 15

Brendan winced as a woman's voice whined through the speakers, accompanied by an acoustic guitar. "What's she so pissed off about?"

"Patriarchy." Erin snapped an elastic around her ponytail and slid her sunglasses on her nose.

"Please don't tell me the whole playlist is like this." He put the rental into gear and pulled out of the parking lot to join the road leading to the highway.

"Nope, I threw in a couple of Broadway hits too."

He groaned. "What did I do to deserve this?"

"I believe it was the forty-five seconds from the first touch to orgasm," she pointed out, flashing him a helpful smile.

She leaned back in the seat as the car joined the highway. She'd had a superb meeting with the Topeka women's team, the Skyline investigation was moving forward, and by the end of today she'd have enough content to make Brendan look like a hero on and off the pitch. She had her favorite tunes, a hot man behind the wheel, and three hours of clear blue skies and wheat-field roadsides. She exhaled happily, unable to remember the last time everything had been going so well.

She smiled over at Brendan, taking in the long legs he'd had to adjust the seat to accommodate, his relaxed posture, green eyes focused on the road ahead. She remembered the way he'd urged her legs to wrap around his waist in the shower that morning, the squeak of tile against her bare back, the muscles in his arms trembling as they came together, gravity forcing him deep inside her. Then she thought of the contrast between the ramshackle assortment of clothes stuffed inside her suitcase and the spare, ordered contents in his, and her smile became a grin.

She crossed her hands behind her head with a contented sigh. This friends-with-benefits scenario had worked out even better than she imagined. Steamy sex, genuine laughs, easy companionship, and the double-edge benefits of shaving down her debt and slowing down the rate at which she added more.

No, not slow—stop. She hadn't opened her slot-machine app in days, not even during the long delay on the tarmac or tucked into her hotel room bed—two situations that normally could've cost her hundreds in bored, restless spins.

Brendan was the first man she would've considered for a medium-term affair, which made his imminent departure all the more disappointing. He didn't bore her like most of her dates. He was good-looking, funny, smart, humble, yet confident enough to stand up to her.

She stole a glance at him across the car. He was leaving, and that meant emotions were off the table. But if he wasn't... If they weren't...

It didn't matter. This would never be anything more than what they'd agreed—what she'd stipulated, in fact. No point getting sentimental about something that was always going to end. By New Year's he'd be in Nebraska and she'd be bed-hopping again, and their fling would be a pleasant but distant memory.

Anyway, she wasn't sure she had the capacity to love a man, not for any significant length of time. She loved her mother and her sister and her dad, but the possibility of feeling something similar for someone outside her family seemed totally unlikely. She could barely muster the emotion to care whether she saw most guys for a second date. At thirty-one, sexually active for thirteen years, she had so many notches on her bedpost she'd lost count. Not once had she felt a romantic tug toward commitment, and that was fine. She treasured her self-sufficiency and independence. Growing old alone didn't faze her. She welcomed it.

And yet growing old with Brendan didn't sound half-bad.

It was a waste of mental energy to even consider it, she decided, sitting up in her seat. Brendan might not want to be with her, anyway—he'd agreed to the same short-term time frame she had. He probably didn't think of her as wife material. She bet he wanted a docile, wholesome, supportive type who baked bread and clipped coupons and kept a holiday decorating schedule. Who wasn't ambitious or prickly or arrogant. Who loved him with the wide-open, uncritical, limitless adoration she doubted she was capable of.

She turned to him with a teasing smile, hoping some playful banter would lighten the weight pulling on her heart. "I bet all of Lincoln's eligible bachelorettes will be there this afternoon, lining up like Penelope's suitors, plying you with homemade jams and hand-sewn quilts."

"Jesus, Erin, it's the Midwest, not the nineteenth century." He shot her a grin. "They'll have Pinterest boards, not quilts, and the jams will be sugar-free."

"Either way, I'm going to do my best to screen them for you. Any sign of extreme religious fervor, excessive cat ownership or sexual inadequacy will get them removed from the event."

He arched a brow. "Sexual inadequacy?"

"Don't pretend I haven't spoiled you for all but the most sexually dynamic of my species. I'm a hard, if not impossible, act to follow."

"I won't argue with that."

"No, but you'll say goodbye to me when the time comes. You'll sleep with other women and I'll sleep with other men. You'll never forget me, though," she told him, then snapped her mouth shut as what was meant to be a silly, triumphant statement came out wistful and full of longing.

He heard it, too. "I never said I would."

"I know," she replied shortly, trying to think of a way to change the subject.

"You brought up these imaginary bachelorettes, not me. Is something bothering you? Because—"

"Look, there's a casino at the next exit," she exclaimed, pointing to a sign on the side of the highway. "Can we stop, just for a few minutes? Please?"

"I hate casinos on reservations. They're depressing."

"Have you ever been to this one?" When he shook his head she continued, "Then you have no idea. It could be great. There's only one way to find out."

He sighed exaggeratedly, but she could tell his gambler's instinct was as piqued as hers. "Twenty minutes, not a second more. We have to get to Lincoln by noon."

"Deal. I can do a lot of damage in twenty minutes." She flashed him a bright smile, but his brow furrowed.

"No one will recognize us, right?"

"At eight o'clock in the morning in middle-of-nowhere Kansas? Not a chance."

Apparently satisfied, he indicated to take the exit.

The casino was one of the smallest she'd ever seen. A handful of pickup trucks and one ancient Lincoln Town Car huddled in the narrow parking lot. They both glanced up at the peeling sign as they walked through it, quickening the pace in case the hinges were as loose as they looked.

"The Golden Gate," she read aloud. "Odd to name this place after a landmark a thousand miles away."

"Maybe they mean it's a gate to wealth and treasure." He pushed open the door, and the watery autumn light washed over a threadbare carpet in a faded orange pattern. As a black-clad bouncer roused himself from a chair at the other end of the long room, Erin made out a row of ten slot machines, three empty card tables, and a roulette wheel. Half of the slot machines were dark, so potentially broken, and the median age of the people playing the rest was at least seventy-five.

"Grim," Brendan murmured as the bouncer reached them.

"Can I see some ID?"

He squinted at their driver's licenses, then waved them through. "Good luck."

Erin wrinkled her nose as they made their way toward the slot machines. "I didn't think you were still allowed to smoke inside commercial premises."

"We're a long way from Vegas," he observed mildly. "Do you want to waste some money on your one-armed bandits?"

She glanced at the beeping, blinking, colorful row of money eaters. There was a time when her mouth would be watering, her hands itching—hell, there was a time when she would've already lost ten dollars by now. On her worst weekend she'd taken the cheapest bus down to Atlantic City on Friday night, then the latest bus back up to Manhattan to avoid paying for a hotel room, slept three hours at her apartment before boarding another dawn bus to a casino. She spent eighty dollars on bus fares, fifteen dollars on food, and lost three and a half thousand dollars on slots.

At the time it felt unlucky. Now, having dragged the patient, accommodating man beside her into this shabby, depressing, smoke-filled room, she realized how totally unhinged she'd been.

She slipped her hand into Brendan's and held it tight.

"I can't believe I'm about to say this, but I think we should go."

He turned curious eyes on her. "Are you sure?"

She nodded. "I've been so committed to staying off the slot app and chiseling away at my debt. I don't want to ruin all my good work. Not here, anyway."

He slung his arm across her back and squeezed her against his side. "Let's go."

They walked hand in hand back to the car. Erin exhaled heavily as she slid into her seat, averting her eyes from the temptation of the entrance as Brendan started the engine.

"You okay?" he asked as he reversed out of the space.

"That was harder than I expected," she admitted. "But, yeah. I'm fine."

"Good. But also a shame. If ever there was a blackjack table where I had the chance to bring down the house, that was probably it. I doubt those decks were even full."

"You can't count cards," she scoffed, then added uncertainly, "Can you?"

"I'd like to try."

"Next time," she promised, leaning back in her seat and resolving once and for all that next time would never, ever arrive.

* * * *

"Good, but if you lean over from the waist you'll hurt your back. Better if you can drop down, like this." In slow motion Brendan bent one leg and put his knee on the grass, scooping up the ball.

His two trainee goalkeepers nodded avidly, mimicking the motion.

"Got a great one," the photographer murmured at Erin's elbow, and quickly angled the camera display for her to see a perfect shot of the three of them on bended knees. Delighted, she stuck up her thumbs as he raised the camera again.

"Much better." Brendan glanced to where Erin stood on the sideline and tapped his wrist. She checked the time on her phone, then flashed ten fingers to tell him how much longer they had before the match started.

"Pretty soon you'll be facing off against each other, so there's one last thing for us to review." He rubbed his gloved hands together. "Intimidation tactics."

Brendan's two students—both men in their early twenties—exchanged wide-eyed glances.

He motioned for one of them to take his place in the net, then positioned the ball at his feet. "Ty, you're first. I'm going to take a penalty, and you're going to do your best to put me off. Ready?"

Ty nodded, separating his feet and raising his hands.

Brendan looked over his shoulder. "Erin, can you give us the cue?"

"Gladly." She stuck her index fingers in her mouth and did her best approximation of a referee's whistle.

Immediately she saw Brendan's hesitation, deliberately delaying the lightning-quick instinct to shoot to give Ty time to react. Ty sneered and growled, cupping his hands with his knuckles facing his chest, and Brendan's shot curled around him to hit the net.

"Dang." Ty slammed his fist into his thigh but perked up when Brendan came forward to slap him on the back.

"First-class theatrics, but don't forget to jump for the ball. Next time you might want to put your arms out, too. Your catch form is perfect, but in a penalty situation you want to cover as much of the goal as possible."

"Got it."

Ty moved out of the way to give his counterpart, Jamie, a try while Brendan reset the ball. He'd barely gotten it into position when Jamie extended his arms to the sides and planted his legs wide, his face a bug-eyed, tension-lined mask of toughness.

Brendan rubbed his chin, attempting to hide the endeared smile Erin could see clearly from where she stood. She replaced her fingers and whistled.

Brendan shot quicker this time, and to the right instead of the left. Jamie reacted instantly, throwing himself to the right, arm outstretched. He fisted his hand and Erin's jaw fell open in astonishment as he punched the ball clear, saving the penalty.

"Yes!" Ty screamed from the sideline. Jamie picked himself up and brushed grass off the knees of his uniform, his expression shifting from shock to delight as the accomplishment registered.

"Wow," Brendan remarked openly, hands on his hips. "Jamie, that was awesome."

Jamie shrugged exaggeratedly. "All in a day's work."

The three goalkeepers—two in their respective teams' uniforms, one in his Skyline training kit—exchanged a series of handshakes, thanks, and congratulations. Brendan put his gloved hands at waist height and the two boys piled their hands on top.

"Outstanding session today, gentlemen. I look forward to seeing you both in action. Play fair, play well. Keepers on three."

In unison they recited, "One, two, three, keepers!"

After a few high fives Jamie and Ty ran down the pitch to join their teammates. The photographer followed and Brendan turned his grin on Erin.

"That was great," she told him emphatically as she stepped closer, instinctively reaching for his hands before remembering where they were—and who was watching—and stopping herself just in time.

"Good photos?" Brendan stripped off his gloves and tossed them on the grass beside the ball.

"Well, yes, but I mean you and the guys. That was great," she repeated. "You were so patient and clear in the way you explained things, but not patronizing, and you gave them a lot of really useful, technical advice."

He lifted a shoulder, plucking up a bottle of water and taking a long drink. "Young Legends is about making sports inclusive, not easy or low-quality. Those guys may not be facing off against Pelé or Maradona anytime soon, but that doesn't mean they don't take their matches seriously or shouldn't be equipped to play to their full potential."

"Exactly. Oh my God, Brendan, exactly." She pressed her palms to her heart. "I know this is the soapbox I always climb onto, but this has so many parallels to the women's game. There's so much complacency around women's soccer, it's like a day-one acceptance that none of the players will ever earn as much or play as well as the men so let's be happy with what we've got and not waste resources on making it better."

His smile changed, became inward, like he was thinking something he didn't plan on saying aloud. "You'll change that."

"I hope so."

"You will," he echoed firmly, leaning down to gather up the pieces of equipment they'd used in the training session. "I need to stow this stuff and get changed. It's almost time for the whistle."

While Brendan changed she found a seat on the front row of the metal bleachers, relishing the crisp, early-autumn air beneath a clear blue sky. She recognized Brendan's parents at the opposite end but didn't have time to walk over and introduce herself before he reappeared in jeans and a brick-red Skyline polo. He offered a few pregame remarks—thanking the parents, the Young Legends staff, and the principal of the high school whose field they were about to play on—then handed over to the referees and joined the two coaches on the sideline.

As the match got underway Erin realized that Brendan's brother, Liam, was up front as striker for one of the teams. Though one of the older players on the pitch he was also one of the most capable, scoring two neat goals in the first half hour, following each one with a careening, arms-outstretched celebration that put a smile on the face of every spectator, whether the point went to their team or not.

The watching crowd was enthusiastic and she joined them in cheering every attempt on goal, every clean tackle, every counterattacking sprint down the field. Brendan paced up and down the sideline, one hand in his pocket, the other gesturing to illustrate the instructions and advice he called out to each of the two goalkeepers. She smiled fondly at his furrowed brow, the sincerity of his shouted encouragement, his firm applause even when the keepers fumbled or made mistakes. His passion showed in every movement, and she wondered what it would be like to be the recipient of all that bone-deep commitment, that intense devotion, that palpable, unwavering love.

She blinked away sudden, silly tears from the edges of her eyes. No point in speculating—she would never know. She'd drawn the line in the sand between them and he'd faithfully stayed on his side. She couldn't start blurring it now.

At halftime she made her way to Brendan's parents. Marie insisted too forcefully that she remembered Erin from their college days, which made Erin think Brendan had jogged their memories, but she smiled graciously and complimented Liam's performance and Marie's sequined Young Legends sweatshirt.

Erin was about to return to her seat when Marie invited her to dinner. She balked. For the sake of appearances the plan was for her to spend the night at a hotel, then meet Brendan at the airport for the flight from Lincoln to Atlanta. She wasn't sure whether a CSL executive ostensibly supervising event coverage should accept a dinner invitation from a player's mother, or whether declining would draw more attention given they did have a public, former-college-buddies friendship.

Thankfully Brendan appeared just as her indecisive silence was about to become awkward. Marie reiterated her invitation in a tone that dared Brendan to contradict her, and he shrugged in dutiful agreement.

"Sure, if Erin doesn't have other plans. Should I invite Leo, too?" He indicated the photographer, who was taking artsy-looking shots of water bottles lined up on a bleacher.

Genius, Erin thought with relief, as Brendan's quick thinking gave the situation a professional angle. "I think he said he wanted to drive back to Des Moines tonight, but I'll ask him. I'm free either way."

"Then we'll see you at the house," Marie decreed. Erin thanked her and moved to take her seat for the second half, exchanging a coded glance with Brendan as they split in separate directions. This whole trip had brought their private affiliation dangerously close to their public pretense. They had to be careful not to push it over the edge.

Erin pulled out her phone as the second half kicked off and scrolled unseeingly through her work emails, her mind churning. What would she do if this really were just professional—if she actually had followed a player to his hometown to show his rehabilitation for the ethics section of the year-end report?

She opened the latest email from Prinisha, scanned it, and hit Reply. She began the message with an answer to the question Prinisha had asked, then continued, *Superb weekend in the Midwest. I'll relay fully on Monday, but the meetings in Topeka couldn't have gone better and we're getting great content in Lincoln. Brendan's mother has even invited me to dinner tonight, so if you never hear from me again, it's because I got drunk on wholesomeness, bought a minivan, and married a farmer.*

She sent the email and stuffed her phone back in her purse. She could already hear Prinisha joking with the rest of the team on Monday morning, imagining their urban-chic boss scraping mud off her designer heels. She would hide this in plain sight. No one would suspect a thing.

Chapter 16

Erin groaned as Marie plopped an enormous scoop of vanilla ice cream on top of the slice of homemade pecan pie she'd just set in front of her. "I'll have to buy a second seat on the airplane after this."

"With a figure like yours you can afford to eat dessert." Marie shot her a wink made saucier by the three glasses of wine she'd had since Erin arrived late that afternoon. Erin had to bite her lower lip to stifle a giggle, and across the table Brendan's eyes flashed with a look that said he agreed with his mother's complimentary remarks on her body.

She lowered her gaze to the table as heat rushed into her cheeks. Although he'd remained responsibly sober, she'd joined Marie in draining more than one bottle of wine, and with each sip it got harder to make sure any attention she gave Brendan was strictly impersonal.

The close quarters of the packed house hadn't helped. Brendan's childhood home was a two-bedroom split-level in which the semi-basement rec room had been sliced in half to raise the bedroom count to four. With his parents, Liam, Liam's girlfriend, his older brother Aidan, Aidan's wife and two kids, and a random aunt stuffed into the open-plan kitchen and sitting room, the ground floor seemed full to bursting. She found herself physically close to Brendan more often than not, and at times the temptation to brush her palm over his thigh or press her fingertips to the small of his back was almost unbearable.

If he fought the same urges, he gave no sign. In fact he'd hardly said five words the whole evening, despite being the guest of honor. He responded politely and affably to anything he was asked, then withdrew into quiet observation—a role his family seemed happy to let him occupy, having no trouble filling his silence with jokes, jibes and good-natured arguments.

She peered at him over her rapidly melting ice cream, remembering his similarly aloof manner when their families shared a table on that long-ago day in college. She couldn't say it was uncharacteristic—he wasn't exactly Mr. Party Animal at the best of times—but amongst his family he seemed to extract himself more than usual.

She let her gaze rise above his head, where family photos clogged the half-wall separating the kitchen from the family room. Teenage Aidan in a high-school football uniform. Liam in a cap and gown. Liam playing basketball. Aidan on the altar with his bride. Liam and his dad in hunting camo. Aidan and Brendan as children with baby Liam propped between them. And on one end a photo she remembered from when it happened—Brendan signing his first professional contract, the famous club's logo looming over his nervous smile, an even more famous manager standing behind him with his hands on Brendan's shoulders.

An awkward pause in the conversation around the table alerted her that someone had spoken to her and she hadn't been listening. She found Liam's gaze two seats down from Brendan, eyebrows raised expectantly.

"Sorry, I was so high in pie heaven I didn't hear you. What did you say?"

"I asked when the Championship League will be launching programs for athletes with intellectual disabilities?"

She smiled, but Liam pinned her to the spot, his sharp expression demanding a legitimate answer.

"Not next year, or probably the year after, if you want the truth," she told him, stowing her spoon and folding her hands on the table. "Trying to get them to properly fund the empowerment programs they already have—not to mention the whole women's side of the sport—is an uphill battle. But I'm working on it."

"Disappointing," Liam remarked, then arched a brow. "When you do convince them that people with intellectual disabilities deserve to play, I suppose I'll agree to be the face of the game. If you beg."

She blinked, only realizing he was joking as chuckles rippled around the table.

"I'll keep that in mind," she assured him, picking up her spoon.

Marie prompted Liam to tell everyone—presumably not for the first time—about the hilarious photo shoot he'd endured when a local retailer asked him to appear in their new signage. Liam launched into the funny but clearly rehearsed tale, and her attention drifted back to the man across from her.

Where do you go? she asked Brendan silently, watching him carefully portion his pie with the edge of the spoon, tilting melty ice cream into the crevices.

No, scratch that—she knew where he went, maybe better than anyone. Into his stats. Into the looping, spiraling tunnel of numbers and facts and probabilities that he transformed into neat lines and columns, and then into absurd sums of money.

The question was why, not where. His family was as embarrassing as anyone else's—his mom a little too loud, his dad a little too right-wing, Aidan not as smart as he thought he was—but by all appearances he'd grown up in a stable, comfortable household with parents who loved him and were proud of him.

Or were they? She scanned the wall of photos again, making a quick mental tally. Pictures of Liam dominated by far, with Aidan a relatively distant second. She could count the pictures of Brendan on one hand.

Maybe they weren't proud of him, she realized with a jolt. Maybe the gambling scandal had rocked this Catholic family to its core. Maybe his mother had tearfully plucked photos off that wall and packed them away.

Or maybe they just thought he should get a real job.

She bit the inside of her lower lip, halting its sudden, unbidden trembling. Every time she returned to her parents' big house in New Jersey she crossed the threshold feeling like a triumphant emperor back from the wars. They'd supported every decision she'd ever made and held on tight for even the sharpest twists in her life's journey. Although the thought of them finding out about her gambling occasionally kept her awake at night, deep in her heart she knew they'd love her just as hard as they always had, backing her through the worst times and the best.

Maybe Brendan hadn't had that unconditional backing, she considered, looking around the table with newly critical eyes. Maybe his trips home were more complicated than hers.

Yet he was moving back here in a matter of months, so it couldn't be that bad. Or did he think he had nowhere else to go?

The clink of a spoon against a bowl lowered her gaze, and she found Brendan's eyes on hers. She smiled, and so did he.

Out of the corner of her eye she saw Marie glance at the empty bottle of wine, and she cleared her throat loudly before Marie could suggest she join her in draining a new one.

"I should get back to the hotel before I pass out on the couch. It's been a long day."

"I'll get the car keys," Brendan announced before anyone could object. "I left them downstairs."

"I think I might have stashed my jacket down there," she lied, knowing perfectly well it hung in the closet near the front door.

With a scrape of chair legs they hastily extricated themselves, and she followed Brendan's thudding footsteps downstairs to the half-basement that housed his and Aidan's childhood bedrooms.

She'd barely drawn breath to make a snarky comment about his subtlety when he shoved her against the wall beneath the stairs, big body pressed against hers, his mouth warm and insistent and tasting faintly of vanilla ice cream.

She moaned, guttural and involuntary. She softened beneath the length of him, sweeping her tongue over his, finding the ridges of his teeth and the heat of his mouth and sharing the air from his lungs.

His palms flat on the wall on either side of her head, he drew back and brushed the tip of his nose against hers. "I've needed to do that all day."

"Find an excuse to spend tonight in the hotel. You can do much more."

"No one would believe anything I came up with. I have to stay here."

"Are you sure? I love hotel sex."

He shook his head, regret plain in his features.

She exhaled her disappointment, running her hands down his arms. "Show me where you'll be fantasizing about me."

He took her hand and tugged her into one of the two rooms. The peculiar angles in the basement bore testament to the process of converting a long, narrow space into bedrooms. Aidan's room took up the larger end, while Brendan's had been carved out of the side made smaller by the staircase.

Wordlessly he flipped on the light. She blinked in the sudden glare, then tightened her grip on his fingers as she absorbed her surroundings.

Tidy, sparse, a faint scent of bleach suggesting the room had been cleaned ahead of his arrival. The bare walls were painted lavender, to coordinate with the darker purple-trimmed coverlet on the single bed pushed into a corner. The surface of the chipped wooden desk was empty except for a silk violet in a glass vase, but the matching bookshelf was full to bursting. Paperbacks, marble composition books, yellowing newspapers presumably containing articles relevant to Brendan's career. And above those, so many medals and trophies and awards the shelves sagged with their weight.

"Did it always look like this?" she asked, puzzled.

"No. I used to have loads of soccer posters, team photos, pennants, lots of teenage clutter. My parents put everything in the attic and made this a guest room."

She dropped his hand and moved closer, reaching up to sift through his accolades. Many of them were from his high school and college days, MVP awards or championship medals. Then she shoved aside a particularly large trophy and her jaw dropped.

"Oh my God." She withdrew the molded gold abstraction of a player diving for a ball. "This is a Golden Glove."

He murmured his assent, his expression neutral.

She held the award higher, shaking it for good measure. "This is one of the highest honors a goalkeeper can get and it's stuffed in a corner of your parents' basement, in a room that shows no evidence you ever lived here."

"My parents redecorated," he said casually.

"When?"

His pause gave him away completely. "Easter, I think."

Her hand fell heavily against her side, weighted by much more than the sturdily mounted statue.

She'd guessed right. They'd redecorated his room after the gambling scandal broke. Their high-flying son had taken a hard fall to earth, and they'd rolled up the safety net.

She turned to replace the award, then changed her mind, her throat thick with emotion. She clenched her jaw as her heart seized and jolted, her balance thrown, her knees unsteady, her pulse pounding as though she'd just nailed a forty-minute workout.

He studied his shoes, and she studied him. He filled the doorway, long and lean, the top of his head almost brushing the frame. Here was a man who'd achieved so much, yet apart from the money in his bank account and the house he was trying to sell, he had so little to show for it.

She hadn't realized how much he lost in that stupid data breach. Forget three months on the bench—he'd lost his parents' respect, and his hero status in their home.

No wonder he was desperate to move back here and try to rebuild what was gone. And no wonder he'd seemed so forlorn and adrift when she saw him for the first time in Atlanta, the lights along the church walkway illuminating every weary line in his face.

He'd lost everything. He was alone. Battered, discarded, unloved.

I love him.

She inhaled so sharply he looked up. She could only imagine how unhinged she must look, given she'd apparently lost the ability to blink or close her mouth, but since it took all of her concentration to stay upright as the earth seemed to lurch beneath her, there wasn't a lot she could do about it.

I love him, she repeated silently, testing the words to see if they still felt as indisputable as in the first second they registered.

Yes, each one was heavy with truth, glowing brightly in her mind and clogging her chest with terror and excitement and shredding despair.

She was in love for the first time—probably the last time. In love with an unattainable man. This love was all wrong.

It wasn't the distance between Atlanta and Lincoln—she could've made that work—or even her job. The Director of Ethics and Advocacy shacking up with a known gambler wasn't great PR, but it could be spun into acceptability, particularly once he retired.

It wasn't miles on the map or the employer on her paycheck. It was what they both loved most, what had drawn them together from the first minute they met. In the end, soccer would keep them apart.

She loved soccer. She lived it, breathed it, worked it, played it. But although soccer had treated Brendan better than it had ever treated her, it was time for him to walk away. To shut the door on the adrenaline and the ecstasy and the unimaginable heartbreak. To look away from his reflection in a black pentagon slick with dew from an early-morning pitch and find himself—place himself—somewhere totally different.

She took one last look around the little room, at the lavender paint flecks staining the window frame, at the bookcase slumping almost apologetically under the weight of a legendary career about to meet a shadowed end. Then she shoved a smile onto her trembling lips and tapped the statue in her hand.

"I'm bringing this to Atlanta and putting it on your mantel where it belongs," she told him firmly, fighting to keep her voice from wobbling. *And I'll love you as well as I can. And I'll protect you with everything I have. And then I'll say goodbye.*

* * * *

"Congratulations. You'll be keeping for Atlanta in the CSL final."

He looked at Erin over his shoulder, and she turned her phone around so he could see the score in the Sunday-night match between Miami and Boise. Unsurprisingly Boise lost, meaning Miami now had enough points that Charlotte couldn't catch them. As the teams occupying the first and second spots in the table, in two weeks Miami and Atlanta would travel to Memphis to compete for the league title.

"Well," he remarked, returning his attention to the key that stubbornly refused to turn in the lock on the front door of his house on the outskirts of Lincoln. "Funny how things turn out."

"Do you see me laughing? There's not a worthier keeper in the country. Your locksmith skills, on the other hand, leave something to be desired." He heard her shoes scuff the wooden boards on the porch. "Are you almost done? It's freezing out here."

He tried the lock one more time, lifting at exactly the right second to throw the bolt. "Got it."

She moved past him into the entryway as he stepped aside to switch on one of the construction lamps hanging from the ceiling. Light flowed weakly down the hallway, illuminating the sanded hardwood floors covered in protective plastic, the flaking floral wallpaper, and the staircase that looked gouged where they'd ripped out the carpet.

"Brendan," she chided. "You can't be serious."

"I knew you wouldn't get it. You're too urban, Erin. This is country charm."

She narrowed her eyes. "Lincoln has a population of two-hundred-thousand-plus. I spent the whole evening in your parents' split-level, ten minutes from Wal-Mart with neighbors they can wave to. I hate to ruin your small-town-boy mythology, but you are not from the country."

"I should've brought you before we went to my parents' house. Now it's so dark, you can't appreciate the potential."

She picked her way down the hall and leaned into the front living room. "Oh, I see plenty of potential. For ghost stories, mostly. Or a horror movie. And don't get any ideas, by the way. Only virgins die in those slasher flicks."

"It's hard to tell now, but this room is huge. Original floors, super high ceilings." He used the flashlight app on his phone and swept the thin beam of light up and down the bay window. "The house is really old for this area, so it repays all the work it needs with great antique features."

"I prefer features like a doorman and a fitness center."

"I'm putting a gym in the basement," he replied, a little defensively.

"You'd have to, unless you want to drive, what was it, forty minutes into town?"

"Thirty-five," he corrected. "And like I said, you couldn't see all the upside of living out here. The approach up the driveway is—"

She spun, cutting him off. "I don't need to see the approach, or the kitchen, or the backyard, or whatever else you think could possibly justify this ridiculous project. Because that's what it is. Ridiculous."

Her reaction didn't surprise him. The sting of it did. He wanted her to like this house, he realized belatedly. On some idiotic, deluded level, he thought if she liked it, she might visit. Just once or twice.

"It's not ridiculous," he told her quietly, switching off his phone and moving back into the semi-lit hallway.

"Of course it is," she said forcefully, following his retreat to the front door. "You're a multi-millionaire. You're going to get another million when your house in Atlanta sells. I refuse to believe there's not a house in the greater Lincoln area you could've afforded that came with land *and* running water."

"I only have another couple of paychecks coming. Then I'm unemployed. I have to be careful with my money."

He motioned her through the door, then shut and locked it behind them. When he turned Erin stood with her hands on her hips, silhouetted by the construction lamp mounted at one end of the wide porch. He could just make out the displeasure turning down the corners of her mouth and the heave of those spectacular breasts as she drew breath to deliver what he expected would be another round of scolding.

Instead she seemed to change her mind. All at once her posture softened and her hands dropped to her sides.

She nodded to the slatted porch swing that creaked slightly as it moved in the wind. "Can we sit for a minute? I'm not ready to face that empty hotel room."

He managed a half-smile. "That single bed in my parents' basement isn't exactly howling my name either. Hang on."

He heard the swing groan with her weight as he crossed through the overgrown front lawn to his dad's pickup. He rooted in the covered bed for a few seconds, then tugged out the camouflage hunting blanket and tossed it over his shoulder.

Erin greeted his approach with a smile, kicking off her shoes and tucking her legs beneath her. "You can't count cards, but I'm sure you just read my mind."

"See? This house has potential for ghost stories, horror flicks, and those slightly supernatural romantic movies where lovers meet across time or whatever."

"As long as it involves a hot man bringing me a warm blanket on a cold night, I'm in."

"Then we're good." He eased down beside her and draped the blanket over their laps, then slipped his arm around her shoulders.

"We are good," she echoed softly. She slid her hand onto his thigh, and again he got the sense she was hesitating to say something.

He planted his feet and pushed the swing into a gentle rhythm, happy to give her as much time as she needed to find her words.

Absently he rubbed his thumb over the curve of her shoulder, watching a lone set of headlights cut through the darkness as a car cruised down the rural road his driveway split off from. Only two other properties accessed that road, and when the trees had leaves and the grass wasn't so dry any passing cars' lights wouldn't even be visible. Nothing and no one to disturb him out here. Total quiet and isolation.

He exhaled, trying to find the peace in that idea. Silence and privacy were all he'd wanted when he bought the house months ago. He'd rocked on this very swing the day it officially became his, drinking beer, grinning like an idiot, so impatient to escape the noise and hustle of Atlanta.

He still loved the house. He loved getting revised plans from his architect, scrolling through galleries of bathroom fittings, imagining the day he'd finally wake up to an unadulterated view of his expansive acreage. He loved Nebraska, the gentler pace, the warmer welcomes. He loved his hometown community and he loved that he'd have so much time to devote to Young Legends. All in all, he still loved his retirement plan.

He just hadn't counted on loving Erin, too.

He closed his eyes and pinched the bridge of his nose, finally articulating to himself the unshaped, ominous thought that had nagged him since they got in the rental car that morning. He'd tried to brush it off as excitement for the day ahead, or leftover adrenaline from yesterday's match, or nerves at how close they were playing to the edge of exposure.

Of course it was none of those things. Of course he'd fallen in love with her.

But then he was always going to, wasn't he? He'd been naïve to think he could ever have a no-strings attachment. Actually, naïve was generous. He'd been stupid. Straight-up, rushed-in, shortsighted, thinking-with-his-dick stupid.

He'd been with women and not loved them. Not one like Erin, though. Never one so smart or sexy or challenging or funny or—what was the word he wanted?—raging. That was his Erin, raging through life like a wildfire, burning everything in her path. It sounded awful, put like that, but it was exactly the freedom and uncontrolled, unapologetic power he envied.

He was stupid to think he wouldn't get torched like everyone else. He sighed ruefully, gathering himself as she shifted on the swing. At least he'd have a nice view while he nursed his heartbreak.

He looked down at the flame-haired woman beside him. Her eyes found his, twin beacons in the darkness.

"You don't have to do this, Brendan," she said softly.

He tilted his head. "Do what?"

"Exile yourself."

"That's not what I'm doing."

"I think you are. I think you're punishing yourself for whatever you seem to believe you did wrong."

He shook his head. "That's not true. Not everyone dreams of climbing the corporate ladder and living in a flashy downtown high-rise. I never planned to stay in Atlanta after I retired."

"Did you plan this?" She swept her hand to indicate the empty stretch in front of them.

He hesitated before replying, wondering what she was getting at. "Actually, I considered Spain. I held on to my house in Valencia for a while, renting it out, but I sold it earlier this year."

"When did you put it on the market?"

"April. Why?"

"And when did you buy this place?" she prompted.

"June, but I don't see—"

"After the dust from the data leak had settled," she cut in, then clucked her tongue. "You're such a good Catholic and you don't even realize it."

"I'm really not," he assured her.

"You are. You're self-flagellating. This is your penance. Your punishment. The SportBetNet leak turned a big, glaring spotlight on a sin you kept secret, and you felt the full force of its shame. Your manager shunned you, your league shunned you, and I'm willing to bet you got some heat from your parents, too. Now you think this is what you deserve, or maybe what you owe—to slink home and isolate yourself out on the fringes while you try to crawl back into your parents' good graces." Her gaze pinned him to the spot. "Am I wrong?"

It took him a second to collect his thoughts, and to parse through the racing stock ticker of conflicting emotions her scarily incisive analysis had set off. He hated that she'd figured him out so minutely, better than he'd figured out himself, giving voice to deeply hidden, ugly parts of his life he shied away from even acknowledging.

But he also loved it. Loved that she could know him so well, understand him more accurately than anyone else on the planet. Loved that she cared. Loved every damn inch of her.

He wanted to tell her exactly that, but that wasn't part of their arrangement. Instead he said pointedly, "Fuck you, Erin."

"I knew it." She folded her arms smugly and sat back. "Don't hate the striker for reading the keeper. We all have tells."

He braced himself for the confession no one had heard before now. "My parents were pretty harsh when the story broke. At first I couldn't understand why—gambling's not that big a deal, in the grand scheme of things. It's not like I cheated, or doped, or had an affair. Eventually I realized it wasn't about me, and that nothing had been about me for a very long time."

She pressed in closer. "What do you mean?"

"It's my fault," he began, but she cut him off with a shake of her head. "Don't take responsibility before you've said anything."

He reframed what he wanted to say, tried again. "Aidan had a late dyslexia diagnosis and always struggled academically. Liam has Down syndrome and needed a lot of attention and advocacy from day one. I am—I was—the easy, low-maintenance, nothing-to-worry-about middle child. Until I started having these racing, obsessive thoughts. Like my brain was a fan with a broken off button, spinning faster and faster and faster."

He glanced down at her wide-open, attentive expression before returning his focus to the horizon. "I still get them. When a player walks up to take a penalty, my brain churns so fast I can't even distinguish one thought from the next. I see everything, or what feels like everything—every possible angle, every strategic choice, every penalty they've taken before this one and what that means for the one they're about to take."

"That's incredible," she remarked. "And somehow not surprising."

He shrugged. "Now I can control it, to some extent. The stats help. Gives me something to focus on when my mind starts to spiral. But when I was a teenager I didn't know what was going on. I couldn't sleep, felt panicky all the time, and eventually I told my mom. She launched straight into campaign mode, running me around to specialists, searching for a diagnosis. She was used to fighting corners for my brothers and couldn't wait to do the same for me." He blew out a breath. "It was too much. I wasn't used to that level of attention and I couldn't handle it, so I lied to get her off my back and totally withdrew, happy to let my brothers be the focus of the family."

"How is becoming a superstar professional athlete evading your parents' focus?"

"All part of being the easy child," he explained. "They didn't have to fund my education because I got a scholarship. They didn't have to worry about my getting a job or helping me with rent because I signed a big contract. They didn't have to worry about anything at all, because I had this perfect, successful life thousands of miles away."

"I get it," she said slowly. "You were the photo they could point to with pride while they dealt with the bigger problems in front of them."

"On point again, Bailey. When the gambling thing came out, I became one of those problems. We'd been so distant for so long, I think resentment came more easily than support."

She didn't respond. His statement hung heavily between them, yet he felt lighter.

"You have to come back here," Erin said finally, her voice thick with resignation. "You have to move home and bridge this gap. You only get one family, and it's time for you to find your place in your own."

He nodded. "It's been a long time coming."

She sighed, resting her head on his shoulder. "I'm going to worry about you, all alone out here, by yourself."

His heart staggered at the notion of her giving him a second thought after they parted, but he said, "No, you won't. You'll work, and go out for drinks, and date other men, and forget all about me."

She shifted at his side, twisting to snuggle closer, pressing her forehead against his collarbone. He moved his other hand to hold one of hers, closing his eyes as he drank in the weight and warmth of her.

"What if I don't?" she whispered.

He gritted his teeth against what felt like his heart tearing loose and careening around his chest, one second buoyed by hope, the next free-falling with despair.

He could tell her right now. He could say he was falling for her, ask her to commit to something—anything—and attempt to tie her up in the strings they'd promised this affair wouldn't have. She might go for it. Clearly she was in a moment of weakness, daring to admit she may actually care about him a tiny bit. Maybe she'd agree to testing the emotional waters between them, and throwing out their strictly sex terms. Maybe she'd even let him call her his girlfriend.

But what would be the point? He'd pack up and leave Atlanta, and she'd come to her senses the first night she spent alone in her apartment. They might drag things out for a while—desperation on his part, obligation on hers—but eventually it would end. They'd separate guiltily, regretfully, and more painfully than if they never really got together at all.

She deserved better. He owed her better. He couldn't let her race toward a stoplight he knew was about to turn red.

"No strings, remember?" Each word felt like swallowing broken glass, but he forced them out anyway. "There's no future for us. You have a hell of career already, and it's only going to get bigger and better. As for me, I want..." *You. I want you. Nothing more, nothing less.* "...I want this, out here. Quiet. Stability. No more attention."

She nodded against his shoulder, and then she straightened, running her fingers through her hair, shifting in her seat, flashing him her wide, confident smile. Her shaky intake of breath betrayed her, though. He couldn't see the tears in her eyes but he knew they were there.

He cleared his throat, shoving aside a swell of pain at her distress. "Getting cold?"

"Yeah." She fidgeted and fumbled, and then a cell-phone screen briefly illuminated the darkness. "It's late."

"I'll take you to the hotel."

He folded the blanket while she slipped her feet back into her shoes. They walked to the car in silence, and he studiously avoided looking at her as he stowed the blanket in the back and then followed her into the cab.

He shut the door, then allowed himself a brief glance at her upturned face.

"Thanks for showing me your house," she said softly, her lips barely curved in a smile.

"Anytime," he promised, and started the engine.

Chapter 17

Erin threaded her fingers on the table. "Anything else?"

Her gaze paused on each one of the men sitting around the boardroom table. Brian Scholtz, eyes fixed resolutely on his lap. Brian's lawyer, glancing sideways at his phone, probably already thinking about his next client. Brian's agent, whose face had faded from bright-red fury to mottled resignation. Randall Morenski, trying to cover his palpable delight with an exaggerated frown. And Roland Carlsson, his expression still as closed and unreadable as it had been the moment he sat down.

One by one the men shook their heads. She glanced at the clock. They would finish five minutes early. Evidently her PA had slightly overestimated how long it took to end a young player's career.

"In that case I'll call the meeting to a close. Our legal department will send countersigned copies of the disciplinary documents."

"Fine." The lawyer was on his feet, phone in his hand. Brian rose slowly, then followed him to the door, bracketed by his manager at his heels. None of the three of them said goodbye, disappearing in silence into the hall.

As soon as they were gone Randall turned to her, his eyes so round and eager she bet he was salivating. "Outstanding work, Erin. The depth of that investigation was incredible. There was absolutely nothing he could say to refute your evidence. It was all there—testimonies from players he'd asked for information, emailed offers to include them on bets, actual written evidence of his attempts to fix matches. You've made a great bust. My only question is how did you know to look at Skyline to begin with?"

She felt Roland's keen stare. No wonder Brendan didn't get along with him. His professionalism couldn't be faulted, but sometimes his demeanor was downright icy.

"An anonymous tip," she replied. "Then Brian's name came up immediately as I began interviewing the players. He'd solicited almost everyone on the team, either to partner with him in betting on the league or to try to influence results. As far as I can tell, though, everyone brushed him off or ignored him."

"Including Brendan Young?" It was Roland's first question in the two hours they'd been in the boardroom.

She turned an unblinking gaze on him. "He never approached Brendan Young."

"So Young didn't have the opportunity to say no," Randall mused, giving voice to what she suspected Roland was also thinking. "Are we still confident he's the right profile for the rehabilitation angle?"

"One hundred percent," she replied. "I'm sure he's here by now. I'll ask Sheila to send him in."

She reached for the phone in the center of the table, but Roland raised a stalling palm.

"Do you need me for this? Technically I'm not sure it was necessary for me to be here for Brian's meeting—his contract expires at the end of this season and he's been aware for months that we won't be renewing it. Brendan will also retire in a couple of weeks, so I don't know that my input is particularly valuable."

She paused. Roland was right—there was no need for him to join this next meeting. But he'd been nasty to Brendan all season. This was her chance to waste his time, and she intended to take it.

"I'd like you to stay. You might have something to add. Maybe some positive commentary on Brendan's contribution to the team in the latter part of the season?"

Roland's lips thinned but he said nothing. She picked up the phone and asked the receptionist to bring Brendan to the boardroom.

After a couple of minutes the door opened again, and Sheila's diminutive figure appeared even more so with Brendan towering at her back. In navy trousers and a crisp button-down he presented exactly the right combination of respectfully professional yet not submissive or intimidated, and she had to work hard to keep a grin off her face.

Sheila showed him to a seat and slipped out, and as he sat he looked between her and Roland.

"Was Brian Scholtz just here? I think I saw him leaving."

There was a hint of distress in his voice that Erin hoped the others didn't pick up on. They'd adopted a strict, don't-ask-don't-tell policy with regard to the investigation, so although Brendan presumably knew the culprit from the beginning he had no idea how far down the line she'd gotten—or that one of his teammates had just been fired for an ethics violation.

"Unfortunately, Brian is going to feature in the same section of the report that you will. I think we can disclose the outcome to Brendan, can't we? It'll be public later today." She directed her question to Randall.

The CFO nodded. "The terms are confidential, but I suspect the fact is already making the rounds through the sport."

"Brian has admitted to betting on the league and attempted match-fixing," she explained. "He's received a one-year ban from the Championship League."

She didn't think Brendan's surprise was genuine as he said, "Wow. Okay," but it was convincing.

"It's an ugly situation, but thankfully one we don't face in our discussion with you this morning." She smiled. "On the contrary, we'd like to use this meeting to finalize the content for our year-end report, in which we'll be highlighting your exemplary conduct following your suspension earlier this year. Your story will be a counterpoint to Brian's—an illustration of the way players can bounce back from ethics infractions to be productive, community-oriented role models."

She sensed him bristle slightly at 'ethics infractions', but his expression stayed even. "I'm happy to be included. I especially appreciate you taking the time to come out to Nebraska and see firsthand the work I've done with the Young Legends programs."

"It was my pleasure," she insisted, letting the tiniest bit of subtext creep into her tone. Brendan's eyes glistened, and she pressed her thighs together beneath the table.

"Let me tell you where I'm at in all of this," Randall began, steepling his hands. "Brendan, you'll remember the last meeting between the two of us wasn't a good one."

Brendan shook his head. "No, it wasn't."

"Being honest, I had doubts about the wisdom of letting you get away with a short-term suspension instead of a ban. I worried about the precedent it set. But I'm happy to sit here today and say my concerns were unfounded."

Randall leaned forward slightly. "I've had several conversations with Erin over the last couple of months about how we should represent your story from the league's perspective. She said early on that it should be a narrative of redemption, and I admit I was skeptical. Now, having read the comments the PR team has taken from people affiliated with the two branches of Young Legends and seen the photos from the event last week, I'm confident we're taking the right angle. I intend to commend you personally in the section on compliance in the CFO's report."

Erin balled her fists in her lap as Brendan thanked Randall graciously. A swelling sense of triumph made her shaky and restless and unstoppable, like she could stand up from this table and effortlessly run a half-marathon in her heels and pencil skirt.

She'd done it. She'd saved Brendan's reputation. He would leave the sport remembered as the hero he was.

"We have the draft content for you to review. I trust you'll be happy with it, but let me know if there are any minor changes and we'll see what we can do." She selected the relevant pages from the stack she'd brought and passed copies around the table.

As they perused the columns of text and photographs, she turned to Roland. "I just realized we don't have any commentary from you. Is there anything you'd like to have on the record? It would be great to get your quote as his manager, and hopefully as the manager of the league champions if Saturday goes your way."

She intended to put Roland on the spot and force him to praise the player he'd been at odds with since they'd met. Instead Roland continued to read the page in his hands, and when he finally looked up his expression was thoughtful.

"I'm embarrassed to admit I didn't know about Brendan's activities outside the club. Not in this level of detail, anyway."

He pivoted to face his goalkeeper. "I'm sorry not to have offered you more support this season. I should've stayed closer to your transition back into the team, and I especially regret that I never got involved with the great work you were doing in your free time."

Brendan stared at his manager, eyes wide with incredulity. After several awkward, silent seconds, he seemed to blink back to the present.

"It's fine," he said softly.

Roland extended his hand. Brendan shook it. As both men turned back to face her and Randall, she got the distinct impression something significant just changed between them.

"Let me think about what I can add to this. I'll email some comments in the next day or two," Roland promised.

"That's fine," she confirmed. "Brendan, any changes you'd like to make?"

He shook his head, leveling his gaze on hers. "It's perfect. Thank you."

She kept her smile steady despite the fluttering in her chest. She loved him, she was proud of him, but she'd get over it. He'd said as much himself, on the porch of his crumbling house in Nebraska. In another couple of weeks they'd be apart, and this would be over.

At least now she could move on knowing she did her best for him in the final hours of his career.

"I don't think there's anything else to discuss," she concluded. "Thank you. And best of luck for Saturday."

All four of them rose and exchanged departing pleasantries. Brendan shook her hand politely, and she tried to give him a look that promised she'd be doing much less polite things to him later that evening. His answering smile assured her he got the message.

She and Randall handed Brendan and Roland over to the receptionist to be shown out. She moved to return to her office, but Randall said her name to stop her, holding up his copy of the draft page for the year-end report.

"This is exactly what I wanted," he told her. "Given you were able to manage this in just a couple of months, I look forward to seeing what you'll do with a whole season devoted to raising the profile of the women's game next year."

She offered him a confident smile which showed none of the emotion roiling beneath the surface. Delight at his praise. Thrill at his commitment to her women's-game program. Nauseating, heavy sadness that Brendan wouldn't be there to see it.

"Watch this space." She ducked her head in farewell and walked to her office on unsteady legs.

Chapter 18

"Well." Erin pushed up onto her forearms and peered down at him with a smile. "That was different."

Still reeling from an abrupt, explosive climax, Brendan didn't bother trying to form a coherent sentence. He put his arm across Erin's shoulders and tugged her onto his chest, tucking her head beneath his chin.

He closed his eyes. His jeans bunched above his shoes, uncomfortably pulling his ankles together. The floor was hard against the back of his head, and the carpet he'd expensively imported from the UK for his basement pub made his bare ass itch. But as Erin sighed contentedly into his neck, he wouldn't have moved for all the money in the world.

He wasn't sure how long they stayed in that position. Long enough for his dick to find its second wind, twitching to life as he slid his hand over the firm mound of Erin's butt and trailed his fingertips down the soft cleft left exposed by the dress shoved up around her waist.

She rolled off him with a groan and rose to her knees, dragging her panties over her thighs. "You are insatiable."

"Have you seen yourself today? That there was any gap after round one is testament to my immense self-control."

She smiled, running a preening hand through her hair. "I figured a man who'll be playing in a league final in less than twenty-four hours deserves something special."

"That dress isn't special. It's sinful." He propped himself up on his elbows. "Take it off."

"I would've said we need to prioritize business over pleasure, but I can't see that you've been up to much on that end." She nodded to the whiteboard, half-empty and mostly outdated.

"I've been distracted." He got to his feet and straightened his jeans, deciding this wasn't a statement he wanted to make half-naked. "I had an offer on the house."

"Really. That's great," she said crisply, rearranging her clothes and perching on one of the barstools.

"Full asking price." He took a seat beside her. "Family with two kids. Dad's some corporate something, and his job is relocating from Chicago to Atlanta. They want to be in before Christmas so the kids can start school in January."

"Asking price and a quick close. Exactly what you want."

"Yeah." He tried to smile. His job was to protect her, now. To convince her he was happy and ready to leave, and never let on that he missed her every minute they weren't together.

"What are they going to do with all this?" She swept her hand to indicate the pub.

"Turn it into a home gym. But that's fine," he said quickly. "I'm going to strip it out and take most of it with me. The house in Nebraska has a cellar. I was going to put in a gym but I think I can make both work."

The corners of her mouth turned down almost imperceptibly before she dragged them back up into a grin. "Just make sure you're not sitting down there alone."

"I'll try."

She looked as though she was about to say something else, then changed her mind, and the subject. "Are you nervous about tomorrow?"

"I don't get nervous."

She rolled her eyes. "Of course you don't. Are your parents coming?"

"My mom's at a Down syndrome parents' conference, so my dad's bringing Liam. They got there this afternoon. Already sent me a photo from Graceland."

"Cute. When does the team fly?"

"It's chartered. Takes off around eleven. When do you go?"

"Nine-fifty flight. Nice that it's only an hour up to Memphis. Means everyone can sleep in their own beds tonight."

"The players, anyway. I was hoping a certain league executive might opt not to sleep in hers." He put his hand on her knee.

"Funnily enough, I was thinking the same thing."

She was leaning forward, eyes bright with wickedness, when her phone rang. She glanced at the display, then did a double-take and picked it up.

"It's Will Hart," she said thoughtfully, naming a local sports writer who freelanced for a few different outlets. "He probably wants a quote for his piece on the final. I'll be quick."

She tapped the screen to answer. "Will, hi. Nice to hear from you."

Brendan had to look away at her coquettish, flirty tone, tugging his hand back into his lap. Would she sleep with Will after he'd left? She had every right. She could sleep with whoever she wanted, whenever she wanted.

That would be hard to get over.

"Are you in Memphis, or—ah, tomorrow. Me too. Maybe we can grab a drink before kickoff, unless—what? Sure. Go ahead."

She bit her lower lip, listening to the deep voice Brendan could only just make out. Suddenly her brows drew together, and then she glanced up at him in panic.

"Whoa, hold on. Do you have proof of this so-called betting, because I'm really not in the mood to..."

Her eyes widened as Will's voice got louder on the other end. Then she clapped her hand over them, her breathing short and shallow.

Brendan leaned forward to grip her shoulder. When she dropped her hand he mouthed, *What?*

But of course he already knew.

"Okay. Okay," she repeated, her voice calm and steady although her face had gone completely white. "What will it take to keep this between us? What do you want?"

Brendan scrubbed a hand over his eyes as after a second she retorted sharply, "Don't give me that right of reply bullshit. Tell me what I have to do."

There was another pause. She began to tremble. "You're going to regret this, Will. This will be the end of your career, not the start. I swear to fucking God."

She cut the call and slammed her phone face down on the bar. Then she flung herself into his arms as she burst into tears.

"He knows," she managed weakly, in between hiccupping breaths. "He says there was another data breach, but I bet he paid people at the betting websites to sell him lists of users. He wants to time a gambling story like the SportBetNet leak with the league final, except he only found one person affiliated with the CSL on all the lists he bought."

"You."

She nodded, eyes round with terror. "He's going to contact all his clients tomorrow morning to sell the story. Highest bidder gets it. This'll go national. My career is over. I'm finally paying for this stupid habit, and it's going to cost more than I ever imagined. Fuck, Brendan, what have I done?"

Her face crumpled as tears spilled down her cheeks. He gathered her against his chest, holding her tightly as sobs shook her.

Instinctively his brain worked all the angles, although it didn't need to. He had no options, no choices, no complex probabilities.

There was only one answer, and he'd known it only seconds after she picked up the phone.

"It'll be all right," he told her firmly. Just as he did during matches, he carefully gathered all of his inconvenient, distracting emotions into a corner of his mind and shut them behind a mental door. He knew what he had to do. No point getting het up about it.

She shook her head disbelievingly, fingertips digging into his shirt. "It won't. Nothing's going to be all right, not ever. My parents are going to find out. Oh my God, they're going to be so—"

"I have an idea. Come with me."

Picking up her phone from the bar, he took her by the hand and led her up the stairs, then through the ground floor to the back door. He didn't dare look back at her—he didn't know if he had the strength not to kiss her one last time, not to pull her close, not to tell her he loved her. He didn't even glance at her as he unlocked the door to the backyard and motioned for her to go through. Her expression was puzzled, he guessed, maybe even wary—he didn't raise his eyes to find out for himself.

"Stay here," he instructed. "I have to make a call."

He sensed her whirl in his peripheral vision, felt the moment she put the pieces together and realized what he was about to do. Too late. He'd already shut the door and locked it, and by the time he heard her pounding her fists against the glass and screaming his name he was halfway to the pub, her phone in his hand.

He paused in the kitchen, retrieving Erin's bag from the counter and placing it inside the garage. He tapped the button to open the garage door so she could get her car out once she made her way from the backyard, and then locked the door that led into the house. Then he descended the stairs into the pub.

The cool, hushed quiet momentarily eased the tension in his shoulders. He propped his hands on his hips and surveyed the space that had served as his personal sanctuary and bunker for years—and been the epicenter for the worst moments of his anxiety and addiction.

His addiction was on the wane—that was something, at least. For the first time in a very long time he felt like he was in the driver's seat of his life instead of locked in the trunk, trying to gauge from the swerving angles where he was headed.

He didn't need the stats now. Hopefully he wouldn't need them again. He was clearheaded. Calm. In control. And for better or worse, in love.

He took a seat at the bar. Touched the stool where she'd sat beside him all these weeks. Breathed in her lingering jasmine scent lingering, that slice of femininity that had so disrupted the course of his life.

A fleeting interruption, already fading. But one for which he'd be forever grateful.

Maybe he would rebuild the pub in Nebraska.

Or maybe it was time to say goodbye to this version of himself, too.

He unlocked Erin's screen by typing in her jersey number twice, then scrolled to her call history. He pressed Will's number to redial it. It rang once, twice...

"Look, Erin, I'm sorry, but there's nothing you can offer me that'll make me change my mind. This is too big, and too important, and frankly that night at dinner you shouldn't have—"

"Will? This is Brendan Young."

Silence.

"Brendan Young," he repeated. "Goalkeeper for Atlanta Skyline."

Another few seconds of silence, and then, "I know who you are."

"Good. We can keep this short. Erin placed those bets on my behalf. I was spooked after the data breach but I couldn't stop betting. I talked her into it—I manipulated her, actually. I have bank statements to show earnings from those bets being deposited into my account. It wasn't Erin's fault, and I'm the bigger story anyway. I'll give you whatever you need to leave her out of this."

Silence again. Brendan sat absolutely still, attentive but unworried, waiting for Will's response.

"How did you get her phone?" the reporter asked finally.

"I took it from her and locked her out of my house so she couldn't stop me making this call. She'll try to take the fall for this, but that wouldn't be right."

"Wait." He imagined Will frowning, shaking his head to get the story straight. "What's your relationship with Erin Bailey? Why should I believe anyone could coerce her into anything?"

"Off the record?"

Will's sigh was exasperated. "I guess."

"She's in love with me," he stated baldly, his flat tone reflecting none of the momentary swirl of emotion the words inspired. "I took advantage of that."

Will's pause was different this time, and Brendan smiled slowly. Will would be jealous of him now, and that much more willing to take him down.

"Back on the record," Will informed him. "If I'm going to spend all night rewriting this then I need a lot of detail. Start from the beginning."

Twenty minutes later Brendan put down the phone and rubbed his jaw. It ached from his tense conversation and the strict attention it had taken to ensure his version of events was as airtight as something left of the truth could be.

It worked, though. Will was probably already redrafting his article, removing all traces of Erin and peppering the tale with the name of the transgressive goalkeeper who, at the time of printing, would be just hours away from playing in the league final.

Whether or not he did would depend on how quickly the story broke, and at what scale. Roland was bringing a youth player as backup in case Brendan was injured. The kid was untried and untested, and would be unlikely to keep a clean sheet for Skyline. That didn't necessarily mean they'd lose, but it would put pressure on the forwards to keep the goal tally high, and on the defense to keep the ball far away.

Then again, maybe Roland would play him anyway. Secure the trophy and then let the door hit him on the way out.

He supposed they'd have to revise his insert in the league year-end report. Oh well, worse things had happened.

And as for his parents… They'd get over it. They'd have to—he'd make them. He'd be there, in the flesh, every Sunday evening for dinner. They couldn't hate him to his face. They'd forgive him. Surely.

He ran his hand through his hair and stood up. He'd have to find a way to get Erin her phone. Maybe he could courier it to her apartment in a couple of hours, when she'd had time to see sense and could be trusted not to do anything dramatically self-sacrificing.

Better to wait until morning and drop it off with the doorman at her building. Just to be safe.

Decision made, he moved behind the bar and opened one of the empty cardboard boxes he'd built that afternoon. Then he wiped the whiteboard clean, sweeping away every last grid, every number, every meticulously calculated probability.

He put the blank board in the bottom of the box. He grabbed a stack of notebooks and placed them on top. Then he began to move around the room, taking down photographs and pennants, carefully and systematically dismantling this part of his life.

Chapter 19

"Brendan! Brendan!" She pounded on the door, more in frustration and anger than hope as she watched his tall form disappear around a corner. She slammed her fists on the door once more for good measure, then pressed her forehead against the glass.

She closed her eyes, tears flowing freely now, breaths coming in gasping sobs. She knew exactly what he planned to do. He would destroy his career to save hers.

"Idiot," she muttered through clenched teeth, not sure whether she meant him or her. Both, she supposed. Her for getting them into this mess, him for sacrificing himself to get her out of it.

Nothing would happen while she stood there with her face against the door, she decided, straightening and taking two steps back. A wave of nausea suddenly overtook her, and she just managed to gather her hair in a ponytail as she leaned over and dry heaved at the bottom of Brendan's jasmine trellis.

Her eyes watered, her stomach cramped and her head spun, but the scent of jasmine was an incongruous, clarifying force, snapping her thoughts into brutal focus.

She would fix this.

She navigated around the side of the house in the dark, finally finding the back entrance to the garage. As soon as she opened it she saw that Brendan had raised the door so she could get her car out.

"Asshole thinks of everything," she grumbled, noting that he'd also placed her bag on the step from the garage to the house. She reversed down his driveway, obstinately gunning the engine.

She drove blindly for a few minutes, not sure where to go or what to do. Eventually, she pulled into the vast, empty parking lot of a home improvement store, where she cut the engine and stared purposefully through the windshield.

She held up her left hand. Reasons to let Brendan take the fall.

Index finger. She wouldn't lose her job.

Middle finger. Her parents would never find out about her gambling.

Ring finger. His career was over anyway—literally within hours—so he had a lot less to lose.

Pinkie. He also had a lot more money than her and could afford to be unemployed a lot longer.

Thumb. She didn't know how to stop him, or what she could do to change this.

She exhaled. Right hand. Reasons to take the blame herself.

Index finger. She loved Brendan.

From there her mind drew a blank. She sat in the silence of the car, disturbed only by the swish of vehicles passing on the main road, staring at her hands. Five fingers versus one. A lifetime spent building her first career and then her second, instantly and easily outweighed by one simple fact. One irrefutable emotion. One man.

"Never mind." She balled her hands, erasing that comparison. There were plenty of self-serving, pragmatic reasons to let Brendan assume responsibility.

And no way she could live with herself if she did.

"Think," she urged, pressing her fingers over her eyes. The solution was not to have either of their names in the article but to have no article at all. How could she stop Will from publishing anything? He wouldn't accept money, even if she had enough to compete with his buyers. He thought this would launch his career to the next level, and she couldn't give him that much exposure. She had nothing he wanted, except...

She sat bolt upright as the answer registered. Then she put her car into gear and squealed out of the parking lot.

* * * *

Credit to her, if Randall's wife had any suspicions about his young, female coworker turning up unannounced on his doorstep at nine o'clock at night, it didn't show in her perfectly polite smile. Her composure was so steadfast she even offered Erin a drink as she showed her to Randall's home office.

Erin thanked her profusely, but her voice evaporated when Randall arrived and his wife left. The CFO's alarm wasn't at all concealed, and his brows rose above his glasses as he asked without preamble, "What's wrong?"

"I'm sorry for disturbing you at home like this. I'll try to be quick. Can we sit?"

"Of course." The desk faced the window, but he motioned for her to take the worn armchair in the corner and rolled his desk chair over to face her.

She took a deep, steadying breath, and mentally apologized to everyone she was about to disappoint. Her parents. An entire league of female players. All those girls who watched YouTube clips of her top-ten goals and dreamed of besting her one day.

I'm sorry. There's no other way.

She told him everything. The weekends in Atlantic City. The sky-high credit card bills. Betting on overseas leagues. The only detail she left out was Brendan—mostly.

"We've been seeing each other for a few weeks," she admitted. "It was never supposed to be serious, but I guess it is, given he's just thrown away his reputation on my behalf. He doesn't deserve that. It's my fault, and I should take the blame."

She glanced at the floor for a second, gathering strength for what she was about to do.

"I'll resign," she offered. "Or you can dismiss me. Whatever it'll take for you to call Will Hart and convince him that I've admitted fault, the league is taking the appropriate action and Brendan Young's name shouldn't be anywhere near his story."

She squeezed her eyes shut, as though waiting for a blow. When it didn't come she reopened them.

Randall peered at her through his thick lenses. They stared at each other in silence for a full minute, the only sound the distant tick of a grandfather clock.

"I have a better idea," he pronounced finally. "I'll call Will Hart and tell him if he publishes an article impugning a player or a corporate employee based on illegally acquired data, he'll lose all access to CSL players, managers, matches, and league executives."

She blinked. Will only wrote about soccer—that would end his career.

"That sounds good," she said dumbly, waiting for the other end of the seesaw to hit the ground with a thud.

He inhaled, crossed his arms and leaned back in his chair. "I have a son. Did you know that?"

She shook her head. "I met your daughter, but I didn't know you had a son."

"You should've. He's twenty-nine, so he would've been your generation. Superstar midfielder in high school. Incredible technical vision, a real cog in the center, able to distribute balls and see opportunities three passes in advance. Won a full scholarship to UCLA and flunked out his freshman year."

She winced. "Sorry."

"Not as sorry as I was, trust me." He smiled bitterly. "He ran out of spending money from his summer job early in the semester, so he started playing poker online. I guess he won a little at first—enough to make him spend hours every night trying to win more. He started sleeping through class, didn't make it to practice, and threw away his future on a website. Of course, we didn't find out about any of it until the bailiffs turned up."

"Bailiffs?" she echoed.

He nodded. "He racked up a load of debt, and used his home address on all the paperwork."

"What happened?"

"We bailed him out. More than once. It took time, but he learned. He pulled himself together, finished his degree, found a job. Gambling ruined his credit rating but not his whole life. It shouldn't ruin yours, either."

Her heart inched into her throat, but she stuffed down the hope welling with it. She didn't dare believe this might all turn out okay.

"Maybe this is why I pushed the gambling thing so hard for the year-end report." His smile turned reflective. "My son's issues were years ago, but they still weigh heavily on my mind, especially when I see a player falling into that trap. I thought the key was to be hard and use punishment as a deterrent. In retrospect—and in fact, it was that piece you presented on Brendan Young that changed my mind—I think second chances can be worth a hell of a lot more."

"I'll phone Will Hart," he concluded, and from the way he sat forward she knew this conversation was almost over. "And I won't accept your resignation, but I will work with you to end this addiction. As a start, I can recommend a great therapist."

She bit her lower lip, fighting to hold back the flood of tears that threatened at the corners of her eyes. "Really? I can keep my job?"

"Only if you continue to excel as much as you have since you joined. Beyond that, I see no need to make this private matter public."

"I will," she promised, the words spilling out on a rush of breath. "And I'm going to kick this gambling thing, once and for all. I'm already halfway there."

"Then I'll help you along the second half of the journey."

He stood, and so did she. She had a sudden urge to fling her arms around his ruddy neck, but her professionalism kicked in just in time. She extended her hand instead.

"Thank you," she said more genuinely than ever before in her life.

"You're welcome. I'm glad you came to me. Honesty is always the right decision."

She managed to hold it together until she said goodbye to Randall's wife, got into her car and drove around the block. Then she parked along the curb and wept.

She didn't cry for herself. Although she was grateful, her relief wasn't selfish—not at all.

Instead, she cried for Brendan. For the man that cared so little for himself and so much for others. For the withdrawal, he'd already put into motion, and the isolation he thought he deserved. For the immense, larger-than-life legacy he would leave behind, and for the extraordinary story that was about to come to an end.

She felt limp and unsteady by the time her sobbing slowed. She'd saved him once tonight. Would he let her save him again?

She'd find out tomorrow. First, she had to do something else, something she should've done a long time ago.

She opened her purse and dug around for her tablet. She brought the screen to life and tapped to her email. She exhaled, then started typing.

Hi Daddy. Sorry to do this over email, but I don't have my phone and this can't wait another second. I have something to tell you.

Chapter 20

Brendan peered suspiciously at his teal uniform hanging neatly in the open-fronted locker. He glanced over his shoulders, surveying his teammates for any sign they knew something he didn't. They were all absorbed in getting ready for the match—as he should be, apparently.

Memphis had been chosen as the venue for the league final before the season started, and as he looked around the dressing room in the brand-new stadium he could see why. The facilities were top-notch and the hospitality they'd received as a visiting team was unparalleled. His spare kit was folded on the bench beside a copy of the match program. On the floor beneath was his cleats, shin guards, flip-flops for the shower, a sponsor-branded towel and a bottle of a sports drink in his favorite flavor.

It was almost like the equipment manager expected him to play.

He scrubbed a hand over his eyes, trying to shed the paranoia that had dogged him since he hung up with Will Hart last night. Although he was relaxed and confident about his decision, he hadn't been looking forward to the inevitable confrontations with Roland, his parents, and whoever else had a minor stake in what remained of his career. He spent the evening with his phone in his peripheral vision, waiting for it to ring.

It didn't. It didn't ring the next morning, either, as he showered and dressed and packed. It remained silent when he dropped off Erin's phone with her doorman, and except for a few pinging texts from well-wishing former teammates, it was quiet from the time he arrived at the airfield to the moment he switched it off for the flight.

Roland acted disconcertingly normal, too, and more than once Brendan had to stop himself from staring at his manager. Was it possible he didn't know? Or was he focused on minimizing disruptions before the big match and saving his hostility for a postgame screaming session?

Neither option seemed likely. As the flight wore on, it occurred to Brendan that the story should be out by now—if it was going out.

But why wouldn't it?

With that in mind, he sat down in front of his tidily arranged uniform and unlocked his phone. He dismissed another slew of messages from Erin without reading them and put his own name into a search engine for what must've been the hundredth time since they'd landed an hour earlier.

Nothing.

He shook his head in disbelief as he cut the screen and stuffed the phone into his duffel. He doubted Erin could've killed the story on her own—she didn't have enough leverage with Will. But he couldn't think of any favors she could've called in that wouldn't have exposed her role in the whole thing, either.

Maybe he just wasn't famous or interesting enough, and Will couldn't sell the story. Again, that seemed unlikely, especially on the day of the final. Maybe Roland had enough sway to get Will to hold off on publishing, but then by now surely he would've given Brendan some indication that he knew—he wasn't exactly the type to keep his opinions under wraps.

He snapped his fingers, the answer arriving with clear dimensions. Will was delaying the story's release until after the match. If Skyline won, the story would be even bigger. What better way to lead than with a photo of the disgraced goalkeeper hefting the league trophy? If they lost he'd get the same impact as if he'd sent out the story in the morning, so he must be taking his chances on a win.

Brendan exhaled and closed his eyes. His thoughts had been going in circles for hours and he wasn't achieving anything except draining his mental energy. All he could do was focus on this final—the last professional match he'd ever play—and trust the rest of the pieces would fall into place exactly as they were meant to.

With his eyes still closed and his hands spread on his knees, he visualized packing up all the shit with Erin and Will and the article and dropping it into a cardboard box like the ones he'd filled last night. Mentally he taped it shut and shoved it in a corner, out of sight, unimportant.

He inhaled as he opened his eyes, letting the scene around him fill the rest of the space in his head. He owed his teammates his full attention, not to mention the fans that had traveled to Memphis. Everything else could wait. For the next couple of hours, he was the goalkeeper for Atlanta Skyline. No past, no future, just the guy protecting the net at one end of the field.

He watched his teammates for a few seconds. Right-back Kojo Agassa bobbed his head in time to the music pumping through his headphones. Winger Rio Vidal hung a Chilean flag and a wooden rosary on the hook, then touched the framed photo of his fiancée he'd propped up on the shelf. Left-back Oz Terim got dressed with one hand and held his e-reader with the other, looking engrossed as he thumbed the screen to turn the pages.

Every player he'd known had their own peculiar pre-match rituals. He touched the goal posts, left, right and center, firmly gripping each white bar. That was it, though. He'd never been superstitious. He supposed he was too aware of probabilities in all their minute details for there to be much mysticism left in his world.

Except for love. He'd barely given it much thought these last couple of years, certainly didn't expect it to materialize anytime soon. Love snuck into his life through the gaps, edging in, coming closer and closer until he had no choice but to acknowledge it.

He smirked as he reached for his match-day top, embroidered with the date of the final below the Skyline logo. That he'd fallen in love with Erin Bailey, a woman immovably married to her career in the sport he was leaving, was definitely a cosmic joke.

He'd only loved once before now, a passion so enduring and deep-seated he doubted he'd ever get over it completely. Soccer. This game had been his refuge, his springboard, his wings, and finally his parachute. No matter how badly he'd screwed up, or how often, or who he hurt in the process, soccer didn't yield. The rules remained, the dynamics persisted, and he could be all the good and usefulness and virtue on the pitch that he couldn't when he took off his uniform.

He finished changing and stood, just in time for the assistant manager to appear in the doorway and give the team a two-minute warning. The atmosphere heightened as nervous rituals were executed more hastily, but he moved slowly to the door, tugging on his gloves as he went.

He caught sight of a tall, lanky figure making his way past the dressing room.

"Pavel," he called, catching the goalkeeper by the elbow.

His teammate greeted him with a tight hug. "I wasn't sure whether I should try to say hello to you before the match. I didn't want to throw you off."

"It's good to see you. How are you?"

"Better every day. Cleared to sit with the rest of the walking wounded."

"Good. Roland and I are just about on speaking terms, but we may have to bring you on."

Brendan meant it as a joke, but Pavel's tone was serious as he replied, "No. This is your day. You're going to be great."

Instinctively Brendan drafted a quip to brush off his teammate's compliment, but then he changed his mind. "Thank you," he said instead. Simply and earnestly.

"Good luck, my friend." Pavel hugged him once more before moving down the tunnel. The final call must have gone out in the dressing room because the rest of the first team trickled past him. He joined their momentum and took his place in the line. Oz was their captain, so he stood at the front. In ascending order of number, Brendan was right behind him.

He trailed his gloved finger down the number printed on his shorts. One.

Each player took the hand of their child escort and walked out onto the pitch, accompanied by the booming voice of the announcer listing their names. Then they lined up side by side while the two captains exchanged pennants and shook hands with the referees. When Oz returned to his position, a country-music star emerged from the tunnel to sing the national anthem.

He pressed his hand to his heart and let his gaze drift over the crowd. He peered up toward the VIP section, trying to remember the row numbers on the tickets he gave his father and brother. He couldn't recall, and he couldn't see them.

They were here. They'd sent him a selfie when they arrived at the stadium, both decked out in shirts with his name, Liam sporting gigantic novelty sunglasses he must've bought from a street vendor. He'd also gotten a text from his mom, full of kissing smiley faces and heart emojis, and a photo from Aidan of his nephews giving thumbs-up in their Skyline shirts. He wasn't unloved. His family cared, even if they didn't always know how to show each other.

He tilted his gaze higher, to the executive boxes. The mental cardboard box into which he'd shoved all his emotional shit popped open and a flashing memory of Erin's fiery hair and dazzling smile peeked out.

She was up there, somewhere, watching him. Probably hating him for taking the fall on the article, but probably quietly grateful, too.

He smiled. The loneliness nipping at the edges of his awareness dissolved. Twenty thousand spectators in the stands, but she was the only one who mattered.

He would play for her. Make her proud. Show her how much he could love something since he'd never be able to tell her how much he loved her.

The song concluded and the audience clapped. He shook hands down the line of his opponents, then made his way to the net that would be his to guard for the next forty-five minutes.

Left, right, center. He clasped each bar, stilling his mind, opening his perception, straightening his spine.

Then he turned to face the last match of his career.

* * * *

Erin sucked in a breath through her teeth, smothering a profanity as Brendan caught the ball and fell on it, saving Miami's shot on Skyline's goal.

"Young's turned out to be a hell of a keeper," the league chairman remarked at her elbow. "Too bad he never got much of a run while he was in Atlanta."

She hummed noncommittally, darting a glance at Randall. Her boss was deep in conversation with one of the directors, but she reminded herself that even if he'd heard, he would've given no sign. His discretion throughout the day had been impeccable, and she had to admit she'd underestimated him. Beneath that socially awkward exterior was a solid man.

Skyline charged a counterattack into Miami's half, and she walked away, trading the luxurious viewing terrace for the mostly deserted tables at the back of the executive box. She accepted a glass of champagne from the bartender and sipped it slowly, gathering herself, making a plan.

She'd spent most of last night talking to her parents, beginning with the painful process of helping them figure out how to use Skype since she didn't have her phone. Once that was up and running they did a lot of listening, followed by effusive expressions of love and support. She welled up remembering their earnest insistence that they were proud of her no matter what, and that they'd do whatever she wanted as she moved forward.

She hung up feeling lighter than she had in years. For the first time in months, she fell asleep as soon as she slipped into bed. No tossing and turning thinking about debt, no icy dread in her stomach keeping her awake.

The next morning started early, but started well, with the doorman buzzing to let her know "her friend" had dropped off her phone. She raced to the lobby half-dressed, hoping to catch him, knowing she wouldn't. She wasn't even fast enough to see the Aston Martin turning the corner. But she had her phone, and she grinned when she noted he'd returned it fully charged.

Even now the flurry of texts she'd sent him was unviewed and unanswered, and her call log was just a long column repeating his number. That was okay, though. She hadn't expected him to respond—in fact, she suspected he didn't intend to speak to her ever again.

"We'll see about that," she whispered into her champagne glass.

She had to rethink her plan slightly now the match looked sure to go into extra time. With only five minutes left the score was goalless, though both teams had given spectacular performances. The forwards drove hard and took creative chances, but the defenders were obstinate and impenetrable. In Skyline's half, Brendan had single-handedly saved at least three potentially fatal on-target shots.

Her breath caught as she thought of him, alone between the posts. Whenever the action raced into Miami's half her gaze snared on Atlanta's goal and the man guarding it. The sentry on whom ten other men relied. Alert. Focused. Isolated.

She gulped the rest of her champagne, shaking off her melancholy. He wouldn't be alone anymore. Not if she had anything to do with it.

She glanced at the match clock. Four minutes left. Time to make her move.

Half the executives had already made their way out of the box and into the lower stands for a closer view, so no one noticed when she slipped into the hall. She detoured into the restroom and rooted in her bag for the Skyline jersey she'd brought. She pulled it on over her dress, briefly admiring the way the hem fanned out from the bottom before fluffing her hair and continuing down the hallway.

The whistle blew while she was clomping down the cement steps of the lower stands, the wall of noise from the crowd nearly knocking her over. The score was still nil-nil. The ref added thirty minutes of extra time.

The players from both teams staggered toward their respective managers and dropped onto the grass. A flurry of personnel rushed onto the field with the precision of Formula One pit crews, distributing bottles of electrolyte drinks, rewrapping limbs, and massaging tired muscles.

She reached the first row and realized Brendan wasn't with the rest of the team. He sat in front of the goal, long legs stretched in front of him, leaning back on his hands.

She propped her hands on her hips. She assumed she'd be able to speak to him when he came near the tunnel. It never occurred to her that he'd remain out on the pitch by himself.

With a heavy exhalation, she made her way along the front row, clambering around people's knees, picking her steps between their splayed feet. Technically she had no right to access this part of the stadium—her

VIP pass only let her into the executive level—but she had to make this work somehow. She wouldn't let Brendan finish his career thinking his legacy was about to be trashed by a single news article, nor would she let him walk out of this stadium thinking no one loved him.

She loved him. More than she ever thought possible. And she didn't care what happened after today, as long as he knew.

Finally, she made it around the curve of the stadium to the line of seats directly behind the goal. She stood in the aisle and leaned over the siding, her breath catching as she got close enough to see Brendan's face. He sat motionlessly, head slightly turned to keep an eye on his teammates.

Drawing a bolstering breath, she bent over as far as she could and called his name to get his attention.

He didn't notice.

Frowning, she tried again. And again. And again, with no response. He seemed so close, yet he couldn't hear her.

Then she looked down the row of fans. At least ten of them were on their feet, also screaming his name.

Dammit.

She had to get closer. She grit her teeth and began sidling in between the fans and the siding, hoping one of them wouldn't mind her standing in their space for the few, crucial seconds she needed.

No such luck. She stopped in front of someone she thought was a nice-looking woman in a Skyline jersey, but she hadn't even planted her hands on the siding when the fan in question spoke.

"Excuse me, what do you think you're doing?"

"League business. I'll be two seconds." Erin flashed her VIP pass.

"What kind of league business gives you the right to block my view?" the woman demanded.

Deciding honey was better than vinegar, Erin whirled with an outstretched hand—which the woman ignored—and a big smile, which also had no effect. "Hi, so sorry to bother you, I'm the Director of—"

"I don't care who you are. I'm a season ticket holder in Atlanta, I paid a fortune for this seat and if you don't move I'll call security."

Erin dug her nails into her palm. If this woman had any idea of the stakes involved...

"I just need to call a message to the goalkeeper. Less than a minute and I'll be out of your way." She tried to make her tone as sweet and polite as possible.

The woman snorted. "Good luck with that. He just moved down the other end. They're switching sides before the whistle."

Erin swore viciously under her breath as she turned just in time to see Brendan making his way toward the center line. She scrambled back through the tangle of feet and legs, but the referee blew the whistle to start the extra half-hour as she reached the aisle.

Panic gripped her. She'd lost her chance—but she had to tell him. She had to.

She should've told him long before tonight, she chided herself, tears welling hot and unstoppable. She shouldn't have been such a self-centered princess, burying her head in her ambition and refusing to see what was right in front of her. Now he was out there, on his own, with no reason not to expect to walk off the pitch into a massive, shaming scandal when instead she wanted him to walk straight into her arms.

She had to think of something. But what? Frantic, rock-bottom tears spilled over her cheeks as breath hitched in her lungs. She'd screwed this up and she was fresh out of ideas.

"Ma'am?"

She spun, coming face-to-face with a security guard.

"May I see your ticket, please?"

She passed him her VIP pass. "Sorry, I know I shouldn't be down here."

"I need to ask you to return to your ticketed area."

"Okay," she acceded meekly. She took one last look at the pitch and the teal-uniformed man at the far end of it. Then she turned and made her way back up the concrete steps, shoulders slumped in defeat.

* * * *

"Up and in. Quick," Brendan instructed his defenders, who obediently ran up the middle of the pitch as he took a couple of steps back for a goal kick. When he was satisfied with the way brick-red jerseys populated the pitch he booted the ball back to the center line.

Skyline's forwards pushed into Miami's half and he checked the clock. Another couple of minutes until the end of added time. Every player on the field ran with heavy legs, desperation, and exhaustion combining to make shots sloppy and passes ill-timed. There was no artistry left, just dogged determination.

Slower players made his job slightly easier, or they would if the mounting tension of this goalless match wasn't sending his brain into a tailspin. If no one scored before the thirty minutes was up, the result would be decided by a penalty shootout. Whether they won or lost would be almost entirely in his hands.

Penalty shootouts were about mental grit, not skill, and the odds always favored the player taking the shot. Saving a penalty required a combination of luck, instinct, and a hell of a pair of cojones.

He was tired, too. Two hours of intense concentration, spiking adrenaline and maximum physical output had taken a toll. As the clock ticked his grip on his thoughts got looser and looser. Already the box he'd shoved his distractions into had slid out of its mental corner, and the tape holding it together was threatening to break open.

At the other end of the pitch, Rio crossed a ball that Deon headed at the goal. The crowd gasped as it arced toward the top of the net, but Miami's keeper got his fingertips on it just enough to push it back into play.

Brendan swore under his breath. He'd briefly overlapped with Miami's American keeper in Spain, and the guy was good. With only a minute left Atlanta were unlikely to get another chance. Unless something extraordinary happened, whether the league trophy traveled to Miami or Atlanta tomorrow was on his shoulders.

The implication of that missed shot exploded in his mind like a firework, and the box in his brain burst wide open. He almost staggered under the rush of anxieties that flooded his mind like a tidal wave.

Maybe the article was out by now. He glanced up at the stands, suddenly reading criticism and disgust in every set of eyes. He'd disgraced himself, his family, his place in this game. In minutes he wouldn't be a professional athlete anymore. He'd be unemployed, unimportant, insignificant. A has-been, and an ill-reputed one at that. Not remembered for the trophies with his name on them, but as the man in the middle of a scandal that broke the day of the league final—maybe the day he lost the league final for his team.

He pressed his hands against the sides of his head as if he could force his reeling mind to still. His breaths came quicker, shallower. He couldn't face the penalty shootout. He couldn't let everyone down again.

The referee blew the whistle on a nil-nil scoreboard and he bent over at the waist, fighting a wave of nausea. He couldn't do this.

He dragged himself upright and made his way to the sideline. Both teams already had their penalty orders determined, and there would be no formal break before the shootout began. A couple of minutes for hydration and then he'd have to face Miami's players one-on-one.

Roland approached as he chugged an electrolyte drink. The Swede seemed to have aged ten years in the last two hours, but as he reached Brendan he smiled.

"I won't bother giving you a pep talk. Just know I'm glad you're here."

Brendan shook his head in objection but Roland didn't notice, slapping him on the shoulder before moving to speak to the players who'd be shooting for Skyline. Brendan lowered the half-empty drink bottle, suddenly feeling sick again, and searched the row of injured players' seats for Pavel. The Czech keeper shot him two thumbs up and a big grin, but it only heightened his anxiety as he realized there was absolutely no way out. He couldn't fake an injury and get Pavel to run on from the stands. There was no one left but him.

"Brendan!"

For the most part, he'd learned to ignore fans yelling his name—they did it all match long—but the female voice ringing over the din caught his attention. He looked over his shoulder, and the plastic bottle dropped from his hand.

Erin leaned over the siding of the front row, a raging fire-haired beacon in the twisting shadows of his mind. She grinned and waved him over, ignoring the furious man whose view she blocked.

He took only a couple of steps closer and didn't shout back, wary of the rules, not wanting anyone to misinterpret their exchange as any kind of coaching or inappropriate communication.

"It's not coming out," she called out, her coded language suggesting she knew the rules, too. "Dead in the water. Randall, of all people."

"You told him?" he shouted before he could think better of it. Immediately he clamped his mouth shut, unsure whether to be delighted that she'd managed to kill the story or sorry that she must've lost her job in the process.

"I'll tell you later, but everything's good. Good," she emphasized, grinning even wider.

"Okay. Well, I have to go," he told her dumbly, not sure what else to say.

"Wait." Her tone was urgent, and her smile dropped. "One more thing."

He turned his hands palm-up.

She inhaled, lower lip darting briefly between her teeth. "I love you."

He blinked. Squinted. Shook his head. "No, you don't."

Her expression moved from determined to annoyed. "Yes, I do. I just said it, didn't I? I love you, Brendan. I love you, and we're going to make this work."

He just stared at her, unable to process what she was saying. Did she love him? Really?

Her face fell, the confidence dissipating, and he realized that she must think he didn't feel the same. Urgency swelled hot in his chest, and the words ran out of his mouth before he registered them.

"I love you too."

Even as it trembled with emotion, her smile was the cooling salve his feverish brain needed. The cyclone in his head calmed to a gentle spring breeze. He inhaled all the way to the bottom of his lungs.

"Fuck's sake, lady, do you know how much I paid for these seats?" The beefy, red-faced man behind her appeared to be on the verge of a heart attack.

"Later," Erin called, edging away toward the aisle.

He raised his hand in farewell. "Later," he echoed, too quietly for her to hear.

"Let's go, number one." The referee was at his elbow. Brendan looked past him to see that Miami's keeper had taken his place between the posts. Atlanta would shoot first.

His whole body felt loose and relaxed as he took his place along the sideline. Never mind the logistics or the complexities that awaited them. Erin loved him. She loved him. The most vibrant, ferocious, lethally sexy woman he'd ever known had chosen him, having never chosen another.

He couldn't stop his smile as he watched Oz step up to position the ball for the first shot. He made a silent promise to his teammates, to his parents, to the woman he loved. We're going to win.

Oz regarded the keeper with the same cool, dispassionate expression that made him one of the most difficult reads in the league. He took a step back, leveled his gaze on his opponent, and delivered a precise, clinical shot straight into the back of the net.

The crowd roared, but Oz's celebration was muted as he high-fived his teammates. Each team got five chances before they went to sudden death. The win was still a long way off.

His turn. He took his place between the posts and locked eyes with Miami's striker. He'd never missed a penalty, but Brendan supposed there was a first time for everything. He widened his stance and spread his arms.

The striker shot left, and he dove left, but not far enough. The ball sailed an inch past his fingers and he heard it slam into the net as he landed hard on the grass.

He pulled himself up and brushed off his gloves as he traded places with Miami's keeper. No point feeling defeated. Still four chances left.

Deon took the second penalty for Skyline, and he made quick work of it, barely taking a second to get into position before he sent a hard shot into the upper right-hand corner. Miami's keeper didn't even have time to dive and walked out of the box less than a minute after he walked in.

Brendan resumed his position, drumming his heels into the grass as he studied the winger placing the ball at his feet. This guy had nerves of steel. No amount of intimidation would work, only skill and speed. He narrowed his eyes as the winger shot, and although he picked the right side, the ball curved around him and into the net, unreachable and unstoppable.

He kept his head high as he walked back to the sideline. Two-two and Miami had used their best penalty takers. All was far from lost.

Laurent Perrin, Skyline's number ten, stepped up for his turn. The French playmaker radiated confidence as he set the ball and stepped behind it. Miami's keeper braced his legs apart and Laurent took his shot.

The ball hit the top post, then bounced over the goal and onto the grass behind it.

A chorus of profanities rippled amongst the Skyline supporters, but Brendan fought to keep his expression neutral as Laurent turned, devastation plain on his face.

"Don't worry about it," he told his teammate as they passed each other, gripping Laurent's shoulder. "I've got this."

I've got this, he reiterated to himself, believing every word. He stared across the box at the Miami defender readying for his shot. He was fifty-fifty when it came to penalties, and Brendan had everything to lose.

The defender took his run-up. It wasn't quite an open book, but it was readable. Brendan jumped the instant the ball left his foot, and just managed to get his fingers on the high shot to push it even higher, sending it over the bar.

The defender swore profusely where he stood and Brendan eagerly vacated the goal, not wanting to give his teammates too much time to celebrate. The score was still even at two-two. Saving one didn't mean he could save another.

He ignored the slaps on his back as Rio stepped up to take Skyline's fourth penalty.

"Not the Panenka," Brendan urged under his breath. Rio was famous for using the ballsy, soft-touch technique to scoot a goal past the keeper and win the South American Cup for Chile. It worked then, but it was too predictable to work now. Brendan prayed Rio realized that.

The little Chilean took his run-up in three slow, easy strides, which totally concealed the powerful shot he sent into the net. The keeper had stayed in the center, expecting the Panenka, and the ball fired way out of his reach into a back corner. Rio fell on his knees in celebration, crossing himself and raising his fist to the sky.

Brendan gathered himself as he made his way back to the goal. Rio's score meant the pressure was all on him. If he saved this, they won. If not, each team took another turn.

He barely knew the midfielder stepping up for Miami. The twenty-two-year-old from Arizona had made his debut this year, fresh out of a college program and bursting with untapped potential. He was fast but he was young. And this was a big moment.

Brendan studied the tension in his shoulders, the placement of his feet, the line of his gaze as he looked up from setting the ball. His mind whirred like a well-oiled motor, analyzing probabilities, reviewing every fact he knew about this kid, recalling each move he'd made in the two hours preceding this moment.

The answer revealed itself with crisp, clear angles as the kid took his run-up. He thought he was being clever, thought he was better than he was, or thought he could make up in bravery what he lacked in experience. Unfortunately, he thought wrong.

He's going for a Panenka.

Brendan remained still as the ball chipped into the air, straight down the line toward the goal. Time slowed, or his mind sped—either way, in the less-than-a-second of that ball's trajectory he saw it all.

His mother grumbling over the sink as she scrubbed out the grass stains in his jeans after a lunchtime spent kicking a soccer ball on the playground.

His feet pounding up the stairs to take the call from the coach at Notre Dame, Liam hanging on his arm as he muttered a one-word acceptance into the phone.

The scratch of the pen when he signed his first professional contract, and the aftershave of the world-famous manager who'd flown him and his parents all the way to Liverpool.

His first game in England, the heaving crowd, the unrelenting rain.

His last game in Spain, applauding the fans before taking a final walk down the tunnel.

Atlanta. Roland. Pavel. The sideline seat digging into his tailbone, week in and week out. Hours spent alone in his pub. Stacks of notebooks piling up along the bar. The day the data breach broke, Roland's fury, and his mother's tears.

And Erin. At once soft and hard, distant yet closer than home. Strong, unapologetic, endlessly passionate. That she'd chosen him, out of all the men who had and would hurl themselves at her feet, made him feel anointed. Extraordinary. Undeserving but utterly ecstatic.

He saw the end, as surely as he saw the beginning, and he was sorry. Sorry that he was about to outplay this young midfielder who had so much ahead of him. Sorry that he would ruin his confidence, maybe even set him back next season. But it had to be done, and anyway, this kid had his whole career ahead of him. Practically a lifetime.

Time regained its normal pace and he squared his feet, holding his position in the center of the net. He bent his knees slightly and caught the ball, its impact knocking the air out of his lungs. Then he cradled it in his arms and fell on top of it for good measure, nose in the grass, eyes closed against the soil.

The stadium exploded into cheering. He heard his teammates whooping, his opponents cursing, Roland's voice raised in uncharacteristic effusion. But he stayed still for just a bit longer. When he stood it up it would all be over. These were the final seconds of his career.

Hands plucked at his shirt before he was ready, and he had no choice but to drag himself to his feet. His teammates pressed around him and knocked him off balance, each one of them vying to hug him first. Someone took the ball from his hands and he felt its absence keenly. He'd never again hold a ball in professional competition.

His throat felt swollen, his lungs scratchy, but he forced a smile. The CSL trophy would be wintering in Atlanta.

As the cluster of his teammates broke apart he glanced around, bewildered and disoriented, not sure what happened now. He exchanged firm, smiling handshakes with Roland, with the other keeper, with the midfielder whose Panenka he'd just stopped, but he did it all numbly. His thoughts moved sluggishly, his tongue thick, and occasionally the earth seemed to teeter beneath his feet.

"Nice save, keeper."

The hand on his elbow lingered, and he turned to see that Erin had joined the other wives, girlfriends, and kids that had rushed onto the pitch. She smiled, and his world found its axis.

She threw her arms around his neck and he held her tightly, anchored by her presence. She kissed him hard, and his shoulders slackened with relief. She was really here. She'd meant it all.

"I came clean to Randall," she gushed when she pulled back. "I told him everything. I thought I would get fired, but he was great—he understood. He told Will he'd lose all access if he published. It worked. There's no story."

"Why did you tell him? I would've taken the fall for you, Erin. There was no reason to put your job on the line."

She shook her head disbelievingly. "Don't you get it? You're worth more to me than any job. I love you, Brendan. Maybe I've loved you since I was eighteen, I don't know. I'll do whatever I have to so we can be together… If you'll have me," she added shyly.

He gripped her upper arms. "I'll have you any way I can get you. I love you."

He kissed her again, and again, and with such intensity that by the time he registered the reporter standing beside him with a cameraman and a microphone, the entire viewing audience had gotten a PG-13 romantic interlude in the middle of their sports broadcast.

The reporter smiled as if it was totally normal to interview a player who'd just been making out with a high-profile league executive, and raised the long microphone connected to the stadium's speakers.

"Congratulations on your win, Brendan, and on that amazing save. This was a pretty spectacular end to your long and remarkable career. How does it feel to retire on such a high?"

He cleared his throat, glancing at the reporter's patient smile, and up at the rows and rows of fans. Then he leaned down slightly to speak into the mic.

"What can I say? I've been so lucky to play the game I love professionally for eleven years, in three countries, and to finish with a CSL league win is more than I ever expected. I owe so much to the coaches and managers who've helped me along the way, to my family, to the fans, to my brilliant teammate Pavel Kovar, and to my...my girlfriend, Erin."

She nodded encouragingly, tears brimming in her eyes. He turned back to the reporter.

"It's been a privilege to finish my career at Atlanta Skyline, where I've played alongside some of the best guys in the sport. I'm sad to say goodbye, but it's time, and I'm..." His voice broke, and he swallowed hard to steady it. "I'm just really grateful."

"Well done," the reporter told him warmly, out of range of the microphone, before she mercifully brought it back to her mouth. "Thank you, Brendan."

Applause and cheering echoed around the stadium before the fans broke into a full-voiced rendition of "Forever Young." He waved his gratitude, taking one last look at what it was like to have tens of thousands of people supporting him.

Then he took the hand of the only person whose support he needed. She squeezed it tightly.

"I'm ready," he told her. "Let's go."

They left the pitch together, hand-in-hand.

Epilogue

Erin swore viciously as she negotiated the rented, two-door subcompact down the snowy driveway toward Brendan's house. She'd already ruined her surprise visit when she called him from the airport to tell him the weather had delayed her flight into Lincoln, so she should've canceled the rental and accepted his offer to pick her up in his four-wheel-drive truck.

She sighed, exasperated, as something clanked against the undercarriage. One of these days she'd learn to let him take care of her occasionally.

After all, she was continually surprised by how much she enjoyed taking care of him. It began the night of the league final when she'd slipped him the card for her hotel room in case he wanted company after the players' party. He'd eased into her bed at two o'clock in the morning with whiskey on his breath and a hard-on between his legs that made her come twice, gaspingly and fiercely, before he finally sighed his release. Then he sagged beside her, put his head on her chest and sobbed.

She wasn't sure how long she held and comforted him as he grieved for the end of his career, but it was long enough for her to know with utter certainty that she would never love anyone as much as she loved him. He was her one and only, her now and her forever.

He'd have to be for her to keep racking up these frequent flier miles on trips to Nebraska, she thought wryly as the lights of the house came into view. Although she had to admit the place was growing on her, and seeing him so happy was worth every damn second she spent on a plane. At Thanksgiving, his warming relationship with his parents had been palpable, and days spent sanding floors and painting walls seemed to be exactly the occupying project he needed as he loosened his grip on his life in soccer.

He'd put in his share of miles, too, either to Atlanta or to wherever she'd traveled for work and had time to spend with him. In the last two months, they'd been together more than they'd been apart, so the distance between their addresses felt more theoretical than real.

"There you are," she murmured as the headlights caught a tall figure with his hands in his pockets standing in the middle of the drive. She pressed the brake and lowered the window. He leaned his forearms on the frame, grinning broadly, snowflakes peppering his ash-blond hair.

"I don't pick up hitchhikers," she informed him, then pressed a kiss against his smiling mouth.

"You shouldn't. You never know who you'll get." He circled around to the passenger side and yanked open the door, folding his long frame into the cramped space, the crisp scents of winter clinging to his barn jacket.

"If you walked out here because you were worried I'd get lost, you're a little late. It's only twenty feet to the house." She put the car into drive and crept up the bumpy road.

"I walked out to make sure you didn't get stuck," he replied pointedly. "And so I could direct you to the parking spot I cleared for you. And because I couldn't wait to see you."

She couldn't halt her smile at his last sentence and quickly squeezed his thigh before returning her hands to the wheel and following his instructions to pull the car into the space he'd dug out.

"Pretty," she remarked as she climbed out of the car, gaze sweeping the Christmas lights he'd wrapped up the chains of the porch swing.

"Sit for a minute. I'll take this inside." He hefted her bag out of the trunk and carried it through the front door.

She did as he instructed, climbing onto the swing and pulling the thick, quilted duvet he'd left out over her knees. Sitting on the swing had become as close as they had to a relationship tradition, and despite the freezing temperature she smiled up into the clear, black sky. Curling up next to Brendan on the porch was one of the highlights of every trip she made to Nebraska.

He returned carrying a bottle of bubbles and two glasses, and she grinned up at him as he set them down and took his seat beside her.

"That glad to see me, huh?"

"It's almost New Year's Eve—officially a year since we had our first, er, encounter. Thought I'd mark the occasion."

"Classy. Almost as classy as that joke you told at Christmas Eve dinner at my parents' house."

"Your dad thought it was hilarious," he countered, the swing shifting as he settled beside her. She pressed into his side as his arm came around her shoulders, and she exhaled her contentment. Nothing made her happier than this man. Absolutely nothing.

"Do you want your Christmas presents?" he asked, and she looked up at him suspiciously.

"Christmas was four days ago, and I drove you to the airport that afternoon."

"Is that a yes or a no?" he pressed.

"Yes," she acceded cautiously.

"First one wasn't confirmed until yesterday." He squeezed her more tightly into his side. "I've accepted a part-time job next season. Goalkeeper coach for Skyline Ladies."

She sat bolt upright, pushing out of his grasp so she could look him in the eye. "You're moving back to Atlanta?"

"I'll split my time," he explained. "But yeah, I'll be in Atlanta three weeks a month. Any idea where I can stay?"

She smacked his arm, delight stretching her cheeks. "You coy dog. I had no idea."

"Good. I'm hoping you didn't see this coming, either."

She watched incredulously as he withdrew a small, velvet box from his coat pocket and opened the lid to reveal a diamond ring so stunning, it dazzled even in the dim light of the semi-lit porch.

Tears tugged down the corners of her mouth as she looked up at him. "Brendan, I—"

He shook his head to silence her. "It doesn't have to be what I want it to be. I know we've only been together a little while, and you might need time to be sure. You can wear it now, or you can wear it when you decide. Or never. I don't care. I just want you to know that I'm ready when you are—if you are."

Air snagged in her lungs. She reached across and snapped the box shut, then linked her arms around his neck.

"It's beautiful, but I don't want you to think it was necessary. Playing or retired, diamond or brass, I love you, Brendan. I want to spend the rest of my life with you."

His grin could've lit up three counties. "Really?"

She nodded, surer of her response than any bet she'd ever placed. "Really."

He brought his lips to hers and she smiled into the kiss. If she was still a gambler—which she decidedly was not—she'd push all her chips forward for this man. He was the surest bet she'd ever seen, as bright and steadfast as the stars over their heads.

Meet the Author

Rebecca Crowley inherited her love of romance from her mom, who taught her to at least partially judge a book by the steaminess of its cover. She writes contemporary romance and romantic suspense with smart heroines and swoon-worthy heroes, and never tires of the happily-ever-after. Having pulled up her Kansas roots to live in New York City, London, and Johannesburg, Rebecca currently resides in Houston, Texas. You can find her on the web at rebeccacrowley.net or on Twitter at @rachelmaybe.

Printed in the United States
by Baker & Taylor Publisher Services